Born and raised in Melbourne, Australia, Edward Shergold's influences of space and light in architecture, the universal realm, history, art and words are entwined in *Jupiter*, his first novel.

He has travelled extensively, visually categorizing the moments of places for some future recollection.

An enthusiast for his native city he currently lives in Melbourne with his family.

For my family

The writer as servant to the story

Edward Shergold

JUPITER

AUSTIN MACAULEY PUBLISHERS™
LONDON · CAMBRIDGE · NEW YORK · SHARJAH

Copyright © Edward Shergold 2023

The right of Edward Shergold to be identified as author of this work has been asserted by the author in accordance with sections 77 and 78 of the Copyright, Designs and Patents Act 1988.

All rights reserved. No part of this publication may be reproduced, stored in a retrieval system, or transmitted in any form or by any means, electronic, mechanical, photocopying, recording, or otherwise, without the prior permission of the publishers.

Any person who commits any unauthorised act in relation to this publication may be liable to criminal prosecution and civil claims for damages.

This is a work of fiction. Names, characters, businesses, places, events, locales, and incidents are either the products of the author's imagination or used in a fictitious manner. Any resemblance to actual persons, living or dead, or actual events is purely coincidental.

A CIP catalogue record for this title is available from the British Library.

ISBN 9781398483613 (Paperback)
ISBN 9781398483620 (Hardback)
ISBN 9781398483644 (ePub e-book)
ISBN 9781398483637 (Audiobook)

www.austinmacauley.com

First Published 2023
Austin Macauley Publishers Ltd®
1 Canada Square
Canary Wharf
London
E14 5AA

The Universe is sustained of its own accord and knowing of itself.

Table of Contents

Chapter 1: How It Began 13

Chapter 2: The Cellar of Silent Pigs 24

Chapter 3: A Knowing 49

Chapter 4: Encomiums 69

Chapter 5: Ezekiel's Prophecy 85

Chapter 6: Aliquis in Viduum (Something in the Void) 105

Chapter 7: The Futuris File 126

    Manifesto: *136*

Chapter 8: The Campaigns 155

Chapter 9: Luteesha's Lament 184

Chapter 10: The Third Confinement 200

Epilogue 228

WANDIN
POST OFFICE

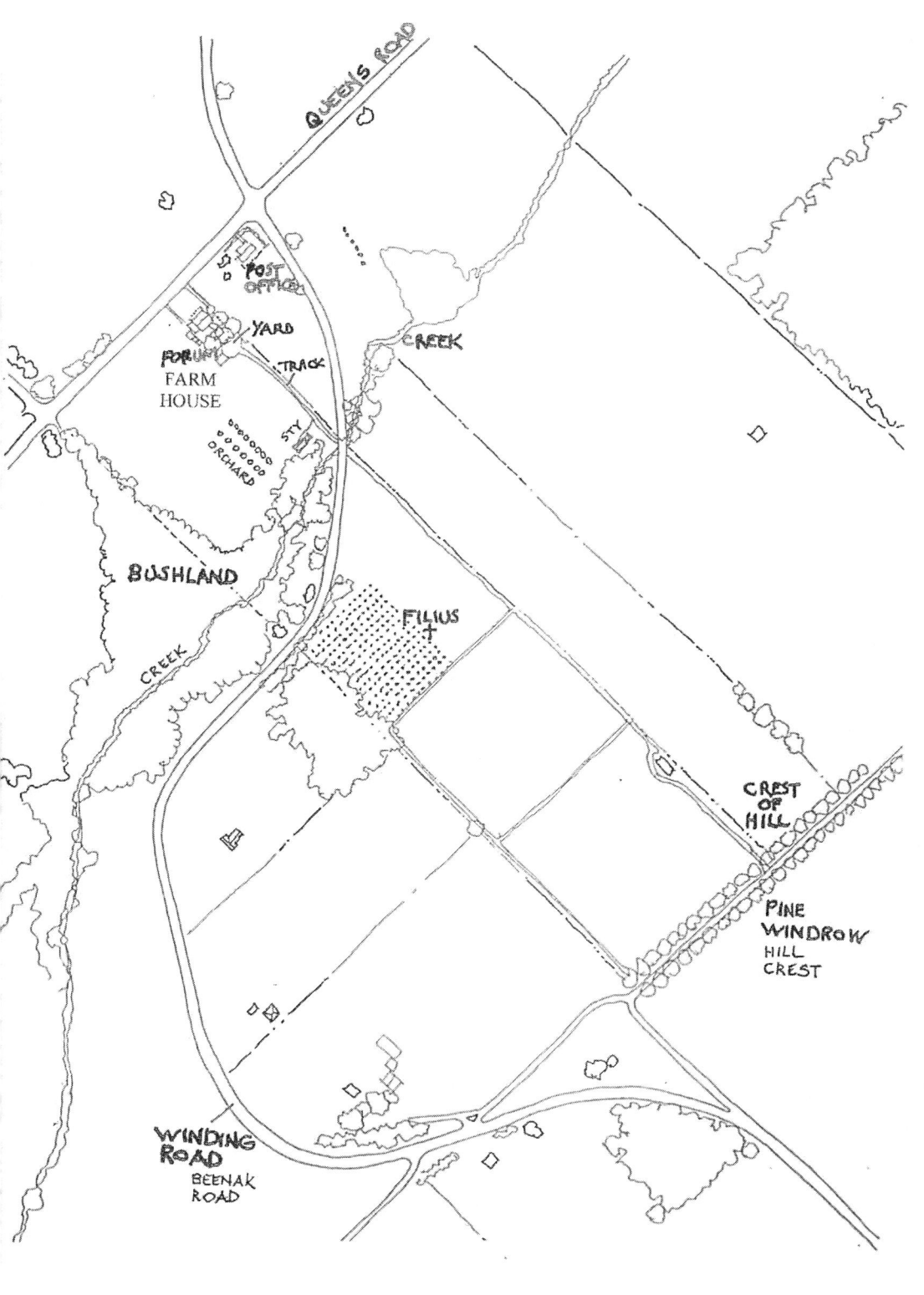

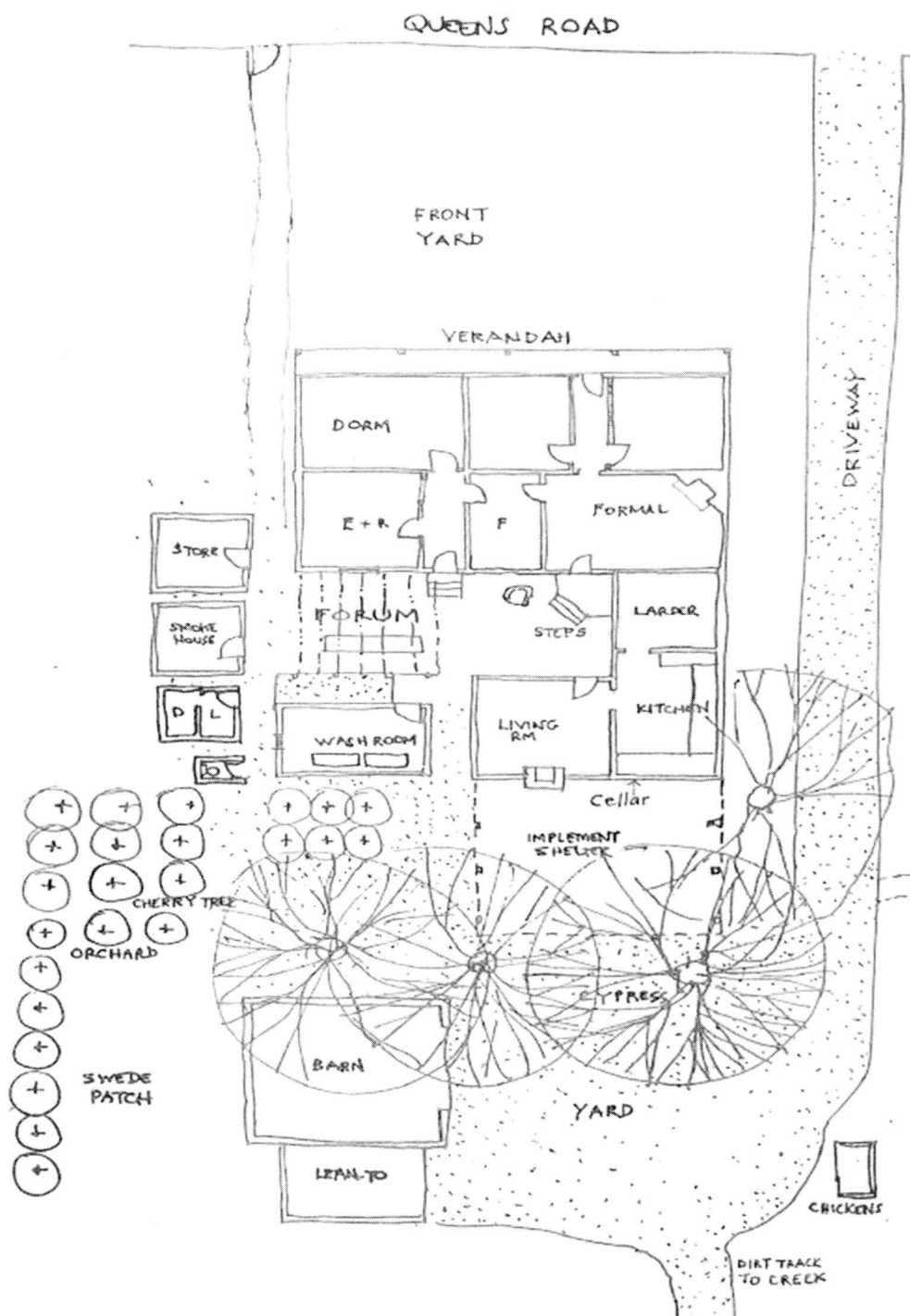

Chapter 1

How It Began

"IDIOT…! Idiot, sav…"

"No! Idiot SAVANT Isaac. That's what 1 said," explained Dr Olga Niesohn.

"As your therapist my task is to help you understand your strengths, not just the disfunction for which you came to seek help."

"What does that mean exactly! It's upsetting it's getting to me."

"OK. As I explained in the last session, it seems you didn't quite get it then, an idiot savant is an extremely gifted person, hampered somewhat by, shall I put it this way, learning difficulties bordering on mental disability.

"In your case, I am concluding difficulty in realising the normal within the societal context."

Isaac Marcu Moritz's mood sank deeper, thinking how best to ask…

"Why idiot? It's hurtful."

"It does have an offensive tone to this description, which is why a more precise term is under consideration, one that is more accurate without implication of a slur. Autistic Savant." Isaac's eyes begged for a reprieve.

"Having said that, not all savants are autistic. Remember, a savant is a knowledgeable person, and you are gifted in your chosen field and have worked diligently to establish a new and recognised science.

"It's not all bad."

Isaac, partly reassured asked,

"Then why do I feel underrated?"

"It's more complicated than that," replied Olga.

"In the time we've worked together, I have detected a condition in you not unlike one of multiple personalities, brought about by a neurodevelopmental disorder. You mentioned previously, an incident in your childhood, where…"

Isaac cut her off.

"Lightning, I was hit by a thunderbolt!"

"And you said, from thereon the visions of long-dead people came to speak with you."

"Yes, more invasive even than that," replied Isaac, seeming to withhold the noise deep inside his mind. He looked up, listening intently to what she was about to say.

"I am coming to understand that it may also be a congenital condition, a propensity to enlarge a perception such as to affect your memory and reasoning."

She looked at him carefully before continuing,

"There may be characters within you from birth, before the lightning strike."

Isaac looked up in disbelief.

"How complicated do you think I can be! It's a wonder I can walk the way you keep throwing jargon bombs at my feet!"

"I'm sorry you find this so distressing, but this is how cognitive psychology works, it's finding your path to wellness, caring for yourself, and in a modern sense, learning to love yourself!"

Dr Niesohn took a moment to write a note, giving Isaac some space.

"Where do we go from here?" he asked pensively.

"From the beginning," and went on to say, "your family background, early childhood, siblings, everyday experiences. Think through these formative influences."

She watched to check his reaction as to whether he had the mindset to process his early life in terms of his life now.

She continued.

"Begin here. Write notes or a diary of what comes to you. It will help you to move forward in understanding why you chose your career, and why you insisted you would not have children. It may help you come to a more empathetic view of how this affects your wife, Luteesha."

Isaac smarted.

"Whatever your background, proclivity or birthright, does not have to be an unchangeable outcome for you. There are mysteries deep within you, that only you can bring to light. I can guide you, but you need to give me the trigger points to elucidate what you are experiencing."

With that much said, Isaac moved to extricate himself from the couch that seemed to harbour the illusions, abuses, addictions, anti-social tendencies and every other disfunction woven into the fabric of 'the couch'.

He mumbled his courtesies and left the room, stopped by the reception desk, made an appointment for who knows when, and descended the grand staircase. He stopped briefly under the arched portico covering the front door, before descending the bluestone steps to the pillared gate, and out into the street.

Again, he paused, fixated on the treed medium strip that divided the roadway in front of him, and turned his gaze to the city skyscrapers.

Did he own the city of his birth, was it an embrace of a mother, or was it responsible for the making of his affliction?

More likely the cause he thought, could lie with the office workers that scurried below its buildings, the shoppers, the slow-moving students, were they to blame?

Did he really belong to this maze?

Still stunned by the session, Isaac looked up at the building he had just left. Medley Hall stood solid, a grey 1892 Victorian mansion, with a double height arcaded loggia perched above the street, and topped by a balustraded parapet, and a tall, weirdly overseeing central tower, replete with statues.

A building of substance, order and authority, the like of which was being shown to be missing in himself.

He walked northwards along Drummond Street, about a mile to his home in Macarthur Place. Long walks bothered him. Too much rhythm, too much time to mull over his troubles. He had grown thin and his ample head of hair was greying, his jacket loose.

He turned into his Macarthur Place address, feeling some comfort in the narrow plantation dividing the north and south frontages to the park.

Trees, and a living green carpet, a welcome sight.

The house, a modest, narrow two-storey Victorian terrace featuring cast iron columns, brackets and lacework supported the second-floor balcony and veranda roof. It was one of a pair joined wall to wall with its adjacent mirrored neighbour.

Above the roof line, a parapet supported two proud triangular pediments, one for each dwelling, separated by the party wall.

He fumbled the key, found the lock and entered the house, placed the keys on the sideboard in the hall, and onward to the kitchen. Without hesitation, he poured a glass of wine, saluted Bacchus, and waited for his wife to come home.

What to tell.

Isaac finished his drink, all the while staring out through the tall, narrow double hung window. The view to the side of the house was not a great deal better than the peeling paint of the window frame.

He had been on paid leave for six months, and had recently received notice that University of Melbourne was about to close his unit.

The front door opened and closed with the familiar clunk.

His wife put her bag and the mail on the sideboard, and hung her coat on the rack above.

One letter was an invitation to her nephew's twenty-first birthday celebration. It was addressed to her family name, Luteesha Veranova.

She had kept her surname for the powerful meanings that she cherished, those of invoking fascination, forgiveness and boldness, in addition to the characteristics of ambition, independence, strength, reliability, determination and professionalism.

Her life with her husband had needed much of the traits of forgiveness, strength and reliability.

She found Isaac seated at the kitchen table.

Seeing him subdued, she approached him and put her arms around his shoulders, and placed a kiss on his cheek, before taking to a chair opposite him.

"How was your session today?" feeling it was probably not the best way to start, and followed with,

"A reasonable day at the State Library today…um…a new guest speaker at the Village Roadshow Theatrette next month, might be of interest to you, we could go together."

"What's the subject?"

"How Amazon tribes deal with mosquitoes," hoping to spark him up a little.

Isaac looked up at her and replied,

"Maybe…1 need to talk through what happens now that the Uni has axed my program, indeed the whole unit.

"I am thinking of approaching Newman College for tutorial work. If I can't have my own research group, I can at least help indigenous nations and international students appreciate how the work I have done can improve the quality of daily life in their remote communities."

Without hesitation, Luteesha encouraged him,

"That could work, Isaac. I think that's a great idea. I can keep my Librarian work going for a few years yet, giving you more time to yourself.

"With all the student accommodation towers going up all over the city, there'd be no shortage of hours."

She thought about what she had just said, thinking, too much too quickly?

"I'm going upstairs to change my shoes, and I'll be right down. Can you have a glass ready for me?"

As she started up the stairs, she halted when Isaac called out, "Teesh…! thank you."

The next day, having made an appointment at the college, he made his way up Elgin Street, towards the university.

On this walk, Isaac thought through his wife's reaction to the advice his therapist had given him. She was supportive of the task of recounting of his early life, but cautioned it might stir up pain he had long suppressed.

In what felt like no time, he reached the intersection opposite Tin Alley. A tram trundled through the bend, blocking his view of the Redmond Barry building, a skinny, vertical tower, slaked in brickwork.

He crossed with the lights and proceeded north towards the residential colleges.

A continuous line of cars hugged the bluestone kerb. Elm trees towered above, gracing both sides of the road, at the end of which was a large roundabout with two tall ghost gums, and beyond, the Melbourne General Cemetery.

The walk past gardens fronting St Mary's College, and the imposing narrow, gothic-inspired Chapel of the Holy Spirit, presented a collegiate and peaceful otherness, and a strong sense of longevity.

Past the Chapel, Isaac found his way into the east residential arm of Newman College, whose motto 'Luceat Lux Vestra', 'Let your light shine', was also a wish that his mother used to bestow upon him when he was little. The sound of it in Latin had a familiarity that still nourished him.

He walked almost the entire length of the wide ramparted walls of the cloister towards the central domed dining hall, when Igor popped out of a room, followed by the thud of an unruly door swing.

"Igor!" shouted Isaac, surprising himself how spontaneously he had reacted to seeing him.

"Isaaaaac! How good to notice you," a common retort he enjoyed using.

"I just finished this tutorial with this undergraduate math student. You wouldn't believe it. A real worry for the future. He's reading quantum math theory, but keeps telling me that music is more his passion. Get this, throwing handfuls of gravel at a harp…it's all in the timing you see, so he says, and the distance. Apparently, it's the sound of spacetime.

"I told him to do more practical math – interplanetary trajectories, fly-bys, gravity assist, that sort of thing. Maybe it's his path to understanding String Theory. I don't know. At least he's paying me.

"Anyway, what are you doing here?"

"Same as you," replied Isaac, "a tutoring, mentorship role. I'm on my way to admin."

"Talk to Shevonne, Roula will give you nothing," advised Igor and continued,

"Oh, I saw your cousin Anton yesterday, what a coincidence. I saw him through the window in Arnold's Pool Hall, leaning on his cue, like a crutch. He had a coffee in his other hand, surveying the pool table like it was his livelihood."

"I've heard he needs a hip replacement," said Isaac.

"That explains everything, and I need to get on."

Igor swivelled and at the top of his voice called out, "Good luck with the tutor position!" By the time he finished talking, he was almost six steps away, his black graduate gown swinging in his own whirlwind. His echo was still trailing down the length of the squat, pleated concrete ceiling of the cloister, when Isaac mused,

"Ah, Igor. More words than a writer's festival."

He found his way to the office, sighted the front desk and thought, *I don't think that's Shevonne*, but asked for her in any case.

The lady behind the counter had straight blue-black hair, cropped squarely at her shoulder line. Black heavy-rimmed glasses stitched both sides of her hair across her 'don't bother me' demeanour-etched face.

This could only be the ill-advised Roula!

"I'm Isaac Moritz and I would like to speak with Shevonne please," Isaac said with a mix of confidence and caution.

"Shevonne is not in today. I'm Roula and you have me!" If omens had a voice, it would come from these lips. The ancient gods would be pleased with her.

"How can I possibly help you?" in a tone just as Igor forewarned.

Isaac summoned his most authoritative, no non-nonsense pitch.

"You have in this College, 220 undergraduate students and 80 postgraduate, 45 percent of whom are of international and indigenous origin resident at this college, half of which have suffered severe insect infestation in their own countries for extended periods in their lives.

"My expertise is entomology, specialising in hand-fly capture, a technique I developed, for arresting Musca Domestica, the multitudinous seriously annoying, disease-ridden housefly." Roula nervously batted one eyelid as Isaac continued,

"I would like an academic tutor and mentoring position that will enable them to apply my expertise in their homeland, as a community benefit program. They can carry this out, while still advancing their chosen careers."

Good point, he thought, and stopped short, sensing he would 'blow out' his presentation.

Roula stared at him the whole time, almost in disbelief, and after an understandable delay said quietly,

"Yes, I've heard of you, standing around the water-jug gossip column."

She paused and continued,

"Your program has been cancelled, what did you call it?"

"SNAP:ZAP Solutions," answered Isaac.

She continued,

"From what I have heard in your favour, is that you are a victim of your own success. The fly population in the state has indeed dwindled, and Melbourne's outdoor cafe culture owes much to your work."

Is it possible that Roula was some kind of kindred spirit, and in a somewhat aghast reaction to what she said next, he understood the connection?

"May Jupiter be with you, Isaac. Take this application form for a Tutorship Authority. Bring it back within two days and the position will be confirmed by the end of next week, after which you can circulate the Expression-of-Interest flyer."

Isaac floated out of the building, such as some oppressive guilt had been lifted off his being. This casual position would leave him with enough time to explore the origins of his condition.

At the age of sixty-three, he now felt secure enough to recount his story.

Luteesha was pleased for Isaac's sake, that he had attracted a number of students at the College.

It was close by, and presented some peaceful moments for him.

She in turn, applied for extra hours at the university in addition to the State Library position.

She approached the Baillieu Library, and the Brownless Biomedical and the Law libraries, all close to home and received offers from two of them.

The Baillieu offer was almost too good to be true.

Being the largest of the eleven branches of the university library, its highly regarded collections were central to research in the arts, humanities and social sciences, subjects with which she was experienced especially art in the Renaissance.

At the age of fifty-one, and coming relatively late to digital technology, she felt blessed to be able to keep up with the pace of change.

Twelve years junior to her husband, their marriage had its upheavals, but she understood the bonds, and the history of their relationship, one that had at first been nurturing, kind and loving, and respectful. In hardship, she remained committed to Isaac, and was not about to change.

They had lost close contact with their immediate families, both sides moving on, married into diverse, extended families. Children and grandchildren filled their everyday, sometimes leaving Luteesha in particular, feeling isolated.

His search for truth or at least some kind of certainty, as he put it, would undoubtedly stir the deep scars of his childhood. She had seen his perturbance, his confused state between the real and the nebulous in the streets ingrained with the characters that haunted him, when she accompanied him to Rome, the Eternal City.

Isaac set about to write. He cleared a space in the upstairs spare room large enough for a long table. He mounted a pinboard on the wall above to display notes he collected on scraps of paper. Books on the history of the Roman occupation of Palestine, the City of Rome and some references on the Latin language he thought might be useful, were spread and stacked across the table. The central location of his keyboard and screen looked a little like a stage set, but that would change with his delving into the unknown consequences of his life, in search of its true place in his life.

On the first page he wrote 2015.

He wrote initially in the first person and after finding it difficult to continue in such a personal framework, changed as if his oldest brother, Ignatius, was the teller of his story.

This disconnect suited him, a way to distance himself from the trauma of recollection, that it would be too visceral, too sickly to the pit of his stomach.

And from this delegation, the recollection began.

***

My first memories of conversation, are of our mother saying how she loved to read books beginning with the letter I.

I was sitting on the sofa with my brothers, Ignatius and Isaiah, and as she spoke in the dulcet tones of a loving mother, my gaze drifted to the mantlepiece above the fireplace.

There on the left of the shelf, the few books in the house were aligned upright so that only the backs of their covers could be seen. In the dim, dust-filled light of the sitting room, their colours barely discernible.

Dried-blood reds, drab greens, blue-greys and an aged yellow in no particular order, were held in place by stone bookends, black and polished in the form of opposing treble clefs.

An arched wooden clock stood in the centre, and a blue and white porcelain vase containing three strands of poa grass wrapped in spider web, completed the composition.

The ticking sound of the clock lulled me into distraction, and it was not until many years later that I realised that in starting her talk with I, she meant I, as in the person to whom the present is attached, and not I as in the first letter of the names she graced her progeny, and the gifts bestowed on them by their calling, and so deemed their inheritance.

In the family, names were essential in conveying the character, traits, inherited values and meanings that could be ascribed to a new-born.

Johanna, meaning God is gracious, had retained her family name by hyphen. Dalca, a Romanian name that means lightning, held the memory of a tragedy that befell her ancestors more than three hundred years past.

She went on to explain to her children, the given names of each, their specific virtues and the year of their birth.

To
Ignatius, the memory of martyrdom to Christ, born 1947.
Isaiah, salvation of God, born 1949.
Isaac, to whom is given laughter, born 1952.

I recall Isaac telling me what happened to him as a child, and it is of him that I now speak, to recount his life as seen through my witness.

The story of Isaac, the third son of Appius Moritz and Johanna Dalca-Moritz, is the story of the greatest flycatcher that ever was.

Chapter 2

The Cellar of Silent Pigs

The southeast corner of Australia where our earliest years were spent, is a region known for dry hot summers, devastating bushfires and sudden changes of weather. Heatwaves throughout the summer of 1956–7 had been more than usually changeable.

On such a scorching day, 1 was perched on a giant bough of the cypress tree, looking down at the head and shoulders of Isaac's singlet-covered little body. From up high I could just make out what he was doing. He rocked his body gently, back and forth as he pushed his hands beneath the soil in front of him.

His eyes followed the paths of his buried hands. As he moved them from side to side, the dry earth flowed over the back of his hands, falling between his fingers when he spread them apart.

Soft and powder-like, the pale brown dust tingled as it piled and spilled over the edge of his hands.

In his play, Isaac conjured unanswerable questions. Why does the soil fall at my will? Could it be that in silence is a place? Through his palms he could feel the cool earth below the surface. As he searched the damp, he varied his motions, exploring order and randomness.

Patterned swirls fell like designs, intentions and revelations. In the circles he saw the correctness of the day, the story of the sixth day of January, the twelfth after Christmas, and the revelation of Jesus as the Christ to the Gentiles, by the persons of the Magi at Bethlehem.

When the circles fanned out and descended into serpentine swales, Isaac mused as to which of the gods the faces manifest belonged. At his choosing, Isaac would allow his fingers to break through the surface as if to clean the slate, before delving once more into the cool below. Even as he watched the features disperse, he remained expectant of new forms that might emerge. What new mythology this time?

The deeper he pushed and scraped below the surface, the cooler he felt, and the deeper he thought about the world.

High in the branches above us, distressed birds rested, wings raised clear of their panting bodies. The guard dog sat, chained at the base of the tree, just marking time. His tongue bounced in parallel with the rapid beat of its breathing, periodically disappearing into his snout to be wetted again. His eyes stayed closed, even when his ears pricked in reaction to some unseen disturbance or whiff of scent. A snake lay curled under discarded sheets of iron not five yards away. Skinks scampered warily around the dog, looking for an injured fly that might have fallen from the snapping of its mouth. The hundreds of flies sheltered beneath the tree also annoyed Isaac, and when a fly stuck close to his eye or the corner of his mouth, Isaac would shake his head or spit air.

The distant sound of an engine reverberated in the hot stillness, shaking Isaac from his thoughts. He scrambled to his feet calling out to his mother,

"Mater! Mater!"

As he scampered from the shade and into the sunlight to look from where the sound came, Isaac disturbed the flies that had settled on his back. The dog stupidly jumped after him until the chain around its neck yanked and he succumbed with a whimper. When his bare feet stepped onto the sun-baked earth, Isaac retreated into the shade. He looked again to the bushland above the creek where he spotted a flicker of reflected sunlight, moving through the bushland.

Most of the flies had regrouped on his back. One still circling wide to the front of Isaac, headed towards him. His right arm lashed out, and with the flick of his wrist, struck the fly squarely on the head with the nail of his middle finger. The impact crushed both compound eyes, forcing the stem of its neck to pierce the body, rendering the fly stiff-solid, and lifeless. The fly's proboscis was reduced to a short, ridiculous trumpet.

The crush jammed the wings at right angles to its compressed body, hurling the fly backwards into the burning red dirt.

It was the cleanest of kills.

Satisfied the fly was dead, Isaac looked over the crops of loganberry, tomato and strawberry to the eucalypt trees rising out of the creek bed. His father's slow-moving truck was now visible through the undergrowth. The hill immediately behind it was dotted with crop pickers, stooped over rows of strawberry bushes. From this distance they appeared to barely move.

This was a working landscape, punctuated by the noise of animals and mechanical things. Isaac would close his eyes and allow his mind's ear to listen and imagine what might be said of them. The warning bark of dogs cut across his sense of peace, while the guttural sounds of disgruntled pigs amused him. The crowing of the rooster was at odds with the conversational clucking of hens, which contrasted with the mournful bellow of the cow. The sound of people calling out, ranging from greetings, instruction, cussing, demanding, and the occasional shrill of whistle carried far across the fields, regardless to whom or what they were directed.

Like an undercurrent in a rural symphony, the buzz of blowflies and the higher pitched zizzer of houseflies droned on incessantly.

At the top of the hill, a row of pine trees lining the ridge formed a windrow, planted long ago to thwart the strong gusts of wind. Isaac focused on them, the brightness of the day forcing him to squint. His mother described them as a sentinel, but he sensed something more, beyond the comfort she hoped he would gain from their protective presence. There custodial quality came at the price of vulnerability, which instilled in him an empathy that stemmed from their immobility. Even though they were fixed and unable to move, he nonetheless absorbed their strength.

A clunked gear change followed by the rattle and prattle of chains drew Isaac's attention back to the truck. He could see people riding on the caged tray of the truck.

This was the latest group of immigrants to arrive from the 'terra mater', the Latin name the family called their motherland. Ever since Isaac could remember, people came from that faraway place. Their arrivals and settlement on his family's farm were a part of his everyday life.

As with others who had come before them, they were to be specially treated to a banquet. This was to be their day. Some of them would remember this year of their arrival, by the age Isaac was on this momentous day, just shy of his fifth birthday.

From this year on, in the comfort of their kindred, their dreams and aspirations would take a confident outlook, the passage of time would temper their doubts, anxieties and loss.

This is how Isaac heard the silent voices of the faces in the distance. As they rounded the bend of the road, sunlight glistened off the sweet pepper and snow pea crops that covered the rich, red soil that lay beneath them. He watched the truck until it disappeared behind the Postmaster's cottage. It would only be a minute before they arrived, and in waiting, Isaac turned his attention to the pigsty perched on the edge of the escarpment above the creek.

The structure was so shaky that it would have taken no more than two large, terse pigs backing in unison for it to collapse. A strong north wind could carry the stench of the sty all the way over the loganberry patch, to the sheds and yard behind the house. When a steaming drum of food was brought down to the sty, he would climb the wooden pen and watch the way the pigs swished, grunted and bumped their way in and around the trough, drooling for the warm stew of boiled acorn and potato.

It was this way with living things, having no understanding of the passage of time, that made Isaac apprehensive. The idea of simple replacement of life without ambition made him restless.

The truck revved hard as it turned left from Beenak Road into Queens Road. In a short distance, it veered into the narrow track and down beside the house, making its way around the corner behind the implement shed. Above the noise of the engine and the squeal of the brakes, Isaac could make out excited voices, that became more subdued as the truck came to a stop in front of him.

The dog barked and yelped as the chain tightened around his neck as he flung forward on his hind legs. The hens scurried as if stricken, and the cloud of dust raised enveloped the boy, clinging to his hair and sweaty skin. He exhaled involuntarily, keeping his breathing to a minimum until the dust settled, then looked up at their faces as they eyed him. The chatter started again as the shade cast by the trees provided relief from the heat and harsh sunlight. Behind the guard rails he could see that their bodies were heavily dressed, looking like unshorn sheep in the heat, and then remembered that it had something to do with winter on the other side of the world. He watched how their heads held still while their bodies shook beneath them before his father killed the engine.

His father, Appius, and his uncle Cato flung the cabin doors open and jumped clear of the vehicle. In a one-two order, they slammed the doors shut, with the sound of certainty and finality that only metal on metal could utter. Whether it was the dust or the heat, his father ignored Isaac, and made his way to the rear of the truck to undo the tailgate. The brothers helped the tired and tried newcomers disembark and helped them lift the luggage off the tray deck of the truck.

As he watched the group sorting their belongings, Isaac's mother touched him on the back of his head, stopping a moment by his side before moving forward to greet the new families. Johanna had a natural sincerity about her, and her welcome was well received.

Isaac watched in what now had become his manner, thoughtfully and without shyness. When the attention was finally turned to him, he was lifted up, beamed at, passed around and prodded with what seemed to him to be an inglorious affection.

Not all of them were so forward, being shy with the newness of their predicament, and if pushed for conversation, a soft-spoken hello and a comment on the heat was all they could manage.

After a short introduction, the group made their way to the nearby shed. It had been cleared out and divided by flimsy partitions and fitted with beds and double height bunks. The windowless interior was cramped and hot. The front and back doors of the shed were left open to catch a breeze. They agreed among them to wait until the cool of the evening to unpack, and were shown to the washroom to refresh.

His grandfather, Ezekiel, was the patriarch of the extended family that were now gathering in Australia. He often talked of letters of assurance and sponsorship papers that would bring more of them from the old country. He had left the Romanian homeland during the nineteen twenties, and when he earned enough money to send for them, he brought his immediate family to the new country ten years later, during the economic stagnation of the great depression, and as fortune would have it, before the start of Second World War catastrophe. It was not until the 1950s that the majority of their community could secure their passage to Australia.

Isaac listened intently to stories of ocean voyages, on ships as long as paddocks, and was captivated by their experiences of war, and the abdication of King Michael of Romania which followed.

Here, at the bottom of the world, Isaac's people found themselves between an old way of life and a new unknown, full of hope for something better. The truck that transported them from the Port of Melbourne and across a city, larger than they had ever seen, also carried with it their dignity and their desire for freedom. This assurance of a better life on this day of arrival, was all they had for now, and all they needed.

Isaac's grandfather had decreed that a banquet and a day of reverence would be held to celebrate this momentous day, in praise and thanksgiving to Saint Adjutor, for the safe delivery of their friends and relatives.

This occasion was to be openly joyous, counter to the hardship of dispossession, when they would become withdrawn and insular. It was through sharing food in abundance that their joy in living was best celebrated. It was a community comfortable with hard work, strong sense of duty, and a long memory of their venerable ancestors.

The midday lunch, that was now the welcome banquet, had been held over, pending their arrival. The women in the kitchen were well into their preparations. Trays of chicken, pork and vegetables were stacked in ovens, the girls at the kitchen table shelled broad beans, peeled peas and boiled eggs, sliced ham off the bone, and laid out cheese and bread on wooden boards. Ready to be taken out to the table were grilled mince-meat rolls, polenta, cabbage rolls, beef tripe soup, pomana porclui, a favourite honouring the pig, sweet bread, salad greens, Jerusalem artichokes, broad beans, asparagus, fruits including water melon, honey-dew melon, strawberries and plums, and lemon and pepper avocado. Sweets included cheese doughnuts, placinta cu ciocolata and a special Joffre cake. Espresso coffee pots, and home-made fennel anise-flavoured grappa, tobacco pouches and rolling cigarette paper were ready to bring to the table, at the end of the banquet.

Wine would be tapped from the cellar by Lazarus, as he was regarded as best and most passionate, when it came to wine making. He could sit for two hours, crouched in the darkness of the cellar, with his ear pressed against each barrel, in turn listening to the hiss of fermentation. The long table in the courtyard had already been extended to accommodate forty-five people. Tablecloths, plates, cutlery, linen napkins, tumbler glasses, and extra bench seats were laid out.

As the workers returned from the fields, Isaac strolled back into the yard to watch them stow their tools, remove the square cornered handkerchiefs they kept wetted to keep cool in the sun, and hose down their heads. It looked like some sort of courtship ritual. When they finished, they walked up the brick pathway towards the opening into the courtyard. With a grinning war cry, Valerius lunged at Isaac, hoisting him high above his head and holding him there until they neared the washroom doorway, all the while coaxing Isaac to come and work in the fields.

"By the love of Jesus, Isaac, your hands *are* dirty! Have you already been working in the fields?" When Isaac finally struggled to the ground Valerius demanded,

"Isaac! Come in and learn to wash like a man!" dragging Isaac inside.

The long rectangular room was abuzz with men washing and changing. The chaotic chatter resounded loudly in the narrow oblong space. The walls and ceiling surfaces of the room, lined with unpainted cement sheets, looked flat and dull.

A single light bulb covered in black fly spots was the only adornment. Isaac's roving gaze had now dropped to the wet timber floor, which was already showing signs of wet rot, and then looked up past the men to the end of the room, where a single dust covered louvre-paned window provided the only natural light. Even without hot water the room was humid. The smell of body odour lingered in this dank space.

High up on one side of the room, fresh singlets, shirts and a bag of socks hung on a line of hooks screwed to a plank nailed to the wall. Below, on two long bench seats sat abluted men, busily dressing. Two wicker baskets on the floor, one for fresh underwear and socks and the other for soiled clothes headed to the wash house.

Valerius and Isaac made their way to the opposite wall to jostle for a position at one of the two bathtubs on the other side of the room. The cast iron tubs that were used as sinks, were rusted where enamel paint had lifted.

They had been stood on timber blocks high enough for them to be used without crouching. Four taps, crudely fitted to a rusting galvanised pipe were all flowing. Men vigorously soaped their hairy arms and chests, slapped foamy water around their necks, and swished into their ears, before lowering their heads under the taps, rubbing the dirt laden soap into the falling water. A slippery timber shelf held cakes of unperfumed soap fat, and above it, a crazed pattern of broken mirrors, covered in a layer of smoke and grime, hung off the wall. The soap shelf also held chipped porcelain mugs containing shaving brushes, razors and combs, their use adding a tinkling sound to the din. Towel hooks and leather shaving strops hanging between, and at each end of the tubs provided a symmetrical order to the room.

Isaac stepped onto an upturned banana box that Valerius had found in the far corner of the washroom, and stretched his hands out under the tap while Valerius reached for a cake of soap.

"Isaac, you have to wash like this! Splash your face, neck and hair first – I'll do that for you. Rub your hands around the soap and then slap it onto your face with your hands…and splash it all off. Keep your eyes closed until the soap has gone, otherwise it will sting. Soap up again and slide over your arms and front and back of your neck and dive into the tub as far down as you can," dunking Isaac's head into the tub under the tap and pulling him out by the hair.

"More soap…and stick your fingers into your right ear and then go around it twice, like this, watch me. And now the other ear. See! If you had three ears and you went round twice, that would be six times."

Isaac watched the wrist action around the ear. When the routine was done, Isaac and others around him were refreshed and drenched. A few of the workers chose not to use towels, preferring to cool off by the evaporation of moisture from their skin. The slow, focused combing of the hair completed the routine.

The place at the tub vacated by Valerius and Isaac, was soon taken by others to perform their ablutions before the broken shards of mirror. Their reflections were dimmed as much by the tarnished silvering that had lifted from the glass as from the sombre light within the room. The reflections of the varied faces told of ancient times, so direct and unadulterated had their lineage been.

Scipio still bore the same full-headed fleshy features of the statue of his namesake. Abraham looked just like Abraham, Tiberius always looked the part and at least once in every second or third generation of the family, an oddity in the form of Little Quincunx would be produced. He was barely five feet high, with short chubby arms, legs and torso, and almost no neck. It was he who made the observation during one wash-up, that the cracks in the mirror held the memories of what it has seen, a comment that impressed many who thought him incapable of any such deep thought.

The washroom block formed one side of a long rectangular courtyard. At one end stood the original cream-painted timber weatherboard house. A long dormitory wing with a number of bunk rooms closed the long side of the courtyard opposite the washroom block. At the far end of the court yard, forming the fourth side of the rectangle were a group of three small, single room buildings, set behind a path that led left down to the yard, sheds and outbuildings, and a path to the right, leading upwards to the road frontage of the property. Like the washroom block, these building were clad in asbestos cement sheets with corrugated iron roofing.

The yard between the front veranda of the house and the road was planted with a small crop of tall sunflower plants. Rose bushes lined the opposite side of the path leading to the front gate.

The first room on the lower side, served as the clothes wash-house that housed two wood-fired copper tubs, and behind a canvas screen, was a hidden distillery. On the side of this room, a low- slung roof covered piles of fire wood and empty bottles. Nearby, cables strung between timber posts served as clothes-drying lines.

Closely abutting, the middle building was the smokehouse where meats and fish were prepared for curing. It was also used to the make tomato sauce, sausages, soap, jams and other commodities.

The third room stored flour, rice, coffee beans, olive oil, bags of salt, pepper and sugar, eggs and noodles. Spices, strings of sausages, filleted dried fish, and legs of pork for long term curing, hung from hooks screwed to the rafter. A board was nailed to the bottom of the door to keep out mice and snakes.

A canopy of green and yellow vine leaves, laden with bunches of grapes, trained along wire strands, spanned the shorter distance across the courtyard, shaded the long table below.

The name the family gave this central courtyard was 'the Forum'.

The name reminded them of their long journey from their beginnings in Latium, to the Middle East, to Romania, and now Terminus, the God of Boundaries, had brought them here, to this place at the end of the world.

The forum was the centre of summer life where, like a stage, people could enter and exit through the gaps between the buildings. The floor was paved in concrete, stained with the red hue of the surrounding soil. Mud grates and shoe horns were scattered all around the farmhouse. In the dry, the dust blown by north winds set off a frenetic round of window and door closing.

The time had come! Many were already seated and in high spirits, taunting the children, and curious about what formalities Ezekiel had in store.

Food platters from the kitchen were brought out and placed across the length of the table. The aromas of salt encrusted dried fish, roasted pork and chicken, beef rolls, eggplant and boiled eggs, floated into the air. Flies sheltering in the vine leaves above became active, and they would soon be joined by the larger blowflies from the orchard.

The last of the tanned men wearing their fresh white singlets left the washroom and took a seat at the table. As he came out, Lazarus called out to Isaac to follow him to the cellar. Isaac caught up with him under the large roof of the implement shed attached to the rear of the house. Its roof had been pitched to cover the large area that extended from the back of the house to the base of the cypress trees. This space was used to shelter the trailer, grape press and other bits of farm gear. The wall of the house was elevated above the ground high enough to cut out a low doorway that accessed the cellar.

As Lazarus squatted to pull on the short, wooden door, Isaac looked into vertical slats of the wine press standing beside him. Mashed blackened stalks still clotted the grooves between the slats. At the top of the rotund apparatus was a tall metal screw topped by turning handles which when rotated lowered the metal pressing plate. He loved to watch the grape juice squeeze out of the sides. The glee on the faces of the men loading the press with a new batch of grenache grapes, and turning the screw to make wine for the next year, was infectious.

After opening the cellar door Lazarus flicked the light switch and descended three tall steps to the cellar floor. It was his job to fetch the wine from the cellar and he wanted Isaac to carry at least one carafe to the table. The small boy carefully descended the steps to the dirt floor and looked around the dimly lit space. The clear height was too low for a man to stand properly. Iron beams replaced the original stumps that supported the timber floor of the kitchen, allowing the earth to be removed to form the cellar. Two rows of French oak wine barrels fitted tightly into available width. Lazarus was crouched by the third barrel on the right. Next to him were two large empty demijohns and a small carafe.

The row to the left contained the new seasons venerated juice, in early stages of fermentation. The round heads of the barrels were fitted with tap fonts. The tops of the barrels had one hole in the centre, plugged with cloth covered rubber bungs.

While a large demijohn was being filled, Lazarus turned behind him and pulled a bung out of one of the fermenting barrels. He raised his voice loud enough to be heard over the pissing sound of wine falling into the container.

"Sometimes we have to remove the stoppers at the top of the barrels, Isaac." And after relieving himself from the discomfort of crouching continued,

"To let the build-up of gasses and froth from the fermentation process…out…so that the wine can become clear."

Isaac looked at the stains on the sides of the barrels left by the trail of seething ferment, oozing down the sides of their rotund bellies. The acrid smell that arose from beneath the barrels was the cause of the pungent smell that confronted Isaac at the entrance to the cellar.

When the two large containers were filled, Lazarus filled the small carafe for Isaac to carry to the table. The boy climbed the steps and crawled out. Laz handed him the carafe. As Lazarus hoisted the demijohns and ascended, Isaac peered into the cellar before the door was closed, and saw how the soiled and much-loved barrels with their steel hoops and small snouts, mounted as they were on wooden blocks, looked like rows of silent pigs.

By the time they returned to the banquet table, there were only two places left on the narrow benches. Amid the din, from somewhere in the middle of the table, Obilius scolded,

"By the patience of Job, Laz, where have you been? We're dying of abstinence. We've had nothing but water to drink!"

The sharp tinkling sound of a spoon on glass rang out across the banter, as the red and gold caped figure at the head of the table rose. The ebullience eased into a quiet observance.

The stout, bearded figure of an ageing Ezekiel, patriarch of the family, paused to survey the scene before him. He brought his hands together to sit on top of his belly, and began to speak:

"I see here before me a happy free place…and a good many of our number, such that it warrants me to pronounce that our people should consider itself transposed to this new homeland of Australia.

"This is a land in which we shall do well, even though 1 fear our heritage may dissipate, and its rectitude and culture eventually, may be lost. I am embattled by this possibility…for we are a special people.

"However, this is a safe haven for us and we should rejoice what this moment brings to us.

"It is at this decisive point, when we pledge our future to this new place…that we should be reminded about who we are, and how we came to be…"

Grand Uncle Felix coughed a polite interjection, and Ezekiel chose not to pursue their history at this time.

"I will begin this rarest of sacred ceremonies for this conclusive day."

The gathering murmured. Like the others seated at the table, Isaac was entranced by his grandfather's decree. The bounty on the table added weight to his decision about the rightness of this new country for their people. It all fitted, and Isaac felt assured.

As the murmur subsided, Ezekiel's head tilted downward to the red velvet veil poised on the table before him. He solemnly removed the cloth covering a wooden box, handing it carefully to Grand Uncle Felix seated to his side. The significance of this observance captivated the onlookers.

Ezekiel placed his hands on the sides of a small wooden box and in a forceful way, raised it for all to see. Without delay he fervently announced,

"Before our God of Boundaries Terminus, I raise this tabernacle of shittah shittah wood, that it may this very day grace our table."

As his breath vented, the old man leaned forward and pursed his lips. The bowing of his head brought a sanctity to the soul of everyone present. It was as though the table had become the tabernacle, and all seated there became its part.

After setting it down gently, he lifted the lid of the humble box and removed a cylindrical silver pyxis. The top of the round container was sculpted with hunting scenes representing Mithras in the role of pursuer of death and evil. A rattle from within the box could be heard as Ezekiel, shaking with religious fervour, chanted its meaning to those gathered before him.

"Mithras, God of Light and Truth, opponent of darkness and evil, has protected us, and we acknowledge him! Mithras has protected us, to whom we now give our mortal thanks."

The gathered repeated this prayer and on hearing the response, Ezekiel raised the lid of the pyxis. Choosing carefully, the old man removed the first of seven Roman coins. He held it between the thumb and index finger of both hands, and he raised it for all to see. His voice was now deliberate and hypnotic.

"This is the first coin of our inheritance, the silver coin of the consul Sulla.

"A tyrant among our people, his proscriptions included, the killing with impunity of opposing political opinion.

"We learn from Sulla that we must accept what we might regard as dangerous to a conquering side, excepting, that by the cautious and patient pooling of considered opinions, we can reach agreement!"

Ezekiel returned the coin to its place and then lifted a second coin hoisting it aloft in the prescribed manner.

"This second silver coin belongs to Julius Caesar.

"It is marked by his wearing of a laurel wreath and bearing the inscription CAESAR DICT PERPETVO.

"The lessons of the first Triumvirate of Caesar, Pompei and Crassos should not be lost to us."

By now Ezekiel was becoming breathless, but vowed to continue.

The younger members of the family were becoming agitated. Too young to understand the lessons, they turned to their elders, beseeching that they be made clear to them.

The third coin was made of gold. It bore the portrait of Pompei whose alliance with the Senate resulted in a civil war against Julius Caesar. It took Caesar four bloodletting years to crush the senatorial rebellion, leaving him the sole ruler of the Roman Empire.

"This coin reminds us that Caesar's great succession lasted only one year, before he was assassinated by the group of senators led by his adopted beloved son, Brutus.

"The lesson, our struggles for supremacy may be short lived more than we might wish."

The fourth coin to be held aloft was a bronze coin showing the head of Cicero's only son, who bore a striking resemblance to the great man himself.

Ezekiel beamed.

"Let us forever uphold the ideals, honesty and integrity of Cicero. His achievements stemmed solely from his understanding of truth, merit and ability."

As nature would have it, some among the gathered were beginning to question the value of the wisdom they were witnessing. In terms of more than lessons, the food they longed for was getting cold.

The silver coin celebrating the capture of Egypt by Octavian was the fifth coin and depicted a crocodile, the symbol of Egypt.

The sixth Roman coin, made of silver and showed the sella curulis, the official chair of Roman magistrates. The Fasces and Secures depicted the rule of law.

Ezekiel was now being assisted by Grand Uncle Felix. He handed Ezekiel the seventh and last coin in their possession.

"This seventh coin of the Emperor Antoninus Pius is gold!" emphasised Ezekiel.

"It is inscribed to Iovi Statori, 'to Jupiter Stator'.

"The God is holding a sceptre in his left hand and in his right hand he holds a thunderbolt!"

The shrill of his last word raced in the hearts of many, including Isaac.

Ezekiel's hands shuddered as he passed the last coin to Felix who placed it reverently into the silver pyxis. He then raised his head and in a strong voice, he made his declaration.

"The Seven Coins of our ancestor's legacy and the Seven Hills of ancient Rome, are today joined by the addition of the Seven Seas. We celebrate this union of sevens for the first time in our history. The passage over the Seas has brought us to this new land, the Terra Firma of our promise.

"The duty has fallen to me, to provide for the safe and complete transition of our people, and our heritage to this new homeland."

The group felt for Ezekiel and the great burden visited upon him. And each quietly reflected on their own responsibilities to observe their traditions and values.

Ezekiel paused in preparation for the welcome part of this ceremony while Grand Uncle Felix repacked the heirlooms of their history.

"This special banquet given to us by the Lord and prepared for us by Rebekah, Nola and Zama, is in honour of our being reunited with more of our family and friends."

A spontaneous cheer of thanksgiving gave Ezekiel a moment.

Ezekiel continued,

"From our homeland of Dacia in Romania have arrived this day in the year 1956 Anno Domini of the Common Era…" he paused, trying to put names to the faces of the people who had just arrived.

He started with those he recognised most readily, from his sister's family.

"The son of my youngest sister, Decius, who I understand has grown much like his namesake, a great and true patriot. And his wife, Sarah, and their three children, Martius, Maius and December."

A clapping of acceptance gave Ezekiel more time to remember the others.

"Also, we have with us today my cousin Regulus, who so much like our forebears is a man of honour, and with him his wife, Octavia, and their two children, Octavius and Miryam.

"The others are distant relatives and have come without their families."

It was common for the men to precede their families, to first find work and to raise enough money to call for them. For some their re-union came after years of separation.

Ezekiel continued to announce them,

"Amaziah, grandson of Quintus Fabius Maximus.

"Marcus Tullius, the son of Seneca and Leah Tacitus, and his sisters Romula and Rema, eldest daughters of Judah and Azariah.

"And finally, Quintus Sulla and his young wife, Ameria.

"A blessed welcome to you all."

"We also give thanks to our beloved gods Ceres and Diana for our bountiful meal, and I now proclaim the land that produced it to be home to our people!"

Isaac sat silently throughout the ceremony and barely moved even after the banquet had started.

He had been transfixed by the mention of the homeland Dacia, the old country he had never seen. Where did that leave him? On pondering this question his mind cast back to the barrels in the cellar that looked like silent pigs. The cellar of silent pigs. What did this mean, and what did it have to do with him or how he fitted into his family?

The image of how it looked would remain with him, and he would come to know it as a metaphor for the subsistence life of his forbears, from which he would grow to make his place in the world.

While Isaac dwelled in his moment of questioning, all that mattered to the assembled around the table was food, wine and fellowship.

Beneath the vine canopy they were each and every one grandparents, mothers, fathers, uncles, aunts, brothers, sisters and cousins, and they were earthy real. In this new land, trial, tribulation and ambition would test their resolve. For the restless, impatience was a virtue. For the contented, impatience was a nuisance. For the simple, life was artless and the tabernacle of food was everything to live for.

As the meal progressed, the clamour heightened. Some of the kids took their food on a run around the table like Indians circling wagons in the Wild West, cupping their mouths to produce bloodcurdling cries. Two small whining dogs that circled the table were either lucky to be given scraps, or scolded. Nervous kittens darted in and out from under the dormitory. These creatures were mostly tolerated. Flies circling, resting, circling and resting, being swiped off, were not. Unlike dogs that could be shown their place by repeated beating, flies just vanished into the leaf canopy above, returning again and again, clinging to the sides of bowls, crawling over platters of food and swimming on the surfaces of wine and olive oil. During the meal, no less than two flies were inhaled and at least five were eaten, causing considerable distress and sobering trauma for the afflicted, generating raucous laughter among those spared. The lack of empathy was a sad digression from the unity sermon they had just received.

When they could eat no more nor drink another drop, those among the women who could, began to clear the table. Orbilius collapsed onto the plate in front of him and could not move. Quintus, followed by Sextus, began the retreat to the dorms as sure as six follows five, and progressively all excised themselves from the table and headed for the oblivion of the sexta hora, the siesta.

Except for the snapping snout of one lone dog, the flies were now free to sup on the soiled table cloth. An average dozen at a time rested unchallenged, on the back of Orbilius's singlet. The heat-soaked sound of the blowflies lessened as they returned to the orchard.

In the late afternoon, the workers whose tasks were to rotate water pipes and stack boxes into the truck for delivery to market, stirred from their nap. The women who worked through the afternoon, washed, dried and stored away all the utensils used for the banquet. It was also an opportunity for the newly arrived Romula and Ameria to get to know their hosts while helping in the kitchen. When finished, they sat down to talk through their roles on the farm, and on this special occasion drink tea rather than coffee, after which they would prepare a light supper.

The evening was warm and still, and in the dying light, the air filled with the scent of eucalyptus, and pinging sound of bellbirds.

Men trudged into the fields to rotate the sprinkler pipes from one crop to another. The lightweight pipes made hollow, clanging sounds as they were carried and placed in different rows, a sound reminiscent of the way church bells pealed in medieval villages.

By the time the last of the pipes had been clamped and positioned, two men carrying torches descended into bushy escarpment on their way down to Wild Dog Creek, the official name no-one on the farm knew, it was just 'the creek'. They brushed aside bracken and ferns along the water's edge near the small pump shed. Nocturnal animals caught in the torchlight would freeze if the bearer so wanted. Bush rats, possums, and the living colours of orange, green and yellow of the frogs, were revealed by torchlight in a way nature had not intended.

By contrast, the small iron shed housing the pump was distinctly unnatural. Its metallic noise and scents of gasoline fumes labelled it man-made. In complete subservience to its maker, the machinery fired into action, pumping water up to the relocated pipes.

The whisper of artificial rain, spraying over crops could be heard from the farmhouse, and the soft beat of the pump muted the sound of croaking frogs and cicada.

The night sky had about it an affluent suspension, giving the impression that it did not want to let go of the day.

After midnight, Abraham and Tiberius checked the truck for any loose stacking, closed the tailgate and headed off for the three-hour drive to the city market. Before dawn, Ezekiel got up from his bed and walked the dormitories and bedrooms like a jail keeper, banging doors and rattling bedrails. His wife, Rebekah, went to the kitchen, the place made hers by gender.

After lighting the wood-fired stove, she screwed together several coffee pots with a carpe-diem grip and placed them on the wanning combustion stove. She loved the smell of freshly ground coffee, and the aroma of it expressing, whetted her appetite. As always, she laid out cups for the men returning from their wake-up wash. Alongside bowls of white sugar and a pile of tarnished teaspoons, Rebekah placed bottles of the homemade distilled spirits to put in the coffee. Breakfast would be at least two hours away and it was essential for them to do as much work as possible, before heat of the day forced them to retire from the fields.

Isaac woke up resolved to spend the day working the crops beside the workers. After breakfast he walked to the tomato crop and there at the end of a row, found a small box. A group of pickers had already worked their way through six rows of plants. They worked in an orderly manner ensuring nothing marketable would be left behind. Isaac selected his own row and began picking tomatoes, placing each one with great care into a timber box. He worked from one plant to the next, being careful not to overlook any fruit ready for picking, and leaving those too ripe or too green. As the box filled, it got the harder to drag along the aisle.

He worked methodically, unaware of the banter and songs sung by those around him. Within the space of his own thoughts, he had no need of others to fill every moment, or every void of his mind. In this space, was his element, and it pleased him.

He sat back on his heels and looked back to a group of pickers converging on him. The work of picking from low bushes was done by kneeling, leaving the hands free to sift through the foliage. Isaac noticed a curious thing about the way Blind Joe was working closely alongside Juliette. After every bush was picked, Blind Joe would help Juliette move towards the next bush by placing his hand on her bottom. Each time he did this, she responded by slapping him on the ear. When this wasn't happening, Joe often had his hand in his pants.

Isaac heard the scraping sound of a case being dragged beside him and turning asked Lazarus,

"Why do they call Joe, Blind Joe? He can see, can't he?"

Lazarus wiped the sweat from his brow and sidestepping the question explained,

"Blind Joe cannot tell the difference between red and green tomatoes, or anything red and green.

"You could say he is colour blind." And seeing how much Isaac had picked, said, "That's great, Isaac! You're doing very well!"

"I'm not very fast," admitted Isaac.

"Remember, Isaac, as Emperor Augustus was so fond of saying, Festina Lente, make haste slowly. Blind Joe doesn't understand that and is all the poorer for it."

"I think I understand," thanked Isaac. Lazarus moved forward to the next bush. The flies converged onto the back of his sweaty, white shirt the moment he stopped moving to fondle the next plant.

Isaac spat at a fly that came too close to his mouth just as Little Quincunx pulled up beside him in the adjacent row. Little Quincunx with the unfortunate squat, pudgy figure that gave rise to his name was thirty-two years old and only a foot higher than Isaac.

"The flies are bad today," puffed Little Quin as a clod of earth thrown by Scipio broke up against his backside, taking Isaac by surprise.

"All 1 can say after that is," mouthed Quincunx, his cupped fingers tapping his chest, "mens sana in corpore sano – a sound mind in a sound body," and winked at Isaac suggesting Scipio's persona wasn't. Quin removed the handkerchief from his head, wetted it with water from a bottle he carried in a sling, and retied it before moving on.

So fond of clods was Scipio, that when the doctor came to visit the farm to advise on the dangers of having an impacted bowel from over-eating, he picked up a clod, pulled the doctor's trouser forward and tucked it behind his belt. The doctor flinched, but Scipio restrained his hand from removing it and said,

"Watch me."

He picked up another clod of dry earth and tucked it behind his own belt, and moved over to the tractor.

He started it and drove the noisy, shaky beast to a patch that needed ploughing. The doctor, wary of causing offense, ignored the discomfort lodged in his well-pressed trousers.

When Scipio finished ploughing, he drove back, climbed down from the tractor, and went straight for the doctor's belt and pulled out the clod.

"See, your lump is still here!" He then pulled his belt forward and said,

"See! My clod has gone…that's why I eat plenty!" gesticulating heartily.

Nearing lunchtime, the workers close enough to the packing yard carried their cases. Those who worked further away, placed them on the nearby trailer, that would later be picked up by the tractor.

Isaac struggled to drag his box, stopping many times, insisting on delivering 'his' box all the way to the yard. Valerius came back from the yard, picked Isaac up and the box.

A section of the yard was kept clear for sorting cases of tomatoes, peppers and carrots, in an order that made best use of the truck floor. Hessian bags filled with potatoes, peas and beans were piled against the cypress trunks. Late at night they would be loaded onto the truck for transport to the market. The soft fruits were packed on the forum table, the same one used for meals.

On return, Valerius put Isaac and the box down. The boy placed his hands on the back of the box and pushed it to where Decius was working. It was his job to sort the order in which the cases and bags were stacked onto the truck. Decius congratulated and thanked Isaac, picked up the box of tomatoes, and lifted it directly onto the truck for him to see. Feeling pleased with himself, he headed towards the kitchen for a drink of lemonade, drank it as fast as the fizz allowed, and banged the glass onto the kitchen bench, before running outside, and through the gap between the house and the washroom, before coming to an abrupt halt.

A gleaming new Holden sedan was parked in the yard. The seductive lines of the vehicle and the glow of its clean, black paint, captivated Isaac. Its very newness was stimulating. The driver's door opened, and a tall man stood up, reached for his suit coat from the back seat, swivelled it on, donned his hat and closed the door. Isaac didn't see that his mother was standing nearby, so taken was he by this unusual event.

As the man took a few confident strides towards her, Isaac's expression turned from being totally absorbed to concerned, and he retreated further into the shade, hoping not to be seen.

On approaching her, he announced,

"Hello, my name is Stewart Parker from the Ministry of Education, would you be Mrs Moritz?"

"Yes, Mister Parker, we received your letter last week," responded Johanna nervously.

"Very good then, you know it is time for your son, Isaac, to attend the nearest State School or a school of your choice. I am here to confirm that transport can be arranged from where you live, so that he can attend school without disruption."

His delivery was by now so routine that he had time to observe her bearing, and her figure. He was taken by her olive complexion and brown-blonde hair, and noticed that her nose, though foreign, had an aristocratic bearing.

"Yes, we have arranged with the local bus driver to stop and pick him up at the corner by the Postmaster's Office, but we will take him to school on his first day."

"Very good then, Mrs Moritz. It's been a pleasure to meet you and if you have any difficulty…"

"Yes, Mister Parker, I have your details."

"Then I shall be off. Good day to you," and tipping his hat, returned to the car.

Mr Parker backed the car around and drove slowly up the driveway, all the while being careful not to raise too much dust, a consideration Isaac would come to know as that of a gentleman.

Although he did not understand all that was said, Isaac instinctively knew the conversation was about him. As it continued towards to its conclusion, its tone of formality hushed-in a dry burning sensation to his throat and mouth. He became still, as if to disappear, blocking out the words he did not want to hear until he heard nothing, and all was silent.

His young mother took a few steps backwards, before turning toward the house. She caught sight of Isaac standing deathly still. She went to him, seeing how delicate he looked. She came to his side to avoid blocking his stare. With her left hand she lightly pressed his head to her belly.

After a moment she persuaded him to move with her, to a quiet place within the stand of fruit trees.

"Sit here with me, Isaac," said his mother as she motioned him to sit against the trunk of a cherry tree. She kept him bundled until he was settled.

"The man who was just here is from the Department of Education. That's where he works, and his job is to help children go to school."

Johanna wasn't sure how much of this Isaac was taking in, but she continued,

"He called in to say that now you will soon be old enough, that you must start going to school." She paused, trying to think of a more inviting way to put it Isaac did not respond. He had no understanding of a place such as a school. Learning was something that happened on the farm. By it being kept from him, he felt that it was something to fear.

His mother continued,

"Isaac, you're different, you're one in a million, precious, and your grandmother knows this too." Still reticent, he looked at his mother as the words became more familiar.

"I think you will like school, and that you more than most of us, will come to a love of learning."

Their eyes held at this expression, then continued to say,

"One day you might even become a solicitor."

'Love of learning' returned to Isaac's mind. They seemed to be the same word, and as he would later come to know, even sensual.

All this was very new to Isaac. He had heard little of this until now, and then only because it had been forced upon him by a visit from an officer of the Department of Education. When were his family ever going to tell him about 'going to school'?

His mother, sensing that his confusion bordered on betrayal, regretted her lack of preparation. All she could do now was to comfort her little boy, to sit with him.

Isaac listlessly swept a bug off his knee. For the first time in his life, he had been instilled with doubt.

Johanna, in an effort to excite him about his prospects at school, sought to change his outlook.

"There'll be lots of children your own age to play with at school, and new games to play. There are so many exciting things to learn about. Isaac, my treasure, I'm sure you will love going to school."

Her assurances, however, did little to ease the deep unease he felt, the fear of being alone, away from the family.

In the years that followed, these fears and eventual loss of innocence, became a threatening and hurtful price to pay for growing up. His response to all of this was to vow that he would never leave school, he would never stop learning, and he would never be left not knowing.

The stroke of his mother's hand over his brow softened his anxiety. With each stroke Isaac found a growing confidence in his ability to cope, to achieve and to do well.

Johanna kissed him on the head, and left him with his new-found being.

Chapter 3

A Knowing

That he would soon start school piqued the boy's innate curiosity. He listened intently to the people around him, how they spoke, what they said, and compared their ways to the old postmaster. He could come across as stern, but committed to remaining approachable, a trait he was not known for before taking the position at the post office. He settled to this new role and felt vindicated, as people in the district came to him for guidance and advice.

A red mailbox at the edge of the road, flanked the path that led through a hedge and down a gentle slope to the post office. The weatherboard and cement sheet building with the red tin roof looked like a free-standing house, except for the odd grandeur of tall double doors. The doors, for the most part glazed, were intended to convey its function as a public building.

The Wandin Post Office consisted of large single room, a counter, and pigeon boxes mounted on the wall behind. A community pinboard hung on the wall beside the door and a range of envelopes and parcel boxes, laid out on stands. In the corner of the room, a discreetly located door to the living quarters of the building, indicated the space beyond to be private.

Located at the corner Queens Road and Beenak Road, the building and its garden setting, occupied a small plot next to the family farm within easy reach of the young Isaac.

It was soon after learning about school that he would wander off to the post office, at first to sit on the grass beside the path to watch the locals going in and out of the office. As his confidence grew, he would go inside and sit quietly away from the counter, and eavesdrop as unobtrusively as his inquisitive nature would allow. His absconding panicked his family until they understood where to look for him. Isaac listened to the worldly conversations the postmaster would strike up with his customers, to hear any word of wisdom he might offer them. Sometimes the gems would be directed to him.

Learning came easily to Isaac. As his awareness developed, a feeling of unease crept in about his place in his family. The language of his family was sounding course, a jumble, unlike the fluid tones of the postmaster. This new language, spoken only intermittently at home, had to come first, and he soon came to use the old language less.

The postmaster often spoke to Isaac about language skills being the key to achievement. If Isaac wanted to set goals, it would be the inability to express them, that would leave him unfulfilled. Isaac wanted knowledge, and to not have it would be a failing.

The postmaster, Manius Campbell Dexter, an Emeritus Professor of History and Languages, recognised in Isaac's language a crude dialect, a corruption of its original Latin form, fragmented and parochial, and only a shadow of its former glory. The words and expressions adapted from Hebrew fascinated him. As Isaac developed his use of English, the professor grew in admiration of the young boy's inquiring mind, and his will to know.

Whenever Harry the Reader walked the path to the door, Isaac would hurry in his wake, making it into the room before the door slammed shut and the doorbell stopped ringing. He would take his usual place in the corner. Harry the Reader, whose passion for books had morphed into his full name, had visited Isaac's family during the winter months, when there was little work to do on the farm. He would entertain them with stories that he had managed to weave from astronomy, geography and science. Sitting amidst the family, Isaac would sit in rapt attention. Harry the Reader lived alone with his books, a repressed extrovert, he enjoyed coming out to the family's hospitality, bringing a sense of theatre to his story telling.

The conversation in the post office always started with Harry.

"Morning, professor!

The exchange with the professor had now long been established. It was philosophical, and every visit provided an opportunity to share and advance their ideas. Both men would pick up where they left off, as if the suspensions between meetings had not occurred. Isaac looked over the postal displays while he listened to their discourse.

Without sparing a moment for small talk, Harry the Reader opened to spout forth one of the professor's dearest beliefs.

"I've thought long and hard about the adherence to the virtue and dignity pre-eminent in classical language, and how these elements should be re-instated and promoted, even honoured, in our modern vocabulary."

The boy was distracted by the professor's wife as she emerged from the back room holding bundles of letters.

"Hello, Isaac, and good morning to you, Harry," she sang as she began sorting them into the private mailboxes. Harry could only give her an acknowledging glance such as was his anxiety.

The professor spoke,

"In all my academic life, I have worried that the disenfranchisement of these very principles is nothing but a betrayal of our precious language, the first and foremost carriage of learning. I take it you agree, Harry?"

Silence in Harry meant nothing less than capitulation. Harry was also a learner.

"And the purpose of this adherence," continued the professor, "the foretelling of a new reality. The overt acceptance of human connectedness by all. In a word, affinity! Affinity, leading to our rightful and final purpose in a new age of enlightened agreement, among all the people of the earth."

Harry drew a deep breath through his nose. Isaac heard it whistling.

"And here is your parcel, Harry – a good deal of reading by the look of it. Before you go, think on this. What is the relationship between the dignity and virtue of classical language and that of public order?"

Having learned something and been given a task, Harry the Reader, left thinking.

The professor long suspected that the roots of learning and its consequences for change, were to be found in the development of newly arrived cultures, how their maturity, assimilated over time, altered the identity of the nation. The pursuit of this goal led him to take the position as postmaster in a rapidly changing community. Direct exposure to the people was the crucible, essential to advancing his inquiry. In Isaac he found an unusually attentive boy, and a mentor relationship developed between them, as well as an appreciable fondness for the other.

The post office and its residence, home to the professor and his wife, Victoria, sat unimaginatively between the front and back yards of the corner allotment. Hedges covered the road frontages and the side and rear boundaries were defined by low wire mesh fences, incorporating two hinged gates. Between the garden bed of hydrangea, planted along the front wall of the building and the hedge, stood a single tree just ten feet from the concrete path.

It was difficult for Isaac to grasp the purpose of this tree. It bore no fruit nor had any function he could see, a tree the professor's wife referred to as 'ornamental'. On Isaac's property, the only trees without a commercial use, with the exception of the bushland in the creek bed, were the cypress trees, and their redemption lay in the shade they provided, and the fact that their size belittled the axe and handsaw.

In this garden, without the interruption and noise of his working farm, he was able to observe the creatures that sheltered there. Small wrens darted in direct lines between hedge and hydrangea, secure in the tightknit foliage. Ants, like tribes descended from Judah, were kept constantly in check by scouts, who peeled back and forth to the sides of the column, searching and directing. Isaac found the spiders to be cautious, dismissive, and keen to move on.

Mosquitoes were hard to see, but their high-pitched presence was as distinctive as their bite. Flies, as always, behaved as if they were welcome to land, lodge and feed wherever they pleased. He embraced the garden, its gentility, dignity and beauty.

Along this path, between the red pillar box and the doorway to the post office, Isaac heard the sounds of his new language, words that seemed to slide over each other. These delicate and seductive elements were missing in his world. The absence of these qualities would make Isaac's life among his people, his present place in the world, feel without purpose.

The professor's company, and the gentle ambience of the postmaster's office, stressed the difference from Isaac's roots. In his early years Isaac yearned for this elusive solemnity.

The professor was a patrician man, Nordic-looking and intensely knowledgeable. The steadfast qualities, first revered in the era of the Emperor Octavius Augustus Caesar, served him well throughout his life. He was tall, lean and slightly bent, his pale complexion bleached by age. The white, wide-brimmed hat surmounting his head, drooped over his grey, dishevelled hair that poked out beneath it.

On his forehead below his hat and above his left eye was a shiny perfectly formed, tight-skinned dome, the size of a small egg, which challenged the politeness and protocols of all those who encountered it. His face was thin and angular, and above his deep-set fading blue eyes, grey wire-like strands passed for eyebrows. The ears which framed his loosely hollowed shaven cheeks, were long and flat and looked tired, as though they had heard too much.

Intended as a means of augmenting his academic knowledge in being among the people, he was surprised by the personal transition his social interaction provided. They had come from Switzerland, Channel Islands, Italy, the Netherlands, and Isaac's heritage from Romania, each bringing their special experience in wine making, animal husbandry, vegetable and fruit production, and floriculture.

The government's post-war immigration policy to populate the country resulted in an influx of immigrants not seen since the gold rush one hundred years earlier.

With his wife, Victoria, Professor Dexter purchased the post office agency with the objective of meeting and influencing the many people of this new and emerging community. Their commitment was in every way genuine. Without wearing out his welcome, the professor continued to lecture across the counter on tolerance as a virtue, the rewards of racial intermarriage and social harmony. His wife shared this vision of her Emeritus and graciously supported him, that he might make his final and lasting contribution to a new society.

In young Isaac, the professor saw his own reflection. The idea of fulfilling his quest for peaceful empowerment of community through one so young, did not sway him from believing it possible.

He resolved to bridge the age difference by whatever means, and if it required him to live to be one hundred and twenty, then so be it. A bond or conduit between them was needed if the professor's quest were to serve humanity. He repeated his tenets to him, those of humanity, humaneness and integrity, and all manner of human being. In turn, Isaac would try to memorise his lessons, even if he didn't fully understand them.

"Isaac, remember, *Faber est quisque suae fortunae,* each one of us is the maker of his own fortune," he would say often, and, "The gift of life, Isaac, is that it's yours," said with great pride, as if having discerned it himself.

"Your desire, your joy, your pleasure, your pain, your ambition is only yours, that no one else can truly know or feel. It is in the passing on of your affinity, that your infinity is assured. If we want to make a difference, then celebrate difference. We only have to want to."

But he did also caution Isaac as gently as he could advise.

"And, Isaac, if you are one to accept this dedication that I now pass onto you, know that people will put upon your grail, all manner of graven responsibility and expectation, tinged with doubt that you will ever triumph. The sceptics will be reluctant to act, to open their minds in order to see."

And with all the love and passion for the reign of Augustus Caesar, mandated and sanctioned by the God, Jovi Stator, the professor welled up emotions he kept secret deep inside him, emotions so tightly held and could not bear to part, for fear of draining of his soul.

"Elegantiarum aeternum,"

And he would follow with its meaning,
"Elegance is Eternal,"
and, ever so slowly, its other side,

Splendidam aeternum,

"Eternity is Elegant."

***

Isaac's grandmother, Rebekah, maintained her short, stocky and too-wide-for-her-height stature for more than sixty years. Her intrigue lay in that she never in her whole life questioned her status or disposition. She was simply simple. Her favourite place was at the long table beneath the vine. There she spent many hours of her day sorting and packing strawberries. She wore a thin black cotton dress in the tradition of mourning, and being a naturally ebullient person, the significance of wearing it no longer held sorrow. She disowned the desert colours of Moses, preferring larger than life floral pink for her aprons, a yellow and crimson scarf and blue and gold headscarf.

Wooden trays filled with strawberries were brought to the table directly from the fields and working mostly alone she carefully selected and packed them into punnets. The top most layer of strawberries were matched to size and placed to form straight lines using the best fruit. As she did this, she thought how attractive the buyer would find her strawberries, and how proud they would be to buy them. She worked happily under the vine singing folk songs, often breaking into laughter at the words that amused her most. For short periods of time Isaac worked beside her, separating the large strawberries from the small. The over-ripe strawberries were to be set aside, as they were destined for processing into jam.

"Exempli gratia Eezak!" thanked his grandmother, pleased that he was spending more time with her at the table. She liked to use what she thought was proper Latin for such appreciation, especially when he had filled two bins for the jam factory.

When he got bored helping his grandmother, Isaac resigned saying,

"Avia, I feel a little tired." He often left the task to play with the skittish kittens, venturing in and out from under the house.

Isaac crept away from the table towards the dormitory wall to lay in wait. The sizeable gap at the base of the plinth boards and the concrete floor was ideal for the hide and seek games. He squatted facing away from the wall, and waited for the little ferals to forget that he was there. Finally, he grabbed one to pet until its contortions, hissing and scratching forced him to let go, and he slumped his legs to the concrete floor with his back to the wall.

There being nothing else to do, he observed the back of his grandmother who was still working at the table. He watched her motions, and the way her body swayed as she worked, and thought her clever, the way she held her chin up to sing, and still keep looking downward on her task. He ignored the whiskers of an inquisitive kitten that tickled his leg. Having not noticed it before, he had fixated on his grandmother's odd behaviour.

Isaac saw a swift movement his grandmother made which had no purpose in her singing or the packing of strawberries. Her arm moved slowly out to her side and after a pause she slowly brought it back towards her body. A giggle followed. Lured by these motions, Isaac got up and took a few slow few steps, to stop just behind his grandmother a little to her right, without disturbing her.

Before long, the movements started again. Her arm reached slowly out to her side and away from the punnet she had been packing. She cupped her pudgy, reddened hand while her arm was still outstretched. After a pause she moved her arm in a slow motion towards a fly that had settled on the table. As her hand neared the surface of the table where the fly rested, she stopped. Then, without warning, her hand swept at the fly. In that sweep, her hand had not touched the table, nor splattered the fly. Sometime during this pass over the fly disappeared. At the end of the sweep, she foisted her clasped fist into the air in triumph, cackling with satisfaction. Like a trumpet voluntary her fist then burst open, releasing a dazed but otherwise unharmed fly back into the vine canopy.

After the release she kept her arm up high, before descending to her routine, unaware her grandson was watching. He retreated in awe of his grandmother, not uttering a word, hoping the see the movement once more. It was becoming apparent to him now, that to add interest to her work she would catch flies. How else could she sit there for so long? The flies were there in huge numbers, circling, landing where they shouldn't, and moving only when they were threatened.

Being the sort of person she was, Avia Rebekah, as Isaac knew her, decided that she would enjoy the pestilence rather than be frustrated and beaten by them. Isaac could flick them in mid-air but what he had just seen was completely new to him. This was something he could do, they were plentiful, and an annoyance to all living things. They were an enemy and Isaac decided, there and then, they were *the* enemy.

Thereafter, Isaac fixed his gaze on their movements, noting how few collisions there were within the swarms. He saw how one or two would break away when diving towards his grandmother. He was fascinated by the way they hovered before landing. When a fly landed on bare skin, the sticky balls on the end of its legs irritated, causing it to feel ticklish and itchy. The tingling sensation varied, depending on the temperature of the day. Isaac would later learn that scratching the skin to relieve the itch served only to give bacterial infections a greater chance of replicating. In his imagination, the fly, beyond its instinct to feed, knowingly sought to cause distress, and this enraged him.

Later that day, Isaac exited the forum through the gap between the washroom block and the wash-house to where his father, Appius, and uncle Cato were digging a trench from the back of the toilet outhouse known as the dunny, and more often than not, the thunder box.

The trench passed the fruit trees and downhill along the rear of the barn towards the bog, where the wash-house, kitchen and washroom water ended up. At the end of the trench near the swede patch he found them excavating a wide, deep pit. Uncle Cato was almost hidden by the growing mound of soil being tossed from the pit.

"Isaac, you've come to help?" the sweaty uncle teased.

His father puffed in to explain, "See the long trench, Isaac? The pipe will follow all the way down from the new toilet and into this pit. But first we have to make a concrete box in it."

"Appius, you forgot to explain about the water," interjected uncle Cato, who knew more about such things and went on to say, "Isaac, it's like this. Instead of sitting on the thunder box bench, you will sit on a big, beautiful white vase with water in it."

"Like a big egg cup, big enough to sit on," corrected his father.

"The cup will be on the floor?" asked Isaac.

"Yes, you sit on the bowl above the water. And on the wall above your head will be a tank of water with a long chain and handle. The drum and the night cart man will be gone for good!"

Cato could not contain himself any longer and took over. "After you've finished, you pull the chain, and the water falls into the bowl and pushes everything in the bowl into a pipe which will go into this trench. The pipe then brings it all the way down into this concrete pit!"

Isaac looked at his uncle's beaming face, both arms gesticulating into the pit.

"What happens after the pit?" asked Isaac.

"Good question, son," and his father proudly continued, "another pipe comes out of the pit. This time only clean water will come out, and the water will then flow onto the cabbage crop half way down to the creek."

The logic of this was writ on the faces of his father and uncle.

"Will that make a new bog?" No response.

"Would this help keep the flies away from the forum?" again asked Isaac.

His father and uncle, perplexed by the question, could only stress the convenience of not sitting on the open drum, even though it was a magnet for the flies, and already effective in containing the forum population.

Over the coming months, as pleasant and busy as the new toilet had become, the flies continued unabated. They were fearless and persistent and Isaac could only wish for what Nemesis, the Goddess of Retribution, Justice and Vengeance might one day visit upon them.

***

In the corner of the forum where the dormitory wing joined the house, an infill roof covered a set of concrete steps. The steps accessed a beautifully detailed, formal sitting room, the only intact room of the original house. An old armchair was placed next to the steps for Grand Uncle Felix to sit and rest during the day. Felix was the oracle of the family, the keeper of the family history and a cousin of Isaac's grandfather, Ezekiel. He was a thin man. The flesh on his head was taught and leathery and covered in a spare, short grey stubble. The edges of his brown eyes were turning milky-white befitting a man in his position.

To Isaac, Grand Uncle Felix was more an object than a person. It was only after his mother told him of his importance and standing in the greater family, that Isaac took an interest in talking to him.

One day he summoned the courage to sit beside him long enough for the old man to take notice of him. When he acknowledged the boy for being there by the raising of his hand, Isaac spoke, "Grand Uncle Felix," and continuing only after a nod, asked, "why are we different to other people around us?"

The old man raised his eyebrows, reminded of how inquisitive the young could be.

"Good, good, young Isaac!" enthused Grand Uncle Felix, surprising Isaac for knowing his name. "We are a people for whom history lives," began the old man in his well-rehearsed verse. "We are the Romano Hebrew people…" and as he stalled, Isaac nodded thoughtfully in polite acknowledgment.

"In our lexicon, our history, our ways and our words, lives who we are."

Isaac had never heard words like this before and began to appreciate his standing in the family. "You know, Isaac, I will tell you everything, many times, so that you may be a keeper of our lives…that wretch, your young uncle Filius took with him all I taught him – when he killed himself!" wheezed the old man in disgust.

"How did he do that, Grand Uncle Felix?" blurted Isaac innocently.

"I knew it, I knew he was too cavalier…brave and stupid. Against all sense he rode the rotary hoe like a chariot, straight up the steepest part of the hill beyond the creek.

With eyes wide open, Isaac couldn't wait,

"What happened then?"

"What happened then was what everybody knew what would happen then," and catching his breath again from despair, continued. "The front wheels of the tractor rose straight up, tossing foolish Filius backwards, and he fell down behind the rotary hoe. The tractor, with the rotary hoe still running slid down the hill, cutting him into pieces and ploughed him back into the ground. His blood, our blood seeped into the earth that feeds us," he mourned.

The old man drew a sharp breath to ease the fool pain. At this point he began to waffle before refocusing on the young charge before him. Regaining his composure, Grand Uncle Felix leaned forward, and explained,

"Isaac, you are born in Terra Australis. This land is a fortunate accident of isolation and timing, but we originally came from Dacia and our history is this, and I will tell you many times in your little life, until I can rest with the dignity and assurance that I have done so."

No one in Isaac's family talked to him this way but Grand Uncle Felix, and Isaac was both entranced and impatient for his story to begin.

"A long, long time ago, before there was air, water, fire and earth, the Gods had a meeting, and they talked about how they could share their abundance and magnificence. Zeus had this idea of creation, and among them some thought it good, but the question was how? The discussion continued and when they realised they could create more Gods for more purposes than they already had among them, they became committed to Creation.

By creating people, who would require a greater number of deities to steer their path in life, they could also enrich their own existence. Some suggestions of how this might be done caused endless mirth, especially the part of the plan which involved, among other things, the planting of herbivore seed, cows, sheep, pigs, buffalo and the like, that would convert grass and water into hundreds of kilograms of red meat. Another involved the covering of a firmament almost entirely with salt water. A giant furnace located high above would evaporate this water from the surface of the oceans, leaving the salt to remain in the sea, and giving rise to fresh water to rain upon the land for these creatures to enjoy. Salt-free water, to quench their thirst and to nourish the grass for the herbivore to eat and so on and on, mirth and more mirth, the Gods, Isaac, do work in mysterious ways."

"Grand Uncle Felix, that's an amazing story. Did that really happen?" queried Isaac.

"Oh yes, it did, Isaac. Yes, it did," promised the old man.

"Why are we?" asked Isaac after a pause.

"Better I tell you first, how, Isaac," never ceasing to marvel at the questions of the young. The questions always the same, why, how, who, when and where and always difficult to answer to their satisfaction.

"Ours was among the first of the great civilisations of the world. The glory of the Roman Empire had a dark side to our origins as a people.

"In August 70 AD, the Roman General Titus besieged Jerusalem, destroying the city and the second temple. He did further massacre hundreds of thousands of Jewish people. For this atrocity, Titus was awarded a triumphal arch in the Forum of Rome. It remains there, in the Via Sacra.

"This was a day of shame for our founding father Septimius Severus, a soldier in the auxiliary regiment under Titus. Amid this turmoil, brave and honourable, and at the risk of the consequences of desertion, he secured the loyalty of half of the 120 members of the auxilia.

"He took the Jewish girl, Rachel, and coerced other women to accept the soldiers as a refuge from their assured destruction. Members of their families joined in trust, and together they fled northwards to the sea of Galilee, passing through the Golan heights and into Syria, a journey well defended by the trained Roman soldiers within their group. They eventually found settlement, far north of Damascus.

"The Consul charged him with dishonourable desertion, punishable by the most agonising death the Roman Empire could inflict, but we, his descendants, see his brave actions as the founding of a new people.

"We arrived in east of Europa, and settled among the subjects in the Dacian Kingdom of Decebaulus. Here we found acceptance and peace, however this did not last long. Just thirty-six years after fleeing Jerusalem, the soldier-emperor, Trajan, having undertaken a triumphant military expansion eastwards into Dacia, annexed our new homeland as the Roman province of Dacia Traiana.

"In this war, knowing the power of Rome, we elected to withdraw to safety, only returning when the new order was established. A column attesting to Trajans' victory, was erected in the Forum in Rome. There it remains to this day.

"And it is from this, whence the Romano Hebrew people came and became, and it is from this that it is who you are," advised the old man.

"Is that how I came to be?"

"Oh yes, Isaac, it is, it is," responded the old man gravely and resignedly.

Isaac remained wide-eyed, and after a time, asked,

"Where is Dac...."

The old man cocked his head forward and adjusted his elbow onto the armrest.

"Dacia," filled in the old man, "we say *Ducsha*," noting Isaac's memory of the word.

"That is a story for another time," teased the old man.

Isaac had brought the first glint to the old man's eye since the untimely death of young Filius. His veined and greying hand moved out to touch Isaac, whereupon he closed his eyes to rest.

Isaac left him, but would return often to hear and learn more from the most articulate man in his family, holder of the living stories of long-gone people, people who never really came to life and who never really died, such is the way of history lost.

***

In the height of summer, scorching dust-laden north winds could be replaced with little warning, by a current of cold air that turned the atmosphere prickly.

Between the burnt breath of summer and the brace of cold air, lay a stillness in waiting, a portent, a messenger without motion and dumb to an impending storm.

The thirtieth day of January 1957 was such a day when the temperature hovered at one hundred and four degrees. Isaac chased a kitten into the pepper field beside the driveway. He followed it joyfully, running the aisles and jumping rows of withering plants, stopping only to look for the little furball. The chase reached the rear of the post master's property, where the young cat vanished under a small bush next to the steel framed wire mesh gate.

Isaac stopped to catch his breath, and as he crouched to look for its wide-eyed hiding, he saw the ground was moving beneath him. A mass movement of crazed ants was taking place. Order had gone, and in its place, a chaotic stampede of ants of all sizes crossed each other, without direction, uniformity or etiquette.

Bull ants trampled their lesser cousins, turning their heads from side to side and occasionally looking upwards. They were so numerous that some had already found their way onto Isaac's legs. In these few seconds it had grown so dark that Isaac had trouble seeing them and panicked.

He jumped madly, slapping his legs in the hope of brushing them off.

Lightning seared the darkness, lighting the ghost-white figure of the professor approaching the gate. The boy, frozen by terror, was unable to call out or scream, his stare locked onto the old man. The professor did not see Isaac. His frail, lofty spectre looked upwards into the black, swelling plumes of clouds, driven by wind.

He began to speak just as his white floppy hat was ripped from his head by the storm's undignified fury. The long strands of his white hair dancing on end as the charged atmosphere took hold. The professor grabbed the top rail of the gate to steady himself, his trembling lips tightening to form his declaration to the tempest. With rain belting onto his old wizened face, his shaking jaw cried out,

"*AdFulminare!* I, Manius Campbell Dexter, beseech you to surrender!"

Isaac blinked the drops of water from his eyes, he thought he heard him say "to the flash with thunderbolts!" The professor continued to scold the storm, despite being pounded by thunder and lightning. He continued to berate until he physically weakened, and his cheeks quavered to the more subdued, and imploring words of Papinius Statius.

"Crimine quo merui, iuvenis placidissime divem, quove errore miser, ... donis ut solus egerem, somne, tuis?"

With these words the professor sought to placate the storm as if it were a violence of and against men, but the buffeting continued until he flapped like a loose sail in the wind.

Isaac watched awestruck as the professor, lit ghostly by the lightning, choked on his saliva. *"Tacet omne,"* and another clap of thunder silenced him.

The storm did not yield, and in his belittlement the professor could only plead,

"Unde ego sufficiam…" I've had enough!

Ezekial's words describing the thunderbolt on the coin of Antoninus Pius flooded into Isaac's head. A restless bull ant climbed onto his foot.

"Iovi Stator!" screamed Isaac to warn the professor, and before his scream was done, Jupiter, the God of Lightning and Thunder, discharged a column of jagged electricity. The bolt tethered itself to the atmosphere and made its way towards the iron railing the professor was holding.

The strike seared the meat of his hands onto the rail, and blew the rest of him up and backwards until he hit the wall of the cottage like an unwanted toy. It pulsed through Isaac's body, just as the bull ant sank its pincers into his foot. Before Isaac could shriek, he heard the last resounding scream, torn from the professor's killing,

"NOSCITA – BUNDUS!" Look to Grow!

Through wet narrowed eyes, Isaac watched the professor until he had fallen out of sight and then squealed. The pain of the strike, dulled by shock had not yet registered. Large drops of rain, mingled with tears, streamed down his face. In the grip of fear Isaac ran, slid and crawled through the mud towards his house. His foot throbbed, and the deep penetrating thunder had torn his ears. He was numb and out of his mind. The foul stench of his own burning frazzled and frightened him. The further he ran, the worse he smelled. Not knowing what had happened to him, his little heart pounded.

In his burning, fuelled by thunder and lightning, Latin, knowledge and history begat Isaac. This new Isaac that would see and feel what was not possible in this world, and from this time on, he would become privy to history's secret visions. This not-possible world was now part of his inclination, disposition and complexity, from which he could not escape. It was a descent into destiny.

Isaac appearing out of the field squealing and bewildered, ran straight past his drenched mother unable to respond to her frantic calling.

Her hand slipped off his arm, as he scampered under the cypress trees and up into the forum, unconscious of where he was going. He just needed to run.

He headed to the steps beside his great uncle's chair and staggered up and into the bedroom he shared with his parents, throwing himself onto his mother's bed, writhing in pain, breathless and suffocating.

Not far behind, Johanna rushed into the room and grabbed him to her, embracing his muddied and shaking body, causing Isaac to hit out. Unable to calm him, Johanna looked more closely at his condition. What she could see of his skin was chafed, bleeding and blistered. The burnt smell frightened her.

"Isaac, what happened to you, poor baby boy, what happened?" not really expecting an answer.

"I'm going to take your sandals off, Isaac." Wiping some of the mud off his skin, she noticed a swelling on his foot. Even if he had been bitten, it could not have been the whole reason for the torment of her divine son. She ordered Rebekah who was now beside the bed, to bring a bowl of warm water, clean napkins, aloe gel and bandages.

With her composure returning, she carefully removed his sodden singlet. The material did not slip easily off his skin. Isaac was still thrashing about in pain. His mouth was open as if screaming but no sound came out. His mother worked cautiously to peel the material away from his skin.

Rebekah returned, first with a bowl of warm water and towelling. As they washed and cleaned him, he calmed to an unnerving still. In his terror, his eyes darted randomly without seeing, his vision and his thoughts internalised, firmly embedded in the interior of his mind.

When she had finished dressing his wounds, she wrapped him loosely in fresh clothing, and held him to her.

While she gently rocked him, she sang words in high pitched assuring tones, hoping to bring him to a quiet state. Isaac sucked on the bittersweet taste of aspirin and honey.

As the storm subsided, rumble after receding rumble, his mother's voice comforted him,

"Isaac, precious Isaac," repeated over and over, all the while petting his brow and, in the refrain, as much as it was for Isaac's comfort, lay the unspoken lament for her loss to servitude, of her dreams and desires. She now knew her place in the family and what was expected of her. The rocking spoke of resignation and compliance. The subduction by the family was as deep and powerful as it was subtle, and it was at this moment in her son's boyhood, that she bequeathed her baton to him, to make his life as he wished.

The calm blinded him, leaving him unable to see through his open eyes. The internal surface of his sight was now an expanse of red velour, a rich velvet pile, permeated with meandering veins of gold silk. The sheen of red taffeta patches floating passed, gave the impression of a moving fabric.

Voices, loud and clear, spoke perfectly formed words that could only be understood at the time of their speaking, all clear and resounding, and immune to memory.

And the word that repeatedly interjected the errant discourse, was the last to come from the professor's bounty.

Noscita-bundus.

Out of the blood-red tapestry, appeared the pearlescent marble bust of a distant king, borne aloft a wooden pedestal. The water-milk whiteness of its face was looking directly at Isaac, and its curious expression diluted his fear.

As the image floated before him, the luminescent stone lips moved without speaking, and from its same cold light, the lips spoke without moving, as if the message was delayed across time.

"*Ignoti nulla cupido,*" the bell-like voice became clear to him. "No desire is felt for a thing unknown."

Far from no desire, Isaac was now becoming all desire to know.

And the heads, one by one, as cold as winter gravestones, continued to emerge out of the ether. The first solemnly proclaimed to be the founding king of Rome, Romulus, whose likeness this must have been. At the end of what seemed to have been an introduction, it moved backwards, and tumbled into the gold veins embedded in the velvet and out of sight, only to be replaced by another figure.

This time the head of the second king of Rome, Numa, dutifully announced himself and offered advice of his own,

"Ignotum per ignotius," and again the meaning abundantly clear, "the unknown explained by the still more unknown." Numa receded, supplanted by Tullus Hostilius, and he in turn, replaced by Aneus Martius, followed by Tarquinius Priscus, Servius Tullius, and ending with the menacing appearance and pronouncements of the deposed tyrant, Tarquinius Superbus, who brought with him the screams of his deeds.

Throughout this visitation the voices continued to extol, proclaim, console, to buy and to sell and to present themselves, some with words made known, and some without comprehension.

Were these proclamations the promises of demons and benefactors, or the warnings of genius and lunatic alike? Were they the threats of monsters and despots, or the peace of humanists and angels?

Were they foretelling without remembrance, of a time of danger, a time without consoling refrains, a time of no more 'preciousness', with or without the strength of time to become accustomed, or just a tease of unknowable riddles?

In this state of cypher, Isaac would interpret and divine meaning and wisdom, solace and direction. And here and now was its first revelation, that of the final word of the Professor, so fatefully exhumed. Here in this place not real, yet so clearly heard and envisioned, the word was summoned and its meaning consecrated and so delivered.

"Noscitabundus!" Knowing.

In a world where every visionary is in part from the future, Isaac was a visionary who was in part, from the past.

In Isaac, by consummation of force and intellect, nature had begotten a thinker and a visionary, a foundling of knowledge.

A Knowing.

Chapter 4

Encomiums

The night before he died, the professor's last wishes were expressed to his wife, Victoria. He had become feeble and for comfort, he asked her to read to him, passages from the first six hundred years of Latin prose. These were among his favourites from all of the historical literature that he knew, and she read them to him the way he had taught her.

When she looked up and saw his head leaning and eyes closed, she stopped reading. The sudden break of her voice startled him into an admission. He had accepted that his time was soon coming, and that when he passed, his wishes were to have a farewell service, to be held in the sanctity of Isaac's family. On leaving them, he would ride the forty-mile journey to the city, for his interment.

In the days following the tragedy, Isaac rarely ventured beyond the Forum. His mother divided her time between caring for him and assisting the family elders with the difficult task of making funeral arrangements, as conveyed by the professor's grieving wife, herself becoming frail.

This was a difficult task for her, as many dignitaries from the city were to attend, and she had little experience of their manners and graces. The small wooden church that Ezekiel purchased from the Lutheran mission, would not accommodate all who wished to attend, and Johanna had the task of allocating seats. Many of the local congregation would have to remain outside the church, and the doors were to be left open, in the hope that some could hear the service.

By the third day after the storm, the spasms in his eyes ceased and while the visions became less frequent, Isaac found that he could recall them at will. After his evening wash, Johanna would gently towel his skin and leave him to dry before dressing him. The air, heavy with moisture from the storm-soaked soil, mixed with the strong scent of eucalyptus.

The day of the service came, and it was to be held at eleven o'clock in the morning in the church that was now the spiritual home of Isaac's family. He insisted that he be seated in the front seat of the car with his uncle and father and when they had approached the corner, all in the car looked to their right at the Postmaster's Office, and each thought of their experience and affection for the Professor.

Isaac's memory of their life together, still raw, forced tears to well and spill onto his cheeks and he bent his head. His mother's hand reached out to him from the back seat of the car and pressed against his shoulder. The caress of her fingers concealed her anxiety. The near death of her son had been difficult enough, but it was the depth of Isaac's distress at the loss of the professor and their close relationship, more than his injuries, that worried her, and she prayed that he might be young enough to outgrow the trauma.

They drove the narrow road around the foothills, the inclines and slopes of this picturesque valley until they reached the church. The journey had been short and trance-like. Trucks, cars and a tractor had already taken what little space was available on the edges of the road. After parking the car some distance from the church, they walked a worn grass pathway, prayer books in hand. They made their way through the mourners gathered outside, who were dressed in their Sunday best.

Inside the church, the family took the seats Johanna had reserved for them. The professor's wife, colleagues and other dignitaries from the city were already seated. The local Catholic priest, whom Ezekiel asked to officiate in the absence of their own Sacerdos, began the service in Latin.

During the first reading Isaac felt constrained and grew restless. As the priest recited, "A time for giving birth, a time for dying; a time for planting, a time for uprooting what has been planted," Isaac left his mother's side and walked to the front row. As the verse continued,

"A time for killing, a time for healing; a time for knocking down, a time for building." Isaac stood in front of the professor's widow, leant back and pressed against her and she clasped him to her. It was the time for tears.

On completing the psalm, the priest lowered his head and closed his eyes as did the congregation. The altar boy rang the high-pitched bell to dissolve all external presence, until only the memory of the professor remained.

The priest then called upon Dr George Herschel, chancellor of the university, to deliver the encomium. He rose deliberately, in the manner of his profession and with arms outstretched to each side of the modest pulpit, he looked straight and determined.

"The man who lies before us, our beloved colleague, believed in what he knew to be proven, and yet openly welcomed intuition and vision, probing until it became knowledge. His process was deep and sharing. In all ages, men have been as willing to receive gracious encomiums at the very time they are deaf to them, as to bestow them upon others in their time of passing. But I sense that here before this great man, we are stopped at wanting to so receive.

As a young man, Manius, insatiable Manius, determined to know all that could be known. His drive and passion to know history was a mission to know all that had gone before, of having to catch up on all the news he had been born too late to experience. He loved words and chastised himself for being born after the writing of great lexicographer, Samuel Johnson, robbing him of such invention as, 'words are the daughters of the Earth, and objects, the sons of Heaven.'"

William Herschel was now unstoppable, and encomiums in the way they were bestowed and at once received, again became mirrored in confusion.

"Consanguineous, sesquipedalianism, retorique. Etymological amanuenses vademecum. Orthography, orthoepy, orthometry and denouement and the wonders of cosmology, relativity and the four dimensions of space-time. I fear I have digressed," he admitted before continuing, "Our Manius Campbell Dexter's favourite theory was of course, the possibility of a single hybrid society within the confines of a single universe."

Here William rested.

Appius looked at Cato. Felix looked at Ezekiel. Johanna held her head down trying to understand. Lazarus' jaw was hinged open and Rebekah, recognising the Latin and Greek, smiled broadly. Isaac was enthralled.

"These were the pre-occupations of our dearest friend!" bellowed William Herschel.

"If any man could touch another place, another world, it was Manius. All the rage, outrage and venom he had within him, he reserved for the lunatic path of human advancement, for to him 'things', were not 'the sons of heaven'. Too often 'things' were blades made from the earth, blades of bloodshed and destruction, paid for in love and goodness.

"He professed the symbiotic paths to harmony, the child of peace to be words, words woven into language, the begetter of knowledge essential to its security.

"He observed as he prophesied, that the offspring of true power would be wellness and creation. Was he ahead of his time? No doubt. And as every visionary must, he risked ridicule."

After a brief pause, perhaps a prayer, William Herschel assigned the professor to the future, and laid his process to history. He ended the professor's consignment with the words, "His light is clear."

The chancellor then eyed Isaac's family and all the local farming community that could be compressed into the small church and began to speak directly to them.

"And he came to you, to your fledgling community, to make the difference in his life. You must know that he did this not only in summation of his life's work, but out of love for you, his fellow, and in all ways, human. It is we, the lifelong friends and colleagues of Manius Dexter that now salute you, and embrace you in this moment of community brought about by him, as his living proof and testament of the power of human love."

Isaac's people were beginning to understand this strange union that had come to them. Isaac, in his boyhood, knew that his place was among the gifted.

As the priest completed the mysteries of union with the Christ, Victoria, with help, removed the bouquet of flowers, and her husband's hat so dear to him. Isaac's father Appius, uncle Cato, Lazarus and three others stood up and moved toward the casket, and surrounded it.

Together, with the unity the professor so loved, they lifted it to their shoulders, adjusting their bodies beneath it. When they were ready, they slowly and solemnly carried it to the doorway. Isaac followed immediately behind them, almost tripping Lazarus as he squeezed in below the coffin. He held his hand to its underside, even though it was out of reach. The mourners peeled away from the door to create a path. The bearers managed the two steps down from the church, and approached the hearse. Isaac moved out from under the shadow of the professor, and when the sun shone into his eyes, he burst into tears. It was the longest goodbye for a small boy.

**

In the days following the service, Isaac found the courage to return to the fence to see where his friend perished, and saw the damage caused by the lightning strike. The back wall of the house was charred. The fire caused by the lightning was extinguished by the heavy rain, and the smell of ash and cinders lingered. Isaac had to overcome his instinct to run away.

He looked at the ground where he had been crouched in search of the cat, and found the empty shell of the kitten grafted to the bottom rail of the gate. His eye roved to the top rail of the gate that the Professor had been holding. Was that his flesh? How well a job had they done, those who found him dead? Why had they not scraped and collected all the dignity of his mortal remains?

He dwelled for a short time before making his way to the forum of his home. His grandmother was seated at the long table, happily packing strawberries. After a brief exchange with her, Isaac joined his younger cousin who was squatted beside the wall, swinging a stick at the kittens under his grandfather's bedroom. Isaac tired of the game, focused his attention on his grandmother. Her singing, dress sense and bizarre body language cheered him up. Isaac knew it would not be long before she set about to catch a fly. In less than a minute he saw the familiar, calm motion of her right arm moving out to her side. She held it there briefly, before commencing the gentle approach towards the table.

He remembered that during this last movement, her hand was already cupped. Her arm stopped just short of the edge of the table. After a pause, the reason for which escaped Isaac, she swept swiftly across the table, just skimming over the surface. The swing that finished in line with her left shoulder, ended with her gloating with laughter.

As she resumed her normal position, her laughter subsided into a menacing cackle. Rebekah looked down at her fat hand and adjusted her clenched fist. Isaac shuffled closer to see. She opened her hand to release her quarry. One fly flew out, another fell to the table and a third fly was squashed. Three flies in all!

"Isaac," called his mother as she walked from the kitchen carrying a pile of clean white table cloths.

"Can you run off and let the men know lunch will be ready soon?"

Isaac looked back to his grandmother and shouted at her,

"Avia! I want to catch flies! Just like you do!" and then ran out of the forum, through the yard, and out into the surrounding fields. He called the workers to lunch, then on to the road above the creek, and on up to the hillside crops to call those who worked there, all the while hoping the dragon flies would leave him be. He hated the way they could fly alongside him while he was running and nibble at the side of his face, with that frightening chaotic flutter of wings scratching at his skin. In this running state of torment, Isaac's imagination would explode their number. Lizards, spiders and roaches littered the path in front of him, an agoraphobic nightmare of stomping and squashing the predatory creatures he imagined to be beneath him.

A six-foot long trestle, added to the already long table to accommodate the growing family, looked stretched like the stomachs which received its bounty. Lunch this day, being cooler, was pleasant enough for people to linger at the table, rather than take the afternoon nap.

When most had finished eating, Valerius reached for the bowl of eggs. Five hardboiled eggs were left sitting in an inch of extra virgin olive oil with a handful of garlic cloves. He brushed the flies off and with the help of Blind Joe, began force feeding Little Quin. Isaac didn't know whether to laugh or protest at what was happening to his little friend.

The men could not resist games. Once this tussle started, the arm wrestle challenge opened, and Isaac turned his attention to the end of the table. Tiberius, who had one eye and four and half fingers, the top half of which was taken by the water pump in the shed by the creek, and a wild ride on the tractor through the orchard that claimed his right eye, was jostling for position with the handsome new arrival, Decius.

He walked to the corner of the table and sat on the red concrete floor beside Decius, a young man with matinee idol looks, to watch the shaking of flour onto hands and the flexing of the biceps muscles about to be locked in static combat.

Isaac, in his newfound state of inquiry, looked beyond the awe and admiration others held for these pulsating, stretched forms. That this two-headed muscle could inspire such reverence struck Isaac in two ways. First, the way the human body could contort such a diversity of form and second, there had to be a greater purpose in life.

Behind the testing hand grips, Isaac could see the faces of Scipio, Quintus and Sextus, as they looked on the challenge preliminaries. Each mouth had a cigarette squirreled into the corner of it.

The rising smoke trail forced their faces into a squint to avoid burning their eyes, much like bandicoot in a bushfire. Isaac loved to watch how with of a gentle puff, perfectly formed rings, came out through their rounded mouths. He admired their finger skills, how they could hold a tobacco bag, load and spread a layer onto such thin paper, and roll it to an even cylinder. They were clever enough to leave just enough paper to lick along the edge without dislodging the tobacco. Isaac loved the sweet smell of burning sulphur as the match lit up.

An unseen force replaced cutlery, bowls, plates and platters with coffee and aniseed distillate, thanks to the sublime graciousness of the women. They laid out cups and spoons, and trays of vanilla-flavoured waffles, some with chocolate and pig's blood filling. Their disdain in the proceedings at the table begged the question, men or boys?

The tension gripped like a vice as the arms locked. The table cloth slipped, causing the spoons to rattle. Nostrils flared with the strain of it all, as the rocklike forearms engaged in battle. The cigarette smoke intensified as the stress began to take hold. Isaac watched new beads of sweat glisten on their foreheads and noses. As the struggle continued, they were even dripping off the hairs in their armpits. The odour attracted three flies which flew past Isaac's nose enroute to the armpit just above his head.

An argument broke out at the other end of the table about the quality of the wine. Descriptions varied from godlike to vinegar, bliss versus headache, an argument which never was settled.

Decius was losing strength, due to the tingling sensation caused by the flies fossicking under his dripping armpit. As luck would have it, just as Tiberius gained the upper position, an unholy fart weakened him. The waft skewed a smoke ring.

Another argument erupted in the middle of the long table between Appius and his brother Cato over Appius' plan to demolish the smoke shelf in the lounge room fireplace. He reasoned that he could jam a whole length of log up the chimney and save time reloading firewood. Cato lost his patience.

"Appi!" he screamed.

"Get this once and for all! The smoke shelf throws the heat out into the room and at the same time creates the draft that takes the smoke up the chimney!"

Tiberius was eroded enough for Decius to straighten the contest once again, despite the tickling sensation under his armpit. At this point, it was going to come down to balls, who would first suffer a hernia. The beads turned into rivulets of sweat.

The tussle with Little Quincunx gridlocked.

"His mouths shut like a clam! Tickle his back!" yelled Valerius. "Just one more egg left!"

Isaac's admiration for the newcomer was one thing, but would he interfere with the outcome? A smoke ring floated between the opponents. Isaac looked up to the armpit, and without anyone noticing, swept all the flies without touching a single hair. The flies moved. Decius detected the slightest breeze from Isaac's wave, and with the tickling gone came an overwhelming relief that bolstered his strength.

Decius overturned the hand of Tiberius, whose nose was beginning to bleed from the broken skin caused by a nasty flare of his right nostril. His forearm gave way and it became pointless to hold it at half-mast and he conceded to Decius.

Isaac was thrilled.

The struggle had been sensational, and the onlookers clapped vigorously. Decius was the new champion, and Isaac's first sporting hero. The afternoon passed with finger games, versions of paper, rock, scissors, finger counts and the ever blood-chilling concealed index finger separation trick. Still more cigarette rolling and liquor swilling, until it was time to stagger back into the fields.

Isaac woke from his afternoon sleep, disturbed by a snoring frenzy coming from outside the open window. He slid off the bed and poked his head through the bottom window sash. Grand Uncle Felix was slumped in his chair at the bottom of the steps. His head rested far back and his gaping mouth faced upwards. His nose quivered as he snorted in air, becoming lifeless for a few seconds, until his chest compressed again. The suspension felt like an eternity. It was the rush of inflowing air rasping against the palate of his mouth that created the dreadful snore that woke him.

Isaac went to him, concerned that he might forget to take the next breath. A group of flies circled and hovered above his cavernous mouth. In the next dead of breath, a fly broke away and dived into his uncle's throat. Isaac blinked. In the following apnoea, two flies emerged from his mouth. Were they feeding down there, he wondered? In the very next pause two flies disappeared into Grand Uncle Felix. He waited for them to re-emerge, then gently prodded the old man to change his position. His head tilted to the side, closing his mouth. Isaac waited to ensure that his uncle was in safer repose, before leaving him to sleep.

***

At his mother's insistence, Appius invited Isaac to join him and Uncle Cato on a drive to the city. They were to pick up three new immigrants at Station Pier, and it would be a great opportunity for Isaac to see an ocean liner.

Johanna had another reason for him going. The killing of the pig was to take place on the same day, and she recalled how disturbing it had been for her son to witness it the year before. The hoisting of the pig by rope from the hind legs was not for the squeamish. The guttural high- pitched squealing of the pig as it hung from the bough of the cypress tree, would end with the slitting of its throat, and the draining of blood into a large milk vat.

Appius elected himself to drive the old Pontiac. His brother, unnerved by his driving, criticised him at every turn. Isaac, having the whole back seat to himself, rarely letting the badgering interrupt his thoughts, unless it directly involved him. At some point he gave in to the rhythmic motion of the car, and fell asleep.

He woke just as they had reached the outer suburbs. He had never seen so many houses. They extended mile after mile, broken only by strips of shops.

Closer to the city, he saw a tram for the first time. It was like a green wall moving outside the car window. It rattled on tracks in the middle of the road, and furiously dinged a bell.

They were moving slowly in a line of cars, trucks, and buses. Bicycles and motorbikes weaved in and out, setting off car horns, and from the front seat, a tirade of complaints about the 'traffic' got heated.

The buildings got bigger, closer and overwhelming, and the cacophony was like the volume dial on the radio at full tilt.

Hundreds of people loaded with bags and trolleys dipped in and out of the shops, and the walls above were punched with windows as far up as he could see from the car. There were no front gardens. The noise, signage and clamour, indistinct, clear, visible and hidden had all the attention Isaac could give. Diesel fumes and cooking smells filled the car. Its complexity excited Isaac's vivid mind, and his visions of antiquity returned to mix with this new reality. Their voices blended and blurred with these new sounds and images.

At the end of this congested street, the road widened as it curved through an intersection, and straightened into a broad, tree-lined boulevard. Trams glided through the plantation separating its divided roads.

Before he could fully absorb this change, the car turned into the centre of city. The grandeur and scale of the buildings so stimulated his mind, that his internal visions became agitated. He slipped across the back seat from side to side like a caged possum. When he couldn't see enough through the sides of the car, he knelt in the middle of the seat to peer out of the back windscreen. The buildings were so tall they framed the street, each building being replaced by another as they drove.

Impatient to see more, Isaac hooked his arms over the front seat between his father and uncle, and heedless of their chatter, stared at the view ahead. The line of cars and buses was several lanes wide, and the moment the traffic stopped, people flooded the spaces between. When the cars moved again, they would just as quickly retreat to a stand-still.

The city looked Roman, the backdrop of his visions. The mass of classical orders, broken by odd looking spikes, scrolled past. With each passing, Isaac became more confused, unsure that what he was seeing was real, or a fragment of his visions, scenes of remote places, remote times and people who might not even exist.

As he stared up at the highest building he had ever seen, the translucent bust of Tarquinius Priscus coalesced amid the massive columns embedded in its wall. The eyes and lips of the great builder of the Roman Imperial Age spoke to Isaac,

"I *gran dolori sono muti."* Great griefs, are silent.

The likeness of Priscus then delivered to Isaac the greatness of the building's features. He was directed to look at the fluted columns, crowned in Corinthian splendour, and how they effortlessly held aloft the entablatures that supported the pediment. Within its triangle, stone horses carried naked, armed men into battle. An oversized doorway, edged by thinly-veiled stone women, separated the mass of its walls. Above this entrance were chiselled the words of state, proclaiming order, unity and the rule of law.

As the visions withered, he saw an unravelling. Like the undoing of a snail spiral shell, a revelation opened up before him. Isaac now understood the meaning of the cellar of silent pigs, as he saw it before Lazarus closed the cellar door.

The cellar as a place of darkness, absent of light, a place unenlightened,

Silent as in the silenced expression of thought, and

Pigs as the absence of Elegance and Correctness.

***

On his first day, Isaac's parents drove him to school. The journey was long, and hardly a word spoken. Not far from home, at the top of a hill where Hunter Road and Quayle Road intersected with Beenak Road, they passed the local state school. The white Arch of the Wandin Yallock

Primary School, celebrating the Jubilee of 1870–1930, faced the corner. A hedge and well-treed garden, concealed most of its buildings and as they descended the hill where the family church stood, Isaac wondered why he would not be attending school there, and how instead, he should have to travel the eight-mile distance to Lilydale. It was not Roman they said.

The edge of the town was like any other rural township. The remnant bushland along road frontages, gave way to concreted gasoline stations, used car yards, farm machinery sales, repair workshops, stock feed stores and timber merchants.

At the end of this utility strip, neat gardens and smartly painted houses, lead the way into the commercial part of the town. Isaac noticed how pretty they looked in contrast to the hacked bushland and concrete that preceded them.

The streets and avenues of the old town were planted with elm and oak. The leafy quilt was breached only by its spires, turrets and towers, and occasional patches of slate and terracotta.

Castella Street, where the school was located, was equal to the finest of its streetscapes. At the top of the hill, his father slowed the car down, stopped and backed it between the trunks of the trees that stood out from the broad open gutter.

Isaac felt scrubbed and overdressed as his mother helped him out of the car. She held his hand firmly, before crossing the road to a red brick, formidable building. Together they walked through a tall iron gate and approached the door to the school's administration office.

Before climbing the three steps to the doorway, Isaac moved to the side of the path, knelt down and picked a small flower for his father. He looked up to him with his arm outstretched, and without a word being spoken, he turned towards the doorway and climbed the steps.

A cavernous echo sounded in the hallway as Appius closed the door. A petite, bespectacled woman stepped out of her room and after confirming who they were, asked them to be seated beneath a large crucifix. Just when Johanna had finished reassuring Isaac that everything would be alright, a sequence of hollow footsteps marched down a corridor they could not see.

The headmaster popped into the entrance hall where they were waiting, and after a courteous but clipped introduction of a disciplinarian, he instructed them to follow him to his office.

Isaac and his parents were asked to sit in a low brown leather couch, strategically placed in front of an oversized blackwood desk. The headmaster took his seat in a high-backed carved wooden chair. On the wall behind him, to either side of his shoulders rose two narrow, tall windows which had the effect of two pillars of light. The glare streaming from the windows darkened the figure of the headmaster, giving him a menacing aura.

Sitting fully upright he stated,

"My name is Mister Patrick Ryan, and I am the headmaster of St Columba's School!"

Then, leaning forward asked of them,

"Moritz, what sort of a name is it?"

Such bluntness astonished Appius and Johanna who struggled to reply.

"It's ah, I don't really know what you mean Mr Ryan."

"Let me put it this way Mrs Moritz. St Columba's is a Roman Catholic School, and on your application for Isaac to attend this school, you state your religion as being of the faith of the Prophet Jesus of Nazareth, and we are having great difficulty coming to terms with this. You have even given our Saviour an address! We would be more comfortable if you were Buddhists!"

Appius swallowed loudly as the headmaster continued, "Perhaps we can persuade you of the truthful place of Jesus in Christianity, and it is in this hope of your conversion, that we take your son into this school of righteous learning."

Isaac's parents could not respond for fear of mentioning the multiple gods of their Roman heritage. They would soon come to query how relevant this Roman school really was.

It came to Johanna to utter the gratitude the headmaster no doubt expected.

"Very well then! We expect Isaac to attend Mass during the school week along with the other children in his class. Now before I show you to his classroom, I shall need to fill out some details on this form. Isaac's full name please."

Again, Johanna did the talking,

"Isaac Marcu Moritz."

"Old Jewish for Gift of God, I suppose," responded the headmaster.

"And Marcu?"

"The Romanian variation of the Roman name Marcus," stopping short of declaring Marcus to be the Roman god of war, Mars.

Isaac sensed that the headmaster, despite his grand office, was not the professor's equal, and that his s's whistled irritated him.

As the headmaster completed his bookwork, Isaac blissfully thought of the professor, his warmth, his charity, honour and his urgency to share his knowledge through the honest love of learning.

The headmaster stood abruptly in a 'I must let you be had' manner and lead them into the corridor and down past the entrance hall. They continued along a tall, wider corridor that contained banks of lockers and rows of benches and coat hooks. Classes were already in session and Mr Ryan headed directly to Room 1C. The top half of the door was glazed, and the headmaster gave it a well-practiced rap.

Johanna stopped Isaac, bent down and kissed him. Appius watched. A woman in a full-length black tunic opened the door. A black veil covered her head and shoulders, her face framed by a white wimple and collar. She smiled at the adults, then looked down at Isaac. Responding to a strict gesture, Isaac followed her into the room and stood on the platform beside her. The door closed and Isaac's parents retreated with the headmaster.

The noise in the classroom hushed as Isaac was introduced. With a push on the shoulder Isaac stepped off the platform and walked to the only vacant seat to join the classroom of small inquisitive faces, aligned in rows.

On her way out of, his mother felt the pain of leaving him there. Her emotions and tensions were knotted.

Appius placed his arm around his wife's shoulder, still holding Isaac's flower between his fingers.

Chapter 5

Ezekiel's Prophecy

In the first week of school, Isaac kept to himself. In the school yard, he sat on a bench with his back to the brick wall, watching others at play. He avoided the school bullies, particularly the twins known as 'double trouble'. They were the first to present themselves to new kids, to ensure that their own enforceable interests be known. Despite his isolation on the farm, their menacing was obvious to him from the start.

In a short while he befriended gentle and like-minded souls, many of whom had similar backgrounds to himself. Through these friendships he thrived.

His mother knew his inquisitive and concentrated ways would serve him well in his pursuit of learning. She felt blessed by the professor's trust in him, and that his mentorship both formed and informed his love of learning. There was no question that he would continue his education beyond any level the family had experienced. His distress of learning about the existence of school from the Ministry of Education fired his dedication.

He spent less time in the crops with the farmhands, preferring whenever he could to help the professor's widow to run the Post Office. Harry the Reader came regularly to talk, to share his wonderment of the written word, something he loved to do as much as he loved to read.

Isaac's use of the family's dialect faded as his conversation skills grew. By the age of nine Isaac could recite the Latin roots of hundreds of English words to the delight of Harry and Mrs Dexter. This life outside his family kept him in touch with the professor's memory and all that he loved about him, his floppy broad-rim hat and his liquid pale eyes, his warmth and his belief in him. Isaac always called his widow Mrs Dexter even as they grew close. Being with her offered a different level of comfort, beyond that of his family. It was the kind of reassurance the bigger world demanded, the confidence to sustain him in his life's work, far from the farm, the family and his religion.

Despite the certainty of the every-day, his visions still owned him. Storms accentuated them, their immediacy, verve and realism. They came alive. The tempests acted like portals to another place, where Roman rulers, no longer ancient, lived in great palaces, commanded cities defined by straight roads, aqueducts, temples and triumphal arches, dedicated to the fortunes of power.

They spoke sayings much like the way Grand Uncle Felix and Little Quincunx recited. They lived beyond their natural time, and he wondered if that could happen to the professor, that he might live beyond his time. With his ability to envision such things, Isaac hoped he could meet him again, that he might not be totally lost to him.

Not all his visions were of brutes, some were beautiful. The elegant universe and the eternity within which it was made, unimaginable as it was logical. Isaac could only glimpse traces of this, the professor's enduring testament, increasingly becoming his own through the intervention of Jupiter, God of thunder and lightning.

In his family, Felix the oracle, was the only one he could proffer such an eloquent thought.

When he was older, the Grand Uncle took Isaac aside and told him that those who strive to obtain acres will not find the Garden of Eden. This impassioned little man wavering in his infirm body, would begin to shake as he unleashed his decree – "This world *is* the garden of Eden!" Isaac had grown accustomed to the ways of the aged. When his great uncle softened his voice, it was like a prayer, extolling the virtues of this world, our home, the only Garden of Eden in all the heavens. At night Isaac looked up to the stars and the space between them. How could Felix know this? Was he more like Isaac than he was telling or was this just something that an oracle understands?

He dismissed these questions as burdensome, going nowhere. He took to his visions actively. They had become part of his learning process. If they led to answers regarding the Garden of Eden or Gardens of Eden as there might be, then Isaac would not live in fear of the despots and their deeds, but follow their path to knowledge.

The psychopaths manipulating the course of history, fuelling our progress to a more humane society, was a torment the professor could not bear. His life's mission had been to propel a new science of society without the provocation of tyrants. History was done, and in some way pure, what happened, happened. Tyrants were vandal delinquents at worst and accomplices at best. This is how Isaac understood the professor's mission.

In the pursuit of truth, Isaac's curse seemed more and more like a gift. Truth is also greed, lust of everything, for power and murder if that is what happens. The lies are true if they are true lies whether they are told or concealed. When their course happens, they become truth in history.

He was beginning to lose the solid ground of his forefathers. In his visions, even though the ground moved or disappeared, the learning was still there.

It was the company and comfort of others outside the family that Isaac's grandfather, Ezekiel, feared most. His responsibility for the cohesion of the family would ultimately be a matter for his personal God in judgement of him. As the patriarch, such fraying of the family weighed heavily on him. He feared the erosion of kinship more than the outcome of his own judgement. His life was dedicated to the protection of their history, their love, their ways and unique evolution, a feat that required godliness, piety and devotion. Yet in spite of all these fears, he presided over their transition to the new world. Would he lose them in this new open foreign land?

Ezekiel's credo, *Eiusdum Generis,* those of the same kind, were his love and duty.

***

When the productivity of the farm could no longer support additional new arrivals, those among the earliest immigrants, who had gained a workable command of English, moved to the city where work was plentiful.

The first group to leave included Valerius, Decius and little Quin. The more physically agile Valerius and Decius found jobs in the construction of a new bridge over the river. Quin found employment in a chain factory. His boss took a liking to him as much for his Latin sayings as for his amusing shape. He also had a number of his own anecdotes. When his employer asked him whether he would like to visit his homeland, he replied in his characteristic slow busy way,

"I have two sisters there in the old country. But a guest is like a fish – after four days – begin to stink."

This insight got him overtime work for which he was grateful.

A week later in the middle of a three-week heat wave when ninety degrees overnight was a relief, Quin quipped,

"Hot days and nights – like this, should stay in cool room."

After being corrected by the boss as meaning in an air-conditioned room, he replied,

"No. Better say cool room, keep cool like meat." This gem got little Quin transferred to the fledgling air conditioning division of the company and a pay rise.

On weekends, for companionship and a little extra cash or vegetables in kind, the city-based workers would return to the farm. Isaac would help on the farm only when he finished school and his work at the post office. When he got bored, he would swipe flies off the backs of the pickers in front of him, shoving the zizzing pestilence under their singlets, hoping they would suffocate in the sweat they so eagerly sought. Isaac laughed when they slapped each other on the back to still the itch, not realising what they were.

When Decius, Valerius and Quin were helping out, Isaac would work alongside them, eager to know about life in the city. As they worked closely, Decius whose muscles Isaac always admired, spoke softly of the pleasures of a big city.

"Women, Isaac, like you've never seen dressed. Now you will be interested as you get older too." For all the brashness they showed Isaac, Quin reminded them of what Publilius said about such things –

"Venus yields to caresses, not to compulsion."

Isaac was captivated by the scale and shine of the city they described, and became restless with his make-do life on the farm. If he could not persuade his parents to move then he would seek a scholarship to study in the city. His appearance was now manlike and he was approaching his mature height of five feet eleven. His pale green eyes turned a deeper green with flecks of light brown. The straight dark hair he had as a child developed a blonde tinge, which matched his darker skin. His neck, shoulders and torso were thickset as if he had caught middle-age spread. The lighter framed teenagers at school teased him for being fat, and he was glad his annoyers missed the porphyry-coloured birthmark on the inside of his right thigh.

His hands were large but refined, with long slender fingers suited more to the professions than a farmer. He developed a tick, springing his hands to his face to gently scratch an itch. At his mother's persistent reminders, he worked at ignoring as many of the itches he could stand, and reasoned they were a combination of the residual effects of the lightning strike and the great fly pestilence. Isaac hated the irrepressible, tricky, tacky hordes.

His grandmother had taught him the one great skill that would sustain him all his life. This gift, the city and his great love of learning triggered Isaac's first pivotal and decisive moment. His great idea materialised. It was now as clear to him as the ground he walked on and as deep as the soft dust he searched through as a child, that he should take the gift of flycatching to the world, to empower people against the great adversary.

Like all great ideas it was transparent and simple. Implementation would require dedication, hard work and persistence. Questions, unknowns, and ideas rushed into Isaac's fervid mind. Once caught, what should people do to them? Squash them in their fingers? Clap them dead? Messy. He thought on. He had to find a way to make it work.

This was Isaac's great moment. The euphoric moment with all the hidden solutions before him. He was young, he had time and he swore to use it. The world needed him.

At the long table in the forum his ageing grandmother still packed and sorted strawberries. Isaac practiced flycatching, challenging her innate knowledge of the creature. He watched carefully, both her hand movements and the movements of the insect. He studied the causes and effects, the stand-off between the hand and the fly, and the sudden rush to capture. A cat and mouse play where the fly's weakest and most predictable manoeuvre was usurped.

When the table transformed into the daily banquet, Isaac would ignore the younger children, preferring to glean whatever he could learn from the men. He listened to what they had to say about their experiences. When they were slow in their telling, he bit his lip for fear of asking too many questions. He had learned the art of listening.

The grandfather patriarch, Ezekiel, was missing at the head of the table. He had been ill for two months and was now too weak to move from his bed. Just one wall separated him from the forum table. Grand Uncle Felix and Isaac's grandmother took turns in taking food and drink to him at this unifying time of day. He rarely ate all they encouraged him to eat.

The stories around the table flourished as the wine flowed. When sitting next to Scipio, Isaac asked him how his driving lessons were progressing.

"Isaac, you ask the most difficult of me. The clutch is damned. The carburettor will never see eternity, and the gear stick is a tool made for the crazed, who seek only virile pleasures."

Isaac was impressed. He hadn't heard Scipio talk so eloquently before, nor with so much passion for disgust.

"When the car moves, I feel terrible. I have even been to the doctor about it. For the first five minutes behind the steering-wheel I get motion sickness. When that eases, I suffer five minutes of blurred vision. Then after that, it all becomes as clear as a polished crystal! It's like watching a film at the pictures on Saturday night. I look at the arms holding the steering wheel and wonder whose arms they belong to!"

Scipio paused for another sip of wine. Isaac saw he was becoming distressed.

"The doctor calls it dis-disa-disassociation– dissociatus, Isaac. And, it gets worse! After that I become so sleepy, my head nods and when I pull it up to see the road, my eyes disappear into the top of my head. I look forward but see nothing, just two boiled eggs to steer by! And then my face turns numb."

Scipio tore at a piece of bread with is teeth. Isaac watched him thumb it into his mouth. Scipio stopped chewing and continued to speak with a muffled talk.

"I asked Felix about it. He said Scipio my great Roman namesake, a man of great valour, courageous, fearless, brave, suffered as I do even when riding on a golden chariot. He could barely make it down the Via Sacra from the Arch of Constantine to the Curia without first fainting and then nearly choking on his vomitus.

"Still, he took his place in the senate, recovered, and was great."

Isaac thanked him and moved to another place on the table leaving Scipio squabbling with another bite from the loaf. He squeezed in between Abraham and Tiberius, knocking a glass of wine over a plate of boiled eggs and eggplant. Abraham winced and Tiberius stuck a fork into an ovum before it became soaked with wine.

Isaac rearranged the glass and napkins as if nothing had happened. Abraham struck a match to light a cigarette. He hesitated. After a moment Abraham titled his head towards the match and began to puff through the sides of his mouth, minimising the effectiveness of drawing oxygen through the cigarette.

The match burnt too low for comfort and Abraham shook it out before the cigarette was properly lit. He tossed the hot dead match aside and took out another, struck the second match until it too burnt out. This was getting too much for Isaac.

"Do you want to smoke the cigarette, Abraham?"

"No, but they tell me I have to smoke – every man should they tell me. I don't know what to think now that women smoke. Do they become a man when they smoke?"

Isaac looked straight at him, knowing more was to come.

"It burns in my throat and when I breathe in, it bloats my lungs and fogs my brain. I can't think! Feels like a rasp going up and down my wind pipe, and now I've got this terrible cough! Sometimes it's so bad I can hardly speak! And they still insist I have to learn to smoke. I bet one day, they will give it up, and 1 won't know how to."

Abraham struck the third match, and with remorseful determination ignited the bent lumpy white cylinder until it billowed smoke.

Isaac turned to see Lazarus grinning on the other side of the table. Next to him Tiberius belched an egg laden burp. Isaac looked at Tiberius, who without prompting offered his driving story, assuming Isaac would listen.

"About driving," Tiberius said.

"I do nearly all the driving to the market. All of it, in the middle of the night while Abraham sleeps! You can't imagine how hard it is to keep awake all that time. Scipio says he can't drive for long either, but he's worse. Poor Scipio will never be able to drive, not until they find a horse that can drive its own chariot! Hahh!"

Then lowering his voice, Tiberius leaned to speak to Isaac and with egg breath asked,

"Isaac, can you keep a secret?"

This is the first time anyone asked this of him and Isaac was not sure what to say or whether he could promise never to repeat what was about to be said. He nodded, accepting, seeing the promise as unstoppable.

Tiberius saw he was ready.

"Grand Uncle Felix is the only one who knows this about me. He explained that I suffer from swooning."

"Is that good when you're driving?" Isaac was bursting.

"Sshhh….No, but I kick Abraham, stop, and make it to the other side of the truck before passing out. He thinks I'm mad with him because he's doing all the sleeping. He doesn't know the truth."

Just as he finished speaking Tiberius' mouth dropped open a little while his cheeks flattened. The pupils of his eyes rolled up. leaving just the whites of eyeballs exposed, like boiled eggs. Again eggs! Isaac squinted in revulsion and wondered if all swooning looked like this. Just as quickly as he had gone into that state Tiberius snapped out of it as if nothing happened.

"Felix tells me it's Julius Caesar's trait that I have inherited, swooning, the falling sickness. It gets worse as I get older and I fear I may not be able to conceal it for much longer. Truth be told, I would be relieved to let it be known. Someone might look out for me just when I need them to."

"Why not tell?" said Isaac wishing to help him.

"There is an unexplained darkness within the swoon which is not understood. No one knows what cannot be known. Sometimes, fear is the lesser evil of knowing."

Isaac thought about his own visions, lucid as they were. He did not fear them to the point of not wanting to go there. Was there darkness and redness behind Julius Caesar's fits? Would Isaac ever know this? What could he do to find out, to know the state that terrorised Caesar, and would that help him to better understand his own visions if he knew?

Isaac pushed away from the table and wandered into the grove of fruit trees behind the washroom. He sat at the base of the same cherry tree where his mother first told him about school. It had a calmness for him, of nostalgia, the comfort of a childhood security blanket. He needed to shut down and dwell on one thing only, to savour a moment.

***

As he got older Isaac thought more about his family and the peculiar nature of the characters in it. He began to compare how different they were from other people in the community. He wished to delve deeper into their history. Their link to the past seemed as alive as it was incredible. The family, in essence, was a living collective fossil.

Whether by inheritance of birth, mentoring or by the supernatural, Isaac exhibited more of the traits of his beloved professor, whose attachment to history was ingrained in him by scholarship. Isaac's living history was garnered by feel.

The great banquet, the one held to celebrate the family's migration to the new world was a profound moment in their history. There, Ezekiel spoke of the lessons to be learned from the treasures of their antiquity. Isaac remembered the tabernacle and the silver pyxis within it. He thought about the seven Roman coins, each with its own story, recounted as grand as the seven hills of Rome. The lessons learned, opposed the tenets of the tyrannical regimes of the time, and underwrote the social rules for their manner of life. Tempered by the Prophet, Reducer of Gods, wanton bloodbaths ceased, fears became private and not the doing of the state. Death was less a duty, and to live out one's life was to be expected.

In the beginning was the word.

Be.

And all created from it was being. In their pantheon, the gods were *near* mortals, living in the purer, less tangible substance of the ether. Hovering above them the lone creator, who had no need to create, did so for love.

These shared wisdoms were the core of the professor's affinity for Isaac and his family. The love of humanity, humanness, humaneness.

Manius pledged these values to a new society. In his belief, the attributes brought to the new world by all people were the essences, the essentials of a boundless future.

The prevailing new-world mantra for immigrants was assimilation. Cultures were to be absorbed and ultimately consumed by the status quo. Against this, he with the support of his gracious wife, set out by their personal example to prove the case for *adoption of culture* into which Isaac's people unwittingly fell.

The professor's last papers and notations revealed much of his relationship with the community around him. His observations firmed into the principles of his new science of social adoption.

The professor thought deeply about the effect of cultural dispersion on the individual, the potential downside of alienation, aloneness and anxiety, and weighed these against the optimistic values of opportunity, learning and cultural exchange.

He studied his community, and saw Isaac's family as a microcosm in action, and the young boy had been pivotal in the evolution of his thoughts. The peculiarity of their beliefs intrigued him as much as it raised doubts about their exchangeability. But he did not doubt that they would survive the faster current of change to which they had emigrated.

The decline of kinship and its potential threat to society occupied the professor's mind, a time when friendship realised greater value than family ties. This process of change might well be a function of emerging affluence, and for some the self-actualisation of the individual. If family were no longer required to play its cohesive role beyond its initial nurturing, protective role, friendships based on individual attributes would then have to form the basis of society.

And he looked further into the future, where friendships survived the male/female dynamic, so far into a future when every new-born would be celebrated as a child of the collective population, each selected, planned and delivered, welcomed and treasured into an Eden. Could human beings come to this?

These were the ruminations of the professor.

The professor's life ended short of his natural term, a term which still would have been too brief to assess the big questions of such a distant future. He knew this, that every great idea if it is to live, must find a new host, a new person in the quest's image and for the professor, it was Isaac.

The blind, hapless lightning strike as callous and mind numbingly stupid as it was, may have had its purpose. The bolt channelled more knowledge and history into Isaac than the Professor could have imparted, even if he had lived the full term of his natural life.

The professor's studies were Ezekiel's fears. The pronouncement his grandfather gave at the transposing of his people to the new homeland carried a warning. It was not couched as such, but he had made it clear that the loss of heritage would cause a great detriment for his people. It was his belief that long term peace came from togetherness, the protection offered by brotherhood. He had no experience of any other way. Their isolation in Romania, from the time of the Roman Emperor Trajan to the abdication of King Michael, seventeen centuries in all, had been blessed and tranquil, a refuge from the biliously violent development of western civilisation. It came in the lateness of his life, that Ezekiel had presided over this migration. The duty and responsibility of the greatest gravity since the flight from Palestine, had fallen to him. It was an honour if all went well and a curse if it failed to secure their place in the future.

Ezekiel, now bedridden, wasted. He devoted his waning energies to speech. Felix, still sprightly when active, sat on the right side of Ezekiel's bed and the chair next to him was reserved for Rebekah.

Her place was also where visitors could sit when they were called by their Patriarch Ezekiel or by the Oracle Felix. It was a tradition that relatives most remote from Ezekiel, were called first and for the closest relatives to be summoned closer to the time of his passing.

As the days passed, Ezekiel asked the most pertinent question of his people either directly or through Felix, that which related to kinship. In these last days, Ezekiel needed to know whether their bonds could withstand the societal pressures distracting them. Each he interviewed, asking over and over, where do you now work? Have you moved to the city? Do you live near each other and work together? Does the city seduce you in favour of your kin?

When the answers were not to his liking Ezekiel fell quiet. Felix continued the interviews, softening the responses by gentle interjection, easing Ezekiel's conscience. Those who dressed too colourfully, Felix asked to change before going to Ezekiel's bedside. In her dutiful way Rebekah served the guests coffee, liqueur and blood-chocolate waffles.

In the last few days of Ezekiel's life, Isaac was drawn to the foot of his bed. He watched people come and go, studiously remembering their diction, manner and what they answered to Ezekiel. When the replies were not to Ezekiel's liking, Isaac felt the hurt.

Each day as Isaac entered the room, the stale, musty odour ingrained itself in his memory, marking itself so as to recall the room, the bed, whenever he could smell it again.

On the morning of the seventeenth day of April 1959, Felix called for Ezekiel's most immediate family. The elongated room had more space beyond the foot of the bed towards the doorway, than at either side.

This morning Ezekiel was propped high on a stack of pillows. Grand Uncle Felix still occupied the place at his left hand. Isaac stood at the foot of the bed.

The sons of the father were seated on the other side of the bed opposite Felix. Rebekah and Johanna, nervously fettered the bedclothes as Appius and Cato watched, silent and stone-faced. Between Isaac and the doorway, sombre men stood respectfully still. As was their custom women quietly sobbed. A shaded light globe hanging from the ceiling above the bed lit the darkening room. The odour of the room was intense.

At 7:30 pm Ezekiel startled from his somnolence and gripped Felix' hand. The onlookers fixed their gaze on him, each one unconscious of the other. Ezekiel's eyes were wide open, as reflective as they were receptive. Light and shade was all he could see and voices gave him direction.

"Are they all here Felix?" forced Ezekiel.

"Yes, they are," replied Felix.

"Firmanicus Incitatus and his daughter Materna arrived yesterday afternoon from Dacia. They feel blessed to be with you here today."

"Felix, our people are now coming here without our assistance…they find work without need of us."

Ezekiel struggled with this closing, bequeathing all his remaining energy to its conclusion. "They are vanishing into the city of a bigger, newer world. Felix, do I die in glory or despair…we will lose them…our kind. Felix, glory or despair?"

Felix consoled him through the firming of his hand.

"In whose eyes am I judged…theirs or the Gods?"

And in the presence of his family, Ezekiel at the age of four score and one died peacefully, as if judged in that moment.

Felix raised his hand to Ezekiel's forehead and gently pressed his eyelids closed, moving his hand down over his nose and onto his beard, respectfully tugging it as Ezekiel had done when he was in thought.

The despondent look of Felix went almost unnoticed, as the tears and wailing followed the death of his other. In this raw, spontaneous outburst of grief, Isaac watched his uncle's dejection, intuiting that it was a questioning of his own demise. Who will close my eyes when I have no need to see? Who is there now that Ezekiel has gone? Who do I want at my last sight?

An hour later, the doctor arrived, minutes before the priest, the first sacerdos of their own religion to lead their church in Australia. Ezekiel's death certificate was being signed as his rites of passage were being read, carrying his spirit on a journey past the Temples of the Via Sacra, overseen by the gods.

The voice of the priest bobbed like wheels of a chariot on the granite boulders that formed the surface of the road. A humble passage of prayer, thanksgiving and forgiving, and above all, love and acceptance, culminated in the word Be. Now, be it known – May Thou Be.

Isaac elbowed his way out of the room and ran across the forum and into the gap that led to the orchard. On arriving at the base of the cherry tree Isaac dropped and wept.

Beneath the yellowing leaves, Jupiter appeared to Isaac. His water-milk likeness faded into the brilliance of the thunderbolt he was holding in his right hand. As the luminance of the lightning waned, the glow returned to his face. Bands of light rippled behind him as Aurora, the goddess of the dawn, accompanied the great god.

Isaac attempted to talk to him as he had tried so many times before. In the six years since the ancient kings of Rome first made themselves known, Isaac had never succeeded in being heard. The cavernous bell-like clarity of Jupiter's voice resounded,

"Ezekiel, namesake of the Hebrew prophet living among the exiled Jews of Babylonia, is received."

"Is he with God the Creator?" asked Isaac.

After a minute Isaac heard clearly,

"Ezekiel has made his passage to the God of Light."

Isaac was stunned. Was this a reply or just more information? Had he communicated? Was this a transmission and not a vision? The head of Romulus, the first King of Rome, tumbled through the image of Jupiter. His face filled the screen like the full width of a coin, and before it had properly settled spoke to Isaac,

"Know your power."

Coming on the heels of Jupiter's revelation, this too could have been a direct speaking to Isaac. It was inconclusive yet sober. It could have been another saying.

But Isaac did think on it. 'Know your power.' Perhaps this was his power, the ability to access another place. He had already deciphered the word, his word, *'Noscitabundus'*, the knowing.

It was now the middle of the night.

The autumn chill woke him and he pulled the second blanket over him. He stared into the darkness, expecting the coming dawn. It had been his grandfather's last day on the surface of this world, feeling a great sadness for the loss of him, yet comfort in his acceptance into the heavens. From this place, would he be released into another body, he wondered.

Moonlight beamed through the curtain. The breeze, gentle and rhythmic, flowed across his cousin's bed, below the open window. In the reflected light of the curtain, Isaac could see the elliptical form of the ornate ceiling rose above the suspended light fitting, and recounted the colours of its flowers and stems, and the *egg and dart* border of its perimeter. The flowers were pink, the stems and leaves green, the twine gold and the eggs were pale blue. The night breeze cooled Isaac's face, ears and nose. His lips stayed warm. Isaac tucked his bare arms under the bed clothes, pulling them tightly to his chin. He could feel the cold of his elbows through his worn singlet. The dead of night could be as beautiful as it could be long, and this was such a night.

Isaac thought about Iovi Stator, Jupiter, and Ezekiel's transition. Received he had said. Received to God the Creator even though his grandfather was not yet buried. Buried, is that what should really happen to him, now that he was received? Not just under blankets but in the ground. Heavy, dark, damp, airless ground. He sensed the feel of it in his hands. Interred.

The only comfort Isaac could find in burial, was that without the need of breath, airlessness could be managed. He grew tired of thinking and before the next flutter of air could fill the curtain, he fell asleep.

***

It was the third day after Ezekiel's passing. Above the dark hollow that was about to claim Ezekiel's earthly remains, the sacerdos prayed on behalf of the mourners.

Isaac stood on the edge of the grave between his father and his mother, Appius in anguish, Johanna distraught, she with her arm firmly around Isaac's waist, and his father leaning against him, his hand resting on his son's shoulder.

The grave site was located on the family property just fifty paces from the escarpment. Two plots away, lay young Filius, whose scattered remains were gathered and packed into banana boxes before being laid to rest in his coffin. His headstone lists his place and date of birth in Dacia and his death date as being laid to rest in Australia. It also proclaimed him as the first of their family to be buried in the land selected by Terminus, the god of boundaries, the first of their kind to die in the new world.

Isaac watched the straps as they tugged at the shoulders of the grave diggers lowering Ezekiel's casket.

At this site, at the last witnessing of Ezekiel, the sacerdos moved into the prayer and response part of the service.

De eiusdem generis Ezekial morire et vivere

Of our kindred, Ezekiel, dies and lives

Deo Volent

God willing

Deus Vult

God wills it

The coffin descended as if in beat with the responses,

Ex vi termini extinctus amabitur idem

By the force of the Word, the same man when dead will be loved

Hic jacet Ezekiel in foro conscientiae

Here lies Ezekiel, before the tribunal of conscience
As the hypnotic prayer continued, Isaac began to hear the responses differently,

Epulis accumbere divum

To sit down at the banquets of the gods

Aquila non capit muscas

An eagle does not catch flies!

Fidei coticula crux

The cross is the touchstone of Faith

Errare humanum est

To err is human

In solo dus solus

An eagle does not catch flies!

In te, Domine, speravi

An eagle does not catch flies!

Fulmen brutum

A senseless thunderbolt; striking blindly!

Nosce te ipsum

Know thyself

Nec scire fas est omnia

It is not permitted to know all things!

Ne Jupiter quidem omnibus placet

Not even Jupiter pleases everybody *Jubilate Deo*
A senseless thunderbolt, striking blindly!

In vacuo

In empty space

Laus Deo

An eagle does not catch flies!

Omnia ad Dei gloriam

All things for the glory of God

In Judicium Dei mors janua vitae

In the judgement of God, death is the gateway of eternal life

In memoria aeterna omnia vincit amor

In eternal remembrance, love conquers all things.

Omnia vincit amor

A senseless thunderbolt…!
Omnia vincit amor

An eagle does not catch flies!
An eagle does not catch flies!
An eagle does not catch flies!

Omnia omnia omnia
Omnia vincit amor

Love conquers all things

Vade in Pace, Hic, nunc et in aeternum

Go in Peace, here, now and forever

The thud of the coffin hitting the base of the pit and the swish of straps being pulled up, woke Isaac from his stupor, to the scene before him. A sudden darkness cast by a dark cloud chilled the breeze.

In procession, one by one, the sods fell to coffin lid. The howling, louder than the pump on the creek bed that wetted the red earth at night, subdued to respectful whispers of prayer that sounded like the soft drizzle of the night spray. At the farmhouse Zama, with the help of Matema, waited to serve food and refreshment, that the living may remember the dead.

As the mourners walked from the grave, they walked into the future, a future without Ezekiel, the Transposer as he would come to be known. As they would take the wider paths, so too would they be dispersed, isolated and in time estranged.

Isaac's path would be stranger, more gifted and altruistic than those of his people. He remembered Ezekiel's plea on his death bed. A plea for mercy, in the fear of estrangement of his people, his *eiusdem generis,* of his kind, his kindred, the fear first confessed at the welcoming banquet to the new homeland of Australia. What he couched in confession, he cloaked in prophecy.

Praedictum Ezekiel.

Ezekiel's prophecy was being fulfilled as the sods fell in his grave. The thuds that rose, also beat the Professor's drum, Isaac's beloved professor's drum, the beat that would accompany the new social order.

Chapter 6

Aliquis in Viduum
(Something in the Void)

"And the earth was without form, and void; and darkness was upon the face of the deep. And the Spirit of God moved upon the face of the waters."
Genesis 1:2

In the teaching of the Romano Hebrew people, *the deep* came to mean the ether, the regions beyond, made of a purer, less tangible substance, invisible, that lay in wait for the word, and upon its voicing, to release into the void, earth, water, fire and light.

The Word was Be, omnipresent and permeating all creation, sentience, perception and thought, to give substance and meaning to the voids of the mind.

In the fire of the lightning strike, whereupon the pronouncement of Isaac's knowing was made, the beginning of something, a substance in his void, was made.

Isaac's first substance was sound of unimaginable clarity, voices not easily confided to memory, and visions whose lips spoke without speaking – *vox et praeterea nihil* – voices and nothing more; sound but no sense, occupied his mind, connecting him to the past.

Could it bring information about the future? Could information about the past bring about a change to the future, and what of the present? These could not be answered by first substance alone.

If first substance carried sound and images from another place or time, a second substance might convey speech for Isaac to be heard and beyond that, a third substance in the void, that of communication, taking the form of conversation perhaps even something physical. *Aliquis,* something, in nothing, bringing meaning to meaningless, form to the void.

At Ezekiel's burial, the prayers that droned into warnings, followed the pattern of first substance in Isaac's mind. It was received by Isaac only in the hearing. The distress of seeing the coffin being lowered into the burial plot, obscured the images which would have undoubtedly accompanied the words.

"A senseless thunderbolt."

Why did *Iovi Stator,* Jupiter, come with this torment at Ezekiel's funeral? And the repetition of, "An eagle does not catch flies."

Who or what was distracting him and to what end? This was the matter of first substance.

Isaac recalled the first change in the usual pattern of one-sided contact when under the cherry tree, he asked Jupiter if Ezekiel was with God the Creator. After some delay a statement, though not conclusive as a response, attested that Ezekiel had made his passage to the God of Light. If Isaac's voice had been accepted, then second substance was real – a second layer of *Aliquis in Viduum.*

A third layer of Something in the Void, if it was accessible, might be capable of carrying information that could be exchanged. This would make conversation possible and allow Isaac to speak directly to his demons, the rulers and gods of ancient Rome, and who or whatever else was present in the void.

In the years following Ezekiel's death, Isaac thought deeply of this presence that occupied him.

He had excelled in his secondary education and qualified for a place at the same university that was the *alma mater* of the professor. He particularly enjoyed the spaces between the nineteenth century buildings of the campus, the small squares, alleyways and cloisters that reflected his visions of antiquity. He imagined walking these places with the professor, of having his presence, as if the lapse of time had not occurred. He was in fact alone.

His course of study was entomology, the study of insects. He would major in his passion for the eradication of the fly for the betterment of humanity. Outdoor eating was banned by local government by-laws, despite frequent submissions by restaurant groups to emulate the cafe lifestyle of Europe. The fly plague in the city was as prevalent as it was in the country.

Education drove a wedge between him and the family values he had inherited, just as his grandfather had feared.

He found student accommodation within walking distance of the University, a narrow double-storey row house used as a student sharehouse, an experience in compressed space for him.

He found solace in the small room he could call his own, and the streets of the city no longer bothered him.

His room, three steps up the from landing to the first floor was ten feet wide and as tall as it was long. Unlike the more elegant rooms of the house, the walls of his room met the ceiling squarely, a plainness he did not mind.

The roommates of his share house stayed much to themselves. Two of them, both named Bruce, were from country towns scattered much further in the state than Isaac's city fringe market gardens.

Sonora, a vicar's daughter, had loud sex often and afterwards, sitting in an eastern meditative position, voiced a consonant for as long as her breath held. Isaac wondered whether the combination was related but was too unsure of himself to ask.

Her search for the mystique included smoking pot in front of a pile of books, hoping the information they contained might be puffed from them, and into her memory. On this, Isaac wondered what kind of use an arts degree might hold.

The country boys, being more used to running with the rabbits when it came to sex, a proposition that disgusted both of them, stayed clear of her as if spooked.

The lean-to roof over the kitchen leaked and at night the cockroaches scoured the floor. The toilet and bathroom were slung along the back wall. Isaac often ate alone in the small yard between the building and the back fence to the cobbled bluestone lane. A jumble of rubbish, an old washing machine and bicycles jammed most of the yard. Makeshift clothes lines spanned the width of the property. He missed the sprinkled darkness of the night sky, the jumble of buildings and the city lights making it virtually impossible to see the stars.

Long before the advent of freeways and fast-food service centres, the capital cities were connected by meandering two lane highways. The roads were dangerous and the traffic that clogged the towns, clung like mussels on a jetty pylon. The journeys were tedious and it was common to pack picnic hampers for stops along the highway to break the journey. Clearings in the bushland by the sides of the road were used as picnic spots. The flat expansive boot lids on the 'Yank tanks' of the day provided an ideal table. As the first sandwich box had been opened, flies appeared by the score. Not even the speed of the traffic passing just feet away dispersed them. The diners persevered until they had eaten as quickly as they could, warding off the assailants in the process. As was the custom, wrappers and scraps were dumped before jumping in the vehicle to minimise the number of flies coming on board. These stops served the flies well and promoted the stigma associated with outdoor eating.

Isaac understood the social consequences of changing this pattern. What he learned of the species gave him greater insight into the human condition. A freer society, unbound by the pestilence, would be less conscious of itself, more skilled at communicating and easier at being. In his learning, Isaac realised the significance of the word 'being'. With the exception of primal personality traits, he rationalised there were no dog beings or cat beings or insect beings, and he felt for very good reason. As much as animals loved the food and shelter their masters provided, they could not build these complex things for themselves. He thought how it would be for several species, perhaps hundreds, to inhabit an abandoned dwelling. Would they cohabit in the shelter at night and go out in the day to feed on each other? Which of the species would abide by such courtesies?

In this Isaac recalled the sayings, so frequently given by his voices,

"Gaudium certaminis" – the joy of conflict, the human trait the professor so despised, was a function of 'being' as distinct from the animal need of conflict for food, shelter and survival. And the rages,

"Furor loquendi" – a rage for speaking

"Furor scribendi" – a rage for writing

"Furor poeticus" – poetic fire

"Furor arma ministrat" – rage provides arms

"Gratia placendi" – the perils of being, versus the delight of pleasing. The professor's battle to change the disposition that,

"Homo homini lupus" – man is a wolf to man.

It was now up to Isaac to take up the challenge, to defuse this destructive impulse of being human.

***

In his visions Isaac was privy to the physical might of ancient Rome, founded by unparalleled force administered ruthlessly, that belied the genius of its age. What they gained by the sword they gave to engineering, civil order, literature and an architecture undiminished by time.

Isaac saw, however, that its authoritative language was as brutal as its force was eternal. It was terse, accurate and without waste. The more they spoke to him the more he understood the expressed Roman mind, the mind of his forebears. For all this, the forfeitable humanity of the Romans remained repugnant to the Hebrew side of him. The Arch of Titus built to celebrate the sacking of Jerusalem, held both wonder and betrayal for him.

The evidence lay in the suspended faces of his first encounter, that of the first substance of his void. The characters, their whims and egos, sounded loud without echo. The visions were specific, and the older he got the more detailed they were in form.

The Roman Emperor Hadrian spoke volumes on the subject of large-scale construction, especially the glory of wall building. He mouthed loudly of the wall he built north of Eboracum to keep out the unruly rabble of northern Britannia, and the great walls of red brick and tufa stone at Tivoli, which he used to segment the landscape into parcels that gave him mastery of his domain.

And from Rabirius, he learned how the use of axis, as he employed in Domitian's palace, was effective in forming magnificent vistas. The clever placement of devices to conceal imperfections in the natural landscape, to mask awkward changes in alignment, also featured.

These lessons were key to earning an income while he was still at university, and in the years after his graduation.

As the city expanded, consuming orchards and outlying towns in its path, new suburbs generated opportunities for wealth. Greenfield land acquisition for eventual subdivision drew a spotlight on quick money, becoming a sport in its own right. The saving grace was that the rising middle-class found larger homes to raise their children, even though services lagged in outlying areas. The motor car was no longer a luxury, but an essential vehicle of modern life.

The workings of this prostrate anthill became a significant part of the economic engine, driving cultural integration as the many ethnic groups sought their own piece of the great Australian dream. The unanticipated social reckoning of this development had in some measure been the professor's quest.

Isaac loved his learning environment and made friends easily with tutors and like-minded students who found him intriguing. His immediacy with Latin description was legendary.

Income from part-time work at a bakery was minimal, and he searched ways he could earn extra money, hitting upon the idea of consulting in land sales.

With the help of Decius, Isaac bought a car reliable enough to drive to the outskirts of the city. It had become popular to purchase small rural plots on the edge of town as hobby farms, seen also as an investment in expectation of growth in value. City dwellers liked open space. The wealthy were particular about views when choosing property, creating dams and enough space for a riding arena and horse agistment.

A country house was the focus of this arcadian dream, and around it, the bounty of water and horses furnished the bucolic realm.

Isaac took a sales position with a Real Estate Agency specialising in rural land sales. With a further year to complete his studies, this job offered weekend work, leaving much of his week for lectures, lab work and tutorials.

It was the kind of work that fitted his research into the behaviour of flies, at the same time providing the greatest income in the shortest possible time. He chose city-fringe real estate, partly for its familiarity with his own rural background, but more so because he could deal with the fly problem. It was a perfect real-world laboratory.

Not all of his plans worked quite the way he expected. The first commission to which he was assigned involved a large commercial zone property. It was located one street back from the main road and was now ripe for conversion to peripheral sales that required larger floor areas.

Standing in brilliant sunshine Isaac looked down the broad frontage to the street. Two figures rounded the corner and swaggered in his direction. Their body language was mischievous. As they approached him Isaac recognised them as the 'double trouble' twins that terrorised the school yard.

The brothers were not identical twins. They simply shared a confinement. Freeman and Horatio 'Ratzarz' earned their acquired surname by their deeds. Freeman Cassidy and his brother Horatio Cassidy loomed large and menacingly enough to cast a malevolent shadow. A small, fat sweaty hand was thrust into Isaacs.

"Freeman Cassidy – this is my brother, Horatio. Do we know you?"

"Isaac Moritz, I don't believe we've met," replied Isaac denying full recollection.

Freeman, the shorter and fatter of the two grew hair like coiled wire which sprung back into place as he pulled it. His thick beard like his hairdo left the barest minimum of skin available for facial recognition. His eyes were in perpetual motion and only ever fixed during the most intensive of negotiations. He liked to be liked. Horatio had grown four inches taller than his twin brother and was thickset. He was clean shaven with straight hair slicked flat and closely over his ample dome. His wide exposed face was like a porcelain dish painted with small fine features. A lascivious, smiling, consumptive look had settled permanently on his face.

The three discussed the merits and size of the property. The brothers were 'between' deals and the sale of half of this property was fundamental to their financing strategy. They indicated the dimensions of the property by a wave of the arm pointing roughly 'here'. Isaac was already unhappy with the documentation and suggested his client understood the dimension to be 'there' rather than 'here'.

At this point Horatio pushed his arm forward onto Isaac's chest and Freeman said,

"Look, Moritz, here are the papers, just get him to sign 'em."

Horatio followed quickly with,

"Or we'll have your guts grow onion weed!"

The twins were still unpredictable. Nothing had changed since the primary school yard when they peddled terror.

Isaac took stock.

"I'll put it to them."

"Yeah," Freeman grunted.

"Just get us the munni!" terminated Horatio.

As Isaac drove away from this meeting, he could not help but recall the classics. In the *Invectivarium in L. Catilinam – Oratio Prima* delivered in the Temple of Jupiter Stator, before the Senate, on the eighth of November, 63 BC, Cicero attacked Cataline for his insolent audacity, and deplored the spirit of the time which allowed this enemy of the state to continue his activities.

Had nothing changed? The Oratio, Cicero's mastery of the Latin tongue was delivered in full measure of his brilliant powers of description and narration, irony and sarcasm. How could this speech fall to its namesakes Horatio's ear and not be heard?

As for his brother Freeman so named by Royal pardon, not even the catholicisation of England as chronicled by the Venerable Bede in 721 AD could soothe his savage breast. Freeman maintained a considerable chip on the shoulder, and a king's pardon for generations of skullduggery, misdemeanour and aggression ensured it would remain there.

This confrontation left Isaac pondering what the development of human history had in common with the battle at Asculum in 279 BC a battle in which the losses on both sides were extremely heavy. As Pyrrus stood in victory over the Romans, the cost of it to his own army was so great that he could only weep. Progress over anarchy seemed to emulate such hollow victories. One hundred steps forward, ninety-nine back.

It was in this thought, that Isaac fully appreciated the professor's torment over human development. In spite of the power of eloquence, it was devastation that remained the actual path of progress, a succession of Pyrrhic victories.

By now his mind was on a roll. The Temple of Vesta built by his ancestor Septimius Severus in AD 205 seemed stripped bare compared with the Tempietto at S. Pietro in Montorio, built thirteen hundred years later. In the former, the vestal virgins kept alight the sacred fire, signifying the hearth as the centre and source of Roman life and power. In the latter an architecture of richness marks the place where Saint Peter was martyred.

After some deliberation, Isaac concluded to his relief, that great leaps in progress can occur, despite the commercially depraved.

Real estate, the grit of life, was the set-piece in the play of multiple lives. Murky waters plied at its edges, the turbidity that trembled between land and water. To Isaac, land for money was like the marriage of clod and vapor, and the 'deal' held little artistic or philosophical interest for him. It seemed only those with a direct interest could exercise the required bone headedness and persistence.

These characteristics were also the trademark of the fly. He had seen important negotiations for settlement terminated in the field, when an emotionally charged party to the contract inhaled a fly and in the convulsions that followed, died of a massive heart attack. The deal was lost.

Exactly five years after commencing his course, Isaac was admitted to the degree of Bachelor of Science – Entomology. The hours that he had spent with his grandmother at the packing table had yielded his celebrated degree, the highest academic honour achieved in his family.

He had fulfilled his promise to his grandmother to catch flies like she did, and committed his doctorate thesis to the practice and improvement of her flycatching techniques.

His awe of the housefly, *musca domestica,* scaled to new heights when an astronaut undergoing centrifuge trials, reported a fly buzzing around his face at a crushing fifteen times normal gravity. The fly was the last thing he saw before his eyes swelled and blackened, before losing consciousness.

The two-winged compound-eyed housefly, found in and around houses and farmland in nearly every country, feeding on garbage, manure and food scraps had mocked the space race.

The real estate cycle that returned to boom conditions, ate into the time required to continue his studies. Owning a country retreat or bush block, had captured the imagination of city dwellers and Isaac was pressured into servicing this market. Without exception every rural inspection would be frustrated by flies. It was becoming impossible to paint an attractive picture of a property when a grand gesture of the arm would turn into a defensive sweep against them. Their persistence often made a sale difficult to close.

Isaac dedicated his thesis to solving this problem. He added the need for discretion to the vast knowledge he had already accumulated, and developed a container similar to a whisky hip flask, split at the sides with a concertina band. This enabled the 'flask' to be opened with one hand. The inside of the flask contained a removable cartridge of grease soaked linen. When folded, the container fitted neatly into the inside breast pocket of his jacket. Mindful that this procedure involved physical contact with the fly, he carried a pack of hand sanitising wipes in the right pocket of his coat, and a satchel for used wipes in the left pocket.

A one-hundred-acre property with grand views was assigned to Isaac, and he made arrangements to meet his wealthy clients inside the gate from where it was possible to make out the main features of the land. It was the ideal location to create a positive first impression.

A gleaming Range Rover four-wheel drive pulled up in the regal manner and Isaac was impressed. The doors opened and all of Isaacs expectations were met. An elegant woman and her successful husband alighted to Isaac's practiced, eloquent greeting.

As soon as pleasantries were exchanged, as if by some cosmic signal the flies arrived as he knew they would. The DZZ-ZIZING sound began softly in the remote key of D-flat, but within seconds had built to an audible annoyance.

Calmly, Isaac gesticulated,

"Please come this way and allow the view to unfold."

Mr Augustus Elkhorn moved forward in an assertion of authority. As the young Mrs Elkhorn moved to follow, Isaac swiped at her back without her knowledge, pulled out the flask and opened it pushing five flies into the sticky chamber. He compressed the flask and hid it from view. As they walked a few paces he pulled out a towel, wiped his hand and pocketed the spent swipe into the satchel located in his left pocket.

"The flies are terrible," sputtered Mr Elkhorn.

"Dreadful, darling," consoled his wife.

"It will improve," assured Isaac. This sale would be hard won.

On the way to a clearing, Isaac had managed three more swipes while he had been describing the lay of the land. He had removed by his reckoning about twenty flies. Already, the fly population was thinning out across all three. Using the principles shown to him by ancient Roman rulers, Isaac made sure his clients were enthralled by the evolving description of the house location, sweeping driveway, parterre, a beautiful pond lawn and even the prime location for a flagpole, all the while swiping flies without their being aware.

As directed by Isaac, the party came to rest at what Isaac had determined to be the best location to develop the Manor house.

"This is a timeless and beautiful place." Isaac sighed.

"Yes!" agreed the young Mrs Elkhorn, provoking a rise in her husband's brow. The remaining flies were soon joined by others. To Isaac's good fortune most of the flies were on their victim's backs.

"I see the view from here as having the hallmarks of the distinguished, classical landscape tradition. The crest of bald, pudding-shaped hill across the valley forms an axis that divides the symmetry of the two slopes to the left and right, which come forward to meet in the gully just below us. The landscape elements you desire should be arranged around this axis."

"Hmm. Yes, I can see that!" agreed Mr Elkhorn.

Isaac swiped again while everyone including the flies were distracted. Ten more in the can!

"To me, the site recalls the formal symmetry of the Temple of Venus at Baalbek built in 273 AD with its excellent forward extension of steps and landings. A fine pair of protruding shoulders should embrace the steps, smaller of course, more of a folly in scale. It would be confident, assured and reaching. With the correct landscape and driveway treatment it would be most welcoming.

"By Jupiter, Isaac, I think you're right!" beamed Mr Elkhorn, Isaac almost shocked by the reference.

"Amazing," echoed his agreeable wife.

"Isaac, how do you envisage this roadway formation?" asked Mr Elkhorn directly.

"Well, if you look back the way we came and along here in front of us, you can visualise a serpentine approach that follows the gentler slope of the land."

Isaac nearly froze. The sudden turning movements had launched a few flies off their backs and he swiped.

"I'd like water and trout, and a small jetty with dome-headed black painted bollards joined by loose, heavy ropes," murmured Mr Elkhorn as if living the dream.

His wife pitched in with, "A pillared arbour towards and onto the water would be nice dear. Ah, on axis of course."

Isaac swiped again, explaining,

"We could get around that by continuing the driveway to the right of the axis and building a high dam wall that would traverse the axis back to the left," advised Isaac, continuing with, "The road would skirt below the wall. The resulting large body of water will conceal the driveway so as not to be seen from the house. The entire length of the wall would act as a level spillway. The vista from the house across the water would appear to be infinite and eternal."

His client leaned forward with his left hand on his chin, his elbow resting on his right arm supported on his belly.

Isaac swiped again. The can was full.

"Look Isaac, we like this property, but…" stalled Mr Elkhorn.

"But Augie my darling, the flies really aren't that bad," enthusiastically consoled his young delight.

"Okay, you've got a deal."

Isaac went on to become the most successful Realtor south of the Tropic of Capricorn. In the brief time he achieved this distinction, he set aside sufficient funds to support himself beyond his PhD, and looked to seed-fund his own research unit. Once established, he could apply for continued funding through the university.

He maintained his position selling real estate only as long as it suited his pursuit of eliminating the fly from the trials of mankind.

Isaac obtained his PhD in Science/Entomology with an exhaustive paper on the INSECT REVOLUTION – Winning the Battle. He explored the idea of starting a company he called SNAP-ZAP Solutions.

His family was overjoyed by his academic achievements and organised a family banquet. They were surprised that his passion for hand-fly-capture had achieved such status for the family name. Uncle Cato danced to a tune he made up about "this must be the Lucky Country" all of which made Isaac cringe. The joy was tinged with sadness as Grand Uncle Felix lay nearing the end of his life. His admiration for Isaac the man, was filial and he summoned him accordingly, to impart the oracle wisdom to the one great child of the family.

In the company of the grand old man, Isaac vowed to pass on the living history of the family. He did so in honour of Felix, that he should find peace in his rest. How he would undertake this great task was not yet made known to him, and he committed it to the future.

His grandmother, his beloved Avia Rebekah, had passed away before she could witness his and her combined achievement.

Having attained an almost cult status among realtors, Isaac continued selling real estate but only at his convenience. A young girl had joined the firm as receptionist and open house hostess, a term that had a sexist ring to it, but it was an acceptable practice of the day. She had taken the job as a temporary position, hoping one day to become a librarian in one of the fine institutions in the city.

Her name was Luteesha Veranova and Isaac found in her, a kindred spirit, and a young woman savvy enough to fend off unwanted advances.

Tall and slender, her bony facial features softened with the look of her deep-set attentive eyes. The curls of her dark hair embraced her face, making her seem tireless.

Where Isaac wavered in his advances, she nurtured the fondness between them. She loved his caring gestures, and was moved by his love for the long-departed professor he so often spoke about. His use of language fascinated her as did his studious and absorptive manner.

She had once replied to him, 'you talk strange', at once implying in a single breath 'I understand', and 'I like it' – the hallmark of a young girl replying to an older man she admired. Over the four years of their intermittent working life, she kept herself aside for him. She loved his passion for learning and his commitment to his research project. It was here that he was at his strongest. Her deepening love for him was measured and not blind. She knew his fragility and that this made him.

In her he felt the mysterious thing unknown about the unknowable, a familiarity that put him to rest. He became more relaxed in her company, aware and unaware of her presence when that was all that was needed in the moment.

Isaac did not share his visions with her for fear of weakening their relationship. He did, however, advise her to study classicism, the Roman period and the subtle role of the Latin language in modern English. He would help her to know history and language the way he felt it. He saw without such a commitment by her, marriage would be predisposed to fail.

Despite wanting to marry her for some time, he had until now withheld the apparitions from her, severe as they were, that increasingly informed him. He did not know the long-term effects on his mental well-being, and decided that with such uncertainty, he would not have children. For her to understand or accept this in marriage, he would have to reveal the torrents of his mind.

His mission and his love would be all that he could give her. Luteesha needed time to accept such an imposition on her life, to forgo having children. She would have to accept his completeness, and his purpose as her own. Isaac granted patience.

He dealt with his achievements easily. They were quantifiable, measurable results and were conclusive. The crowded complexities of his mind were not. They were leading and inconclusive, and Isaac was still unsure if the role they played directly related to his success.

What were the visions and sounds telling him about entomology? Had they so usurped Isaac's mind that they denied him his right to offspring?

The visions and sounds that occupied the first substance in the void, were more than the natural processes of his brain. They were an external intrusion. He trusted his theory of second substance, that of being heard by his unwelcome assailers. In time he would confront, without doubt or hesitation, the faces of his fears. If he could not abandon them, could he bring them to justice, alter their ways to benefit him?

Joop D'Angeli was a self-anointed real estate mogul working out of the same office as Isaac. He was abrupt, brutal and greedy. Luteesha's denials upset him, and for her to favour Isaac was as insulting as it was incomprehensible. He despised Isaac personally, as much as for his success.

His working style included long, alcohol-fuelled lunches during which he 'chaired' strategies. He regularly missed closing deals for lack of sober judgement. Joop had no reserve and spouted whatever came to mind, and Isaac was one of his most frequent prompts.

"How does the bastard do it? He comes in twice a week and gets a ninety percent strike rate for first visits! The nerd doesn't deserve it!" All the while waving the only fly off his plate.

His colleague, Richard Dennis, who liked Isaac, defensively urged,

"Take it easy, you'll burst your face! If you don't listen and learn, you'll have to live with it!"

**

Isaac received a letter from the University Board of Review. He had been both invited and ordered to attend a meeting in the Chancellor's Board Room at 11:00 am January 30. This was to be Isaac's final appearance before the Board and it would be on the merits of his presentation that his research funding would be granted. Without it he could not build the team he needed to demonstrate the practical application of his theories. His application if successful, would allow for two permanent staff members, laboratory access, travel expenses and three five-year options for renewal of the placement.

A robust and difficult character Isaac un-befriended was the bursar, a position that did not advantage him. He had fallen out with him over his criticism of Isaac's 'absurd' hypothesis as he put it. Isaac responded with the same caustic sentiments, sealing their disagreements.

Vent 'call me Vent' Wilberforce, had written a treatise titled 'Flatulence in Society, 1300 to 1900', selling more copies than his clinical research would have suggested. The amusements hurled at him was distressing, as there were many instances of suicide associated with accidental venting at Royal Banquet Receptions over several hundred years.

During the early hours of the morning on the day of the hearing, Isaac lay awake in the first-floor bedroom of the terrace house he bought close to the University. The bust of Julius Caesar tumbled and hovered a while in Isaac's mind. The familiar lucent stone lips moved and as usual Isaac heard nothing. He waited for the clear bell like clarity of the words to follow. As the lips stopped moving, Caesar's expression became nonplussed.

"Id est nunc aut nunguam" – it is now or never

"Observanda" – things to be observed

"Cavere vox et practerea nihil" – beware sound but no sense

"Noli irritane leones" – do not irritate lions

"Aquila noncapit muscas" – an eagle does not catch flies,

and after a pause, in the dawning of light,

"Audentes fortuna juvat" – fortune aids the bold.

With the message given, the water-milk whiteness of Julius Caesar receded into the gold crevices of the velvet red from where it came, and finally Isaac knew. This was a clearer a communication than he could have dreamt. This advice was from his forebears, his *eiusdem generis,* his kindred.

Isaac sat bolt upright as if he needed to reassure himself of consciousness. The daylight lit the stained-glass border on the door leading to the balcony. Isaac needed to prepare for this day.

At five minutes to eleven, Isaac walked the corridor towards the Board Room. He sat on a wooden bench placed in an alcove opposite the tall panelled doors to the room.

The skirting boards of the wide corridor were at least twenty inches high. Fifteen feet above the floor, a huge gutter cornice separated wall and ceiling. Large mahogany honour boards hung from a picture rail mounted on the aged cream painted walls. Among the lines of prominent Alumni, he saw the Professor's name in gold letters, Manius C. Dexter. A metal conduit pierced the cornice and descended to the top of the chocolate-coloured switch-plate. It reminded him of his first day at school and the horrible headmaster. His nerves began to burn.

The door slowly creaked open. An elderly gentleman stepped into the hallway and summoned him. Isaac picked up his case and followed him into the room.

"Mr Moritz, welcome!" called out the Chairman.

He walked towards the table and took the seat as directed. During the reading of his submission Isaac sat patiently and intently. Each board member flipped and fidgeted with their copies and at the end of it being read, the Chairman called for any questions that the directors might ask of him.

"You are asking for a laboratory, two staff members and an operating allowance for this project for a period of potentially three terms of five years. Is that sufficient, Mr Moritz?" asked Sir Robert Robie in a beg to differ manner.

To defuse the thrust of his question, Isaac asked if he might have a glass of water, and without authority got up and went to the sideboard. With his back to the table, he poured water from the jug with his right hand. With a deceptive stance, he took out a cigarette packet and flipped the lid open and shook it, releasing seven spritely hungry flies into the room, tucked the packet away and walked his glass back to the table.

Seven. The seven coins of his family heritage, the seven hills of Rome, the Seven Seas they had crossed, and now the seven flies of his future.

He resumed his seat and leant forward, at first eyeballing Sir Robert and confidently scanning the rest of the board members, including his nemesis, the Bursar Vent Wilberforce.

"I believe it to be a fair and equitable proposition as I have committed my personal funds to establish the program thus far."

Noting a stir on the other side of the table the Chairman beamed.

"Yes, Sir Magnus, feel free to ask questions as you may!"

"Is this a joke, Mr Moritz?" queried Sir Magnus who being of such age and laureate could not recollect a single humorous jest. His query was genuine and not intended to stifle the debate. Isaac understood this.

The flies were now doing their work, and Isaac had to brush one off as he stood up to reply, "Only in that it appears simple, Sir Magnus," respectfully replied Isaac and went on to explain, "The application of the principles to be developed are of world significance and shall empower millions of victims of 'musca domestica', to bring relief from its pestilence and associated diseases. In practical terms I estimate the benefits to be ten-fold that of penicillin as the procedure is safe, preventative and self-administered.

"I can also assure you that the time lines and budget outlined in the submission will be met, and I invite you to share my complete confidence in this most valuable project, and I am certain that the honour and integrity of this great Institution will be enhanced and lauded universally."

A ruckus erupted, cutting Isaac short as Sir Paulus knocked his glasses clean off his face while swiping at a fly. Isaac was relieved by the disturbance, remembering from the morning visions that he should not irritate lions by the overstating and repetition of his case. A young note-taker retrieved the glasses and when he finally regained composure Sir Paulus asked of Isaac,

"I can see this fly thing is a pest but how much do you think you can learn by this placement of University resources?"

"The fly has a fundamental weakness, a flaw in its genetic makeup. It is my belief that unlocking this will lead to new discoveries and opportunities for application in the aerospace industry and quite possibly surveillance technology. This would be in addition to the benefits the World Health Organisation would receive by the eradication of the common fly."

"Precisely what is it that you mean by the term hand-fly-capture I just don't understand this new-fangled phrase!" interrupted Sir Fergus. As fortune would have it, as Sir Fergus drew breath a fly zithered into his mouth forcing him to cough involuntarily. Luckily for him the fly ejected.

Isaac jumped to his feet and before all, swiped the very same fly from the air, walked to the side of the room and pitched it hard against the wall. The banging of the fly against the wall stunned it for long enough to fall to the floor and in the gaze of all, he quietly crushed it below his shoe. Isaac spun around to face the committee and said,

"Gentlemen, an eagle does not catch flies! People do!"

When the jaws of the learned men returned to their speaking position, Isaac walked briskly to a small tea room in the corner of the Board Room and emerged seconds later still wiping his hands with a towel. From the door he tossed the towel back into the tearoom and walked to his chair to once again address the meeting.

"What you have just seen is the power, in its most rudimentary description, of hand-insect-combat, specifically hand-fly-capture, and the procedure of the hand washing etiquette so required for its proper execution. It is this two-fold sequence that will empower the third world among many others."

"Are there any further questions that any member of this Board may ask of Mr Moritz before I put the motion to the meeting?" brokered the Chairman.

"This is ridiculous!" exclaimed Vent Wilberforce.

"Not a question, Mr Wilberforce!" scolded the Chairman.

All were silent.

"Then in the matter of the granting of the Research Placement to Mr Isaac Moritz, those in favour raise your hand," and all but the bursar did so.

"Motion carried. Thank you for your patience, Isaac, and congratulations!"

Isaac concealed his joy by redirecting his thoughts to how he had conducted himself throughout the meeting, remembering what Julius Caesar had said that morning, that fortune aids the bold. His visions had at last proved constructive and he was thankful.

On this very same day, with his future secured, he called Luteesha and asked her to marry him. Wanting him, she accepted. At the age of twenty-three, knowing his fear of having children, she accepted the consequences of a childless union.

He did speak to her of the accident in his childhood in which the professor was killed, but stopped short of explaining the full impact of the visions and sounds that plagued him. She was devoted by nature, and understanding of his mental condition, and committed to whatever social life or society they encountered, to be content to withdraw if he needed her to.

***

Aliquis in Viduum. Something real occupied the void of Isaac's mind. He pondered long on the meaning of this, and as it was a matter of something that just happened, concluded that it didn't mean anything. Usually a jumble of information, at the very best it was advice.

A jumble, such as when Numa, the second king after Romulus, the founder of the city of Rome appeared to him, praising the conquests of Cincinnatus, Coriolanus and Camillus whose campaigns galvanised all of the Italian Peninsula to become the Republic of Rome. Numa, founder of the State religion of ancient Rome, praised the victories of men born three hundred years into his future. How could he know to tell of that which was future to him?

When he became lost in the depths of his thinking, he learned with limited success, to sift and expunge them when they did not contribute to his life's mission. He resorted to the word *nullum,* nothing, to ease the boiling turbidity of his mind, to think on nothing. It was not long before nothing itself became something. Nothing is like you think. Nothing is like you think it is. Nothing is like you cannot think. The space he made empty became filled once again. Even when he had no desire for the thing unknown, it just as quickly, explained itself by the still more unknown.

Isaac's void was real. This he knew and he would use it regardless of proof, knowing that nothing is the measure by which something is valued.

Chapter 7

The Futuris File

An office, two work stations, a small meeting room with a tea bench, a fume cupboard and a single island lab bench were sectioned off the vacant Chemistry Building for Isaac's research team. The ground floor space had ready access to an undercover loading bay and a large, conveniently located store room.

Of the two recent science graduates assigned to the project, Julia was the more absorbed. Her movements and speech were measured, and her manner had the reserve and quiet of a physician. She worked around Isaac's impatience for conclusions, with the same self-possessed assurance that allowed the Sabine women to intervene in the war following their rape and seizure, ultimately enabling them to secure peace.

Rex was as brilliant as his attention deficit disorder would allow. He was quick and with Isaac's help, could snatch flies from space with embarrassing ease, and like his boss had mastered the multiple-grab without harming a single fly caught in the cusp of his hand.

Behind the closed door of his office Isaac would sit motionless for up to two hours at a time, thinking, *An intricate structure or enclosure, containing a series of winding passageways, hard to follow without losing sight of one's way. It has to be logically connective, rather than like a maze that seeks to confound. The fly's eye, a dome of lenses magnified and tracked to the brain, arranged by evolution from a single light/shade pocket on the surface of its body.*

Was it branch-like, leading to a single trunk or were there multiple connections, essential to the interpretative nature of the creature, that made it such a formidable opponent? Does the reception of colour survive the collective path to cognition, or does it lose its intensity to become a grey scale image, and would it make a difference if it did?

In the first month of his placement Isaac had been busy with such questions and devised experiments, some of which required vivisection to assess the impulses and pathways under a light microscope. A small, electric current proved effective in detecting the stimuli under the beam of light, focused through a series of lenses. Julia had mastered the process and was adept at the write-up of data. The long-term aim was to road-map a membrane for use in symbiotic metal surfaces.

Isaac and Rex spent hours at the Municipal dump, practicing single and multi-fly captures as well as the more advanced, combination single fly/multiple fly catches. A key feature of the exercise was to minimise the length of the approach sweep that would improve turn-around times.

The capture of flies unharmed was a doctrine. Nothing infuriated Isaac more than to injure or kill a fly in a capture sequence. The kill was reserved for the pitch and stomp method. The dump also provided an unlimited supply of flies for laboratory purposes. They were cheap and plentiful. Quarantine-bred rats and rabbits were a significant drain on the resources of other research laboratories, and Isaac knew that in this regard, he had chosen his subject well.

The pitch and stomp method best suited younger people as it was so physical. For older members of the community, he needed different solutions, and Isaac put ideas for these on hold for now. As impressive as aerial capture in open spaces was, it drew modest support from Isaac, the problem being the kill. He abandoned the concertina hip flask as it required a skill level much higher than the general public could grasp. The main purpose of research in the initial stages of the program involved the 'lifting' of flies from surfaces, particularly indoor environments. If the surfaces involved the skin or clothing of a person, the technique could only be judged as successful if that person was unaware that a lift had taken place. In Isaac's view, the victim under attack had already suffered enough.

Isaac's terminology had it that the person on whom a fly had landed was to be called the 'victim' and the fly always the 'aggressor'. A third-party rendering assistance is the 'hunter' who may never be permitted to touch, belt, smack or swat the victim. All being in accord with this rule, capture can take place with or without the victim's knowledge.

Rex had the task of plotting the trajectories of a fly's movement in varying circumstances of initiation. This involved a range of movements. The reaction time and direction associated with a simple sway, a determined wave, an aggressive swipe had to be recorded.

Julia would the plot data for each move and analyse the results in relation to the cognitive tracks of the compound eye.

Combat sequences were measured for every imaginable and practical surface. Isaac's classic slow approach, stop and sweep method was tested on solid, opaque and clear flat surfaces. Each flat surface was then inclined from horizontal by five degrees until vertical. When the incline moved beyond vertical where the fly became located on the underside of the surface, Isaac had to reconsider the technique. Adjustments were made to the approach angle, stop distance from target, and speed of sweep. It was concluded that an incline of one hundred-and-seventeen degrees was the limit that hand capture could work. At this downward angle and lower, it was best to dislodge the fly to a more favourable position.

The more transparent the surface the less the standard procedure worked. Clear glass in a horizontal plane complicated the fly's perception of direction such that the likelihood of successful capture was reduced to fifty per cent of the capture rate for a solid surface.

Curved surfaces of varying radii, irregular surfaces and a range of material finishes were also studied. The evidence they were able to quantify proved what Isaac had already intuited.

The fundamental flaw in the fly's genetic structure was, however short, its need for a vertical take-off. What appeared to be random dispersal in any direction was true only above a vertical dimension of six to ten millimetres. On most surfaces a fly needed to vertically clear the surface on which it rested before it could take full evasive action. This clearance was all that a well-timed hand movement needed to clear the surface on which the fly sat and, to bump it unharmed into the cusp of the hand. This flaw was a fortuitous match for the shape of the human hand.

Timing was also vital when closing the hand to form a chamber. A large chamber allowed the fly enough freedom of movement to buzz around provided it could not escape. If the captor wished he could close the chamber. The smaller volume within the hand restricted the available space and so the fly's buzz became a higher pitched intense zither sound.

Isaac found the changing pitch amusing. In his younger days he played the fly like an instrument, closing and opening the chamber in rhythm or pulse. The tingling sensation of the fly's beating wings could also be enjoyed.

Isaac pondered the day he could use this variation in pitch as chamber music to some fit end. The time to exploit this was nigh. Soon, within the walls of this laboratory, housed in a red brick building with white framed windows, he would solve the where and how of ridding the world of the fly.

In the coming weeks, his team would conclude another flaw.

In Australia alone, nine hundred billion flies were bred in one week from three hundred million pats of dung dropped each day, by a mere twenty-eight million cows. Although Australia's fly species ranged from the hairy maggot blowfly, the oriental latrine fly, the flesh fly and the usual bush flies, it was the house fly, *musca domestic,* that Isaac detested most. It was the house fly that Isaac knew best, its taciturn, catch me if you can nature. Isaac knew it all. For every human there were 2.4 million flies.

Isaac scoffed at the work of the dung beetle proponents. He believed the numbers simply too great without tripping yet another environmental and ecological disaster.

American embryologist, Fred Soper dreamt of eradicating yellow fever malaria from the world by raising the killing of mosquitoes to an art. The Global Malaria Eradication Campaign undertaken by him helped eliminate the disease from the developed world, and from many parts of the developing world. Isaac admired his fanaticism and absolutism, and his commitment to saving lives.

Urgency was key to undermining DDT resistance raised by genetic variants, appearing in as little as six or seven years. Soper claimed fighting malaria had little to do with the intricacies of science and biology. In some obtuse moment, Isaac imagined that Soper hired a swat team of men, to go door-to-door, killing mosquitoes.

Rachel Carson's book, *Silent Spring*, quoted a bird-lover from Alabama: "There was not a sound of the song of a bird. It was eerie, terrifying. What was man doing to our perfect and beautiful world?"

But to Soper the world was neither perfect nor beautiful and the question of what man could do to nature was less critical than what nature, unimpeded, could do to mankind.

Isaac sympathised with Soper's bewilderment. The moral ground had shifted beneath his feet. The absolutes that governed Soper's life had suddenly been set aside. Despite saving tens of millions of lives, Soper's beloved panacea had an unusual persistence, and a toxicity that laid waste to wildlife and aquatic ecosystems. In short, saving the present threatened the future, the historical record showing the cycle of extinctions of life to be vigorously regenerative, adaptive and replaceable.

Isaac's hand-fly technique was chemical free with no environmental consequences. The health benefits of the procedure stemmed from the practice of hand-washing after every kill session, was made environmentally responsible by the advent of biodegradable soaps.

One of the tasks he set for Julia, was to coordinate research into biological diversity with interdepartmental colleagues working on closed sustainable systems. This work was required to determine the impact of removing a species from the chain of life. Precisely, would frogs die out without a heavy fly population. What were the numbers required to sustain the frog and spider habitats? Isaac reasoned not many, and came to this conclusion years before the research was complete. He took Soper's chance. Implement.

It was Isaac's dream to go beyond simple eradication, to restore dignity to the people, subjected to an out-of-control species. Over the ensuing months his team settled into a routine, confident and quietly excited about the outcomes of their research. The practical application of the principles in the field, had escaped them. They needed a method or package that would engage those in most need. He had to be sure that people would not take shortcuts or just lose interest.

The worst thing that could happen would be belting, swatting and slapping the victim, in fun or malevolent play. The thought horrified him, as did omitting to wash one's hands. During extended combat sessions, handwashing at regular intervals was recommended. The maximum number of flies for this interval had not yet been determined.

Isaac would need to devise an approach that would excite crowds and individuals alike, to enthusiastically adopt every principle of capture/kill, including their sanitary obligations.

During a tea break Isaac and Julia were discussing an aspect of Julia's research when Rex came into the room, swiped and pitched a fly at the wall narrowly missing his knuckles. The fly was not killed on impact, and fell to the floor intact and stunned. Rex naturally stood on the fly to complete the kill and washed up.

"Of course!"

Rex and Julia responded as normal, in silence. They had been rendered speechless in the past by his light bulb moments, and this was such an occasion for silence, knowing that more information would soon follow. What he was internalising was the first time it had become evident, and they waited.

Rex had released the child in Isaac which had brought forth the 'game'.

"I want you to think in terms of a game," he finally announced.

"A game that will capture the imagination of the young, remove the enemy and encourage sanitation."

"Like scrabble or trivial pursuit?" fished Julia.

"No, like what Rex just did!"

Rex felt he should be able to offer a suggestion but he couldn't think of one and allowed his mind to drift off remembering he had to meet his friend Titus for lunch. Isaac bounced back.

"We set up a whiteboard in the bush, in a semi-circle. We then set up the other elements of the game. The squash board at the foot of the whiteboard, the soiled garment-stand to the right and the wash trough to the left. The washing and hand drying process will give sufficient time for the flies to regroup onto the garment for the next capture session."

Isaac left to think. The interval between hand washing would have to be judged on the regrouping rate of fresh flies.

Julia knew never to drink or eat food when Isaac was at his best. Spraying in reaction or choking on food was undignified. This same woman analysed the creature of their study by careful dissection of wing structure. She brought understanding to the flight path immediately after take-off and the vital moment in which the fundamental weakness of the creature lay, the weakness which could be exploited.

She also defined how solid, translucent and transparent surfaces affected the fly's flight path at the moment of escape. She studied the compound eye with such insight that she was able to calibrate perceived and actual speed relativities. This information was vital in corroborating field observations, when approaching the fly without disturbing its position.

She discovered the mechanism that made it possible at a certain speed to come to within one hundred millimetres of a fly with a cupped hand without the fly perceiving a threat. It was at this distance that Isaac knew by experience to be the 'stop' position. Julia proved that this stand-position related to the fly's span of attention, being limited as it was to approximately 1.2 seconds and considerably less than the memory span of a gold fish. Thankfully for the goldfish, five seconds enabled the fish to find new areas of interest in a relatively small tank. Any more than five seconds would have been a living imprisonment.

Research continued with new discoveries, vindicating Isaac's grandmother's technique from which he developed his hypotheses. The stunning conclusion of the compound eye being made up of numerous simple eyes or *ocelli,* revealed a world of bravado which enabled the fly to see the usual, incoming sweep in slow motion, even though the attacker intended to catch the fly by surprise.

Coupled with the fly's perception of slow motion, the fly also relied on the increase of air pressure being built up in front of a speeding hand. Atmospheric compression was a give-away. The slow approach therefore not only confused the compound eye as to recognising a movement, but it also made little difference to air pressure. The fly remains unsure of danger and after a small delay, it simply forgets. In short, slow motion is read as no motion.

The treatise on capture was now well advanced and set out the principles of approach, stop and attack-sweep. Vertical take-off measurements were recorded against a variety of surfaces, and all above-surface approach dimensions were documented. This data was essential in ensuring a victim would not be touched in the process of capturing the fly.

Cupped hand dimensions were given their minima and maxima openings. So advanced had the work become that the formulae revealed complex matrices for multiple catches. It was now possible to calculate how far apart two flies could be caught by the same sweep. Isaac had practiced repeatedly, using theses distances. Clusters of flies were relatively easy, but two spaced 120 millimetres apart required great control, concentration and alignment of approach. The first fly had to remain caught in the cup of the hand while the sudden attack motion alerted the second fly to lift off, and in so doing fly directly into the path of the incoming cupped hand containing the very confused first fly.

Once captured, the only way to dispose of this quarry and conform to the new found etiquette in such matters, was to toss, as in pitch, the flies at a suitable vertical surface, releasing the flies at approximately ten millimetres from the wall surface. This ensured first, that you would not damage your hand against the wall. Secondly, that the flies should be temporarily stunned, so as render them disorientated, unable to fly and fall to the floor. Thirdly, any distance further from the wall would allow the flies to take evasive action and escape.

Isaac was comfortable with serious research, but it was difficult for him to visualise a game, the purpose of which had to be fun. To refine the concept of fun he proposed for flycatching, he learned to play board games that were popular with children.

Isaac needed to gain a broader perspective, a view of make-believe rather than pure science. He hoped that a useful idea to come from such an oblique view, would foster a technical solution. He recognised the need to understand children in this game of lateral thinking.

To Luteesha's surprise Isaac finally and willingly accepted her requests to go to the theatre.

Isaac saw Shakespeare's Julius Caesar twice in the same week. The drama fleshed out the character of his scaleless visions, bringing an immediacy and intimacy.

The struts of its multifaceted introspection, and segmented view of power was not unlike the traceable paths of the compound eye of the fly. He was now familiar with both.

The toga was more than clothing. The civility apparent in its draping, the exposing the head and right shoulder, invited drama capable of great tragedy and irony.

Where rightfully earned power ruled, the void judged in absentia, slaying a tyrant no matter how benevolent or riddled by moral corruption, fear and guilt. The void was soulless, a place of no comfort until something occupied it, whereupon it could be fashioned anew.

Isaac pondered devolution of authority and its role in a future reduced to less than it what might have been. What could Archimedes have brought to the future had he not been conscripted to help defend Syracuse against the Romans? As he sat beneath a tree, engrossed in a mathematical problem, an iron blade wielded by a centurion ended his life. Fallen, his blood filled the lines of a circle he had scribed in the sand.

Isaac could empathise with those befallen by tragedy.

Fun, Isaac found difficult. He could not grasp its relationship to meaning, nor that others could distil insight from it, and its spontaneous enjoyment.

In this sense he did not readily exhibit the traits of his given name, Isaac, to whom is given laughter. He did understand, however, that the young learned well in an environment where happiness and laughter were present. The professor's beloved civility relied on this to build the new society the young would deliver.

Luteesha worked hard to relieve him of his ceaseless internalising. During the period Isaac was developing the flycatching game rules, she would drive him to the outer suburbs to watch her sister's children play sport. Suetonia and Antony's children were growing so fast that Isaac no longer remarked on their progress. The eldest, Livy, was already fifteen and vying for selection into the State Hockey program. His sister Diana at fourteen, had a great love of learning, inquiry and independence.

"Learning becomes her," Isaac used to say.

Suetonius was still a toddler and made up the point three of the statistical family. He had an inexplicable love of the outdoors and seemed in perpetual motion. Being fast asleep for him was a race towards the dawn of a new day.

Between innings, Isaac caught flies with the intent of understanding children's reactions. He swiped a fly off the hat of a noisy disgruntled parent seated in front of him, and turning to his niece asked,

"Can you guess what I have in my hand?"

"Okay, Uncle Isaac, what is it?"

"Well, I'll hold it up to your ear and you can have a listen," Isaac said as he moved his arm into position and continued to say,

"You should be hearing something now."

Diana heard but did not flinch, wondering what it could be.

"Now I'm going to change the pitch."

"It's the rubbing of two coins," guessed Diana intelligently.

"Then how am I changing the pitch to the sound higher? I'm not moving my fingers in a way that could do that," advised Isaac.

By this time two other young friends had joined them. They looked on and were curious and serenely quiet as they looked on something they did not understand.

Isaac moved his hand away from Diana's ear and watched the other children's eyes following his motion. He opened his hand and released an exhausted fly into the air. Gasps were all that could be heard within the group until Diana broke with,

"That's pretty impressive, Uncle Isaac."

"Remember where you were when you first saw it, Diana," replied her uncle.

The other two children peeled away. Isaac noted how daunting the experience had been for them, yet he felt confident that the 'chamber music' option could be of additional interest in the game to contain fly populations the world over.

***

Manifesto:

The procedure involves the standard slow-motion approach with cupped hand coming to rest one hand width from the fly. Following the fly's lapsed memory span, a brisk forward swipe will initiate vertical take-off. The sweep must clear the deck and be fast enough to collect the ascending fly.

If it is too fast, the bottom of the hand will knock the fly sideways to safety. If the sweep is too slow, the fly has time to take evasive action away from the incoming hand.

It is important to remember that at this moment the fly has approximately eighty five percent of three-dimensional space at its disposal. In this circumstance it is almost inevitable that the fly will escape, and live to annoy again.

A very close encounter involving contact but not outright capture, will trigger the release of adrenaline in the fly significantly increasing its

memory span. After such an experience the fly will retreat for some time before re-engaging.

Once the fly is collected into the cusp of the hand, the fingers are to be drawn into the palm of the hand, forming a tight chamber. If the procedure is correctly carried out there is no risk of squashing the fly.

This new etiquette would have the fly safely tucked in the chamber of the hand, with the fingers bunched closely enough to prevent the fly from climbing out through the space between them.

***

It was in this standard 'set' position that Isaac held the fly when he put his niece Diana to the test. Before he raised his arm to her, he loosened the grip between his fingers and the palm of his hand thereby increasing the size of the chamber. This enabled the fly to move its wings enough to produce the low, terse DZZ-DZZ sound emanating from the chamber.

This manoeuvre required great skill, as loosening the grip might allow the fly to escape. This was the sound that Diana heard and that she described as two coins rubbing together.

The change of pitch was created when Isaac released his grip even further, creating a chamber large enough for the fly to rotate freely and produce the higher pitch sound DZIZ-DZIZ-DZIZZZ. This frenzied movement produced an extraordinary sensation in the hand. Isaac could feel the impressive energy and strength of the creature. He recalled even as a boy, the power of the fly to create a significant enough air turbulence, that he could feel it on his face as it flew by.

Isaac called a staff meeting of to discuss the relationship between the fly's body strength and its ability to generate kinetic energy through the atmosphere.

"We must correlate this phenomenon in scientific terms but I have yet to decide whether such a quantitative investigation is within the allocated research fund."

After some consideration, Julia spoke, "I have a friend in the School of Biology. They are doing research into the manipulation of simple organisms. They're very excited about applying this research to larger creatures such as crickets and roaches. The objective is to see if it is possible to direct the creature left or right, stop and go by remotely stimulating implanted sensors. They foresee organic machines being injected, to code their genetic structures."

"Check out whether air turbulence is part of their investigation, otherwise we won't be following up that line of inquiry. If we can't at least extrapolate a model from their findings, I'd like to stay on course," concluded Isaac.

"We can arrange a transfer of funds if necessary," he added.

"If you have any difficulty with her, I'll take it up directly with the Head of Department. I'll give you three days," resolved Isaac, and continued.

"Now, in the coming week, we need to resolve the game plan, the rules of how it should be played. We need to resolve what the contest is about, how it will be contested and how it is to be scored. We also need to account differently for degrees of difficulty, and decide where the trials are to take place so that we can match the clinical data we have collected, to actual field conditions. I believe we are not far from consolidating our findings in the form of a manual, a modus operandi if you will."

He closed the meeting, being comfortable with the general position of the program.

Isaac took a short break to privately dwell on the substance of his visions, those he thought of as second substance interaction. His visions were either interfering or guiding his progress. He now had reason to believe that his visions of a living past might even be intruding via some adjunct parallel of space and time.

Through the energy and stimulus of the fly held in the hand, Isaac could feel the harmonic parallels between the animate and inanimate of a void. He was sensing that stuff-of-a-void, which could explain tactility within a void. The theory so derived postulated that, energy influenced stimulus and vice versa. This reciprocity gave meaning to Isaac's life, real meaning in the form of a dialogue between matter and space time, and the kind that he hoped could further the professor's beliefs of societal paths to human dignity.

At times, the link confounded him. Science had no plan to help him understand it. Something in nothing, an imbroglio of gods, a perished professor and long-dead emperors.

Communication, exchange, execution?

***

Lutetia and Isaac married within two months of Isaacs granting him the research placement. They moved into the terrace house Isaac owned in Macarthur Place. The outlook over plantation in front of the house was a welcome reminder of the space of his rural upbringing.

Isaac intrigued Luteesha from the day they first met. Love had been long in coming and she had been intentionally cautious. It was not an expressed passion so much as a construct, like a smile that revealed a need. In time, that caution grew to a want for him, to belong to him, his compassion and his aberrations. She had difficulty understanding if Isaac belonged to the past, present or future but she was prepared to be a part of it for a lifetime to find out. If mathematics could ever be described as romantic, then Isaac and Luteesha would be the abscissa and ordinate of dependence in an equation. She accepted that the children of their union would be other than human. She consoled herself by will, that a child of her own would have been inconsistent with her life with Isaac, and resolved to be a devoted aunty to her sister's children.

Her child would be more like the children of men, like the machines men made to travel to the planets and beyond, perfectly obedient man-made children, rejoicing in the remoteness and frailty of a child that would not tire, a child that would obediently return to signal its maker.

This is what the children of men were expected to do, and it was this for which they were loved.

Isaac, in his convoluted way, was fascinated by her natural inquiry and spirituality, and her instinct for the creative. For Luteesha, creation was a mix of randomness and order, absurdity and surprise that would always test and freshen the intellect. And the subtleties, the sensual pleasure of lying on a bed, as simple as to rest, to allow the natural force to heal the bones, the sensing under the covers of darkness, of hands moving on her body like the flow and ebb of a tide the goddess Diana made possible.

***

The rules of the game were finally drafted and Isaac confirmed the Outback of Australia as the location for field trials. If the rules worked in the settlements and townships of the outback they could be applied anywhere on the globe, where the unwelcome bond between people and flies needed to be broken.

Rex charted a six-week program. The itinerary included a rodeo, boxing carnival and a travelling freak show which had long past its social use-by date, all in the tri-state area of central Australia. The Birdsville horse race meeting and a tour of the Top End of the Northern Territory were also included in the schedule along with detailed estimates, circuit timetables, maps, vehicle hire, generator for the new elder-generation funnel and insect zapper, and aircraft links. Isaac could not resist describing Rex's enthusiasm as having a dog-like tenacity, a rare attempt at humour.

The estimates exceeded the research budget and as Isaac had no intention of curtailing the program it was necessary to apply directly to the Minister responsible for the additional funding. This he did and the Ministry replied,

"You are called to meet with the Honourable Sir Henry Afterwood, Minister for Innovation and Rural Affairs, at the place and time herein prescribed.

Place: The Minister's private summer residence; Howqua Inlet, Victoria.
Time of Arrival: 11:00 am Friday 30 September;
Depart: After breakfast Sunday 11:00 am
Dress: Semi-formal tweed daily, Black Tie Formal wear at dinner.

The tone of the notice seemed curt and Isaac's calls to the Ministry seeking more information gleaned nothing as to the Minister's position on the application. He had been given time and that was all the Minister's personal assistant would offer.

This all made Isaac nervous and as he sipped tea, vivid images of himself as Flaminius jammed between the Apennine mountains and Lake Trasimene flashed before him, the very moment in 217 BC when he looked up and saw Hannibal's elephants and troops, rendering him sick with fright that devoured his stomach.

Howqua Inlet, Lake Trasimene, ambush!

The unsettled weather patterns of spring arrived and the meeting with the Minister was fast approaching. Isaac became increasingly troubled. Two nights before his journey to the Howqua, Jupiter brazenly thundered into Isaac's mind and as the last tingling charges of electricity dissipated from Isaac's brain, the god of lightning mouthed the following words.

"Ars est celare artem" – It is true art to conceal art
"Ars long, vita brevis" – Art is long, life is short
"At spes non fracta" – But hope is not crushed

And in the cauldron of Isaac's occupied mind, the advice of second substance again took on meaning. In his meeting with the Minister, art would have to play a role if his hopes for a positive outcome were not to be crushed. He looked to the only thing that was common in his visions of Rome's tyrants. Lucence. The kind of translucence the marble heads of emperors that shone when they tumbled out from the redness of his interior, water-milk whiteness as he called it. Isaac rummaged through

Luteesha's art books until he found what was familiar to him. Michelangelo's Pieta.

The draped limp body of Jesus, lucent, as it lay across his mother's lap. The body looked as though it was about to fall. It was this way of Michelangelo's capturing of the moment of things. Isaac studied the shining. He absorbed the reflections and saw the emotions well up from deep within its translucence.

The beautiful, youthful countenance of his mother placed her no older than her son Jesus, a girl, possibly younger than him. Her head was heavily caped, making it appear larger and more caring. The folds of garments that hung from her right arm, fell in motion as her right hand grappled to seize him. No greater flight of grace had Isaac seen. From behind, the composition resembled a lovers embrace. The face of Jesus expressed that his work was done and her lips, about to break into a smile, spoke of a rejoicing in what he had achieved.

Isaac saw in the nascency of the moment that the mother, embodied with eternal youth, was disbelievingly amused in that she had been selected by God to bear his mortal son. Her brow bore testimony to the gravitas of this, while the tilt of her head belied the deeper emotions.

The glow of light that reflected off the body of her son, lighted the shadows of her face. In the changing angles and shadows, she appeared to cry. It was as profligate and sexual as it was fluent, and filled with knowing. This was power and Isaac knew this.

On the morning of his departure to meet with the Minister, Isaac awakened tired from a night disturbed by anxiety and the clamor of the voices living in his head. Luteesha carefully packed all that Isaac needed for the three days he was to be away. Among his papers Isaac included an abridged version of his most precious file marked 'FUTURIS'. It was this file to which he would resort if all other manner of persuasion failed.

Isaac left the city before the sunrise. The rhythm of the highway was soporific and before long Isaac had to pull over to rest. A section of the road passed through the mountain range that divided the flat interior of the continent from the eastern seaboard. A straight section of the road through the tall eucalypt forest reminded him of the corridors of the kings, the red carpeted hallways of houses of power. Wigs, wigs, big wigs and more wigs.

Isaac Marcu Moritz, of no great standing, was to meet with a Minister of the Crown in no less than his own private residence. The thought of the position that he had come to was daunting, and he preferred not to dwell on it. His origins were humble, something Isaac had to put behind him, to hide, as he had done on so many occasions, and this he would do again as the moment dictated when before the Honourable Minister.

These doubts dissipated as the mountains gave way to an undulating fertile valley. Sunshine lit the green pastures and he remembered Grand Uncle Felix's story of how the beasts came to be, and how the sun shone upon the oceans to give rise to salt-free water to once again rain upon the land. Isaac wondered if he would ever be able to fulfil Felix's promise. Could he be the family oracle? And in so asking he was reminded how little he had seen of his family. His obsession for work prevented him from taking up the mantle bestowed upon him, of succession, order and duty, relegating any such commitment well into the future.

Isaac felt suddenly neglectful and stricken with nostalgia for the loss of his birthplace, his grandparents, the farm hands, the post office garden and the professor, and realised how much of his world revolved around his childhood. In those early years, the new immigrants referenced themselves to how old he was when they first arrived, the first born in the new land. This memory brought him even greater discomfort about his isolation from the family. Given his mission, he could see no easy way to redress this imbalance in his life. His estrangement also owed much to his not having children. Such a deep commitment to the family seemed onerous and incompatible with his life.

At Macs Cove, he spotted the waters of the Howqua Inlet and continued on to the crossing. As he drove over the bridge, he saw two canoes emerge from the narrow river that flowed into the inlet. On the other side of the bridge, he turned right onto the southern bank of the inlet and followed it until he could see the larger body of water in Lake Eildon.

Fishermen added a quiet timelessness in this remote place that he found disturbing.

The road veered left and up into bushland. It was not long before the turn-off to the right appeared. The gravel surface sounded harsh after the asphalt road surface. The track meandered as it descended, closing in on the shoreline of the lake.

A clearing revealed the way forward to a narrow neck of land not much wider than the road. He crossed over. A late-Victorian mansion, commanded a surround of brooding pine and cypress trees. It was located on the water's edge near the end of the isthmus, in the shape of a tongue that entered a small bay. Several boats were moored on a jetty, some with masts. Further around was a ramp leading to a barge.

Isaac parked in the gravel turning bay in front of the building. In the open view of the water, sunshine sparkled off countless wavelets like a sea of flashing light bulbs. The power of this place overwhelmed him. The sense of floating on the water cut him adrift, lost, the present on hold, with barely a thread to his childhood.

Like the cypress tree under which he burrowed his hands on the family farm when he was a boy, the trees above drove him into a state of being solely for himself. The sun barely penetrated the tangle of massive branches. The darkness above was seductive, at once mythical and imaginary, strong and protective. It was custodial.

Isaac sat in the car for a few minutes, taking in all before him. A man-servant appeared on the portico at the appointed time. He was briefly welcomed and shown to his quarters, tucked away on the ground floor.

Over a painstakingly meticulous lunch the Minister showed his affable side, less forbidding than he might otherwise have been behind his office desk. During a walk through the rose garden Isaac demonstrated his hand-fly-capture technique going to great lengths to explain the gentility and elegance of the procedure. He revealed the secrets of the equipment he used as a real estate agent, the split hip flask and replaceable sticky cartridges. He used it to swipe flies from the Minister, pocketing the container and drawing out the medicated towel to wipe his hand. The

Minister was amused, and he could see the propriety of the hand-wiping sequence and said he looked forward to discussing it further at dinner.

Isaac felt a little stiff in his new collar and butterfly tie, but not as choked as the Minister looked. He was sitting opposite Lady Mary, Sir Henry at the head of the table. Their daughter and her new husband were also dining. A candelabra hid him from Isaac's view.

A frequent guest, the robust, spider veined, retired Commander Arnold Drinkwater embellished the space across the table.

Sir Henry opened the fly discussion halfway through the Duck-a-l'Orange and the fourth glass of wine, catching Isaac by complete surprise.

"Isaac! We've been discussing, or should I say, laughing about your project for the past week! It is a surp…"

Sir Henry stopped mid-sentence, and started fidgeting about the plate with his knife and fork looking like he had lost something, leaving Isaac suspended.

"Look! All this stuff about flies will probably make interesting and doubtless amusing reading in a library…compound eyes, attention spans and whatever else, but, Isaac, who's going to take it seriously?"

Isaac's mind began to race. It was clear he would need to delve deeply his into survival instinct. His experience in real estate led him into what were at the time, unchartered moral territories. Ambivalence, double standards, coercion, collusion and deception. It was in this environment that Isaac learned to engage and disarm.

With a wry smile, the Minister looked to his friend, and loudly cajoled,

"What do you think Drinkwater?" and turned back to Isaac.

"I'm not going to mince words. This project of yours is becoming unbelievably difficult to justify. Look at it from my point of view - an opposition ready to carve up anything, everything, everyday! If they find out about the funding you've received thus far, never mind what's currently on the table for your field trials, they'll go into a frenzy. Think of the headlines!" Before Isaac could reply, Lady Mary brokered a respite.

"Gentlemen, surely this is something you could take up after dinner Now, I believe we have a wonderful dessert to enjoy."

And all agreed.

As they settled into the club lounge interior of the drawing room, Isaac looked upwards and saw the most adorned female cornice he had seen outside of the upper-house chamber of State Parliament. He counted eight vestal virgins emerging from the egg and dart wreath braiding of the cornice, hovering at a height of some sixteen feet above the floor.

The older men nestled into the padded Chesterfield arm chairs while the butler filled glasses with the finest dry-earth muscat liqueur in the world.

Isaac sat in a tall upright chair beside a huge mahogany desk. He thought carefully, waiting for the opportunity to speak first and so control the course of the evening's discussion. He wanted to avoid detailed conversation about his project as there was still time to deal with agenda items the next day. This was the moment to bond. During this pause Isaac recalled the last communication he had with Jupiter Stator when he was advised that hope would not be crushed in the wake of art, that art was long and life short. Jupiter further implied that great art was never obvious and that its appeal to the eye looked effortless.

"The vestal virgins on the ceiling remind me of Michelangelo's Pieta," stated Isaac as he sipped his muscat. Caught by surprise, both pairs of wiry eyebrows raised before settling above sharpened eyes.

The Commander retreated into his double chin while Sir Henrys head tilted backwards, peering up to the ceiling.

"How perceptive of you Isaac. In what way do you connect the two?" said the Minister in a high-pitched gravelled voice of inquiry.

"Well, apart from theistic differences, Michelangelo's Pieta captures the essence of moment, whereas the cornice is controlled by caution, wary of the many deities that guide the continuance of Roman life. The burden of maintaining the fire vigil subdues the moment to near stillness."

"Yes! But what's the connection, Isaac!" The Minister beamed as Drinkwater frowned the deepest furrow.

"Motion, Sir Henry, motion," said Isaac now more comfortable referring to the Minister by name. "The vestal virgins emerge from the cornice as intently as the mother of Jesus that hovers above her inanimate son. Each is a caress and both are represented in slow motion."

"Yes, I see that, go on," snapped Sir Henry.

"In both re-creations if you will, stillness or no motion reads as slow motion, liberating the frozen or capture state of the stone. This ability to discern stilled motion is the great attribute of the human eye. In this regard it is far superior to the reading of movement by the compound eye."

Isaac's defining moment could well have come straight out of the fly catching manifesto and it served him well with the Minister. As the conversation sank deeper into the mysteries of perception, the retired commander submerged into slumber. A rasp-like noise grated through the roof of his mouth and Isaac wished he would just snore.

When they could no longer add to the warmth of understanding they had developed between them, Isaac rose from his chair and helped the older gentlemen to the grand staircase, where they were met by the butler. It was all he could manage to do for them. The alcohol was now master.

Isaac made his way through the dimly lit interior of the manor to his ground floor bedroom. The brass door handle squeaked as he wrenched it to open the heavy wood-panelled door, uncaring whether he shut or slammed the door. A full moon shone through the tall narrow window lit the interior. He slumped into the leather sofa beside the bed, pulled his tie open and released the shirt collar. In the darkness his head spun and he tumbled into an oblivion.

At 3:00 am a thunderclap crashed through the open window. Lightning was the only light. The plume of the chiffon curtain swirled around Isaac's head, waking him from his infused stupor.

He leapt off the sofa waving his arms and gasping for air, trying to locate himself. It came to him. The guest-room. Howqua Inlet. Another storm. Restless and stressed Isaac hurled himself out of the room, and headed for the front door of the mansion. He fumbled with the lock until it released, pulled the door open and slammed it shut behind him. In his haste Isaac lost his balance, tripped on the steps and fell onto the gravel driveway. He rolled onto his back in the belting rain. He opened his dry, stale mouth to receive the water in a single primordial action. Sheet lightning lit the clouds above him and Jupiter Stator appeared to him.

"Filius Terrae" – Son of the earth, the victim of the senseless thunderbolt lies in wait across the water!

"Brutem Fulmen!" Isaac remembered *Brutem Fulmen,* the senseless thunderbolt that killed the professor.

Isaac twisted onto his side, rose on all fours and staggered through the garden to the water's edge, following the sound of a steel halyard cable clanging against the flagpole. In the bursts of lightning, Isaac could make out a small cove across the water. He had to cross the water as instructed.

Under the light of a single marine lamp Isaac righted an upturned dinghy and pushed off the ramp ploughing the boat into the water and awkwardly started to row with the double-ended paddle, eventually getting the feel of alternate movements.

It was two hundred yards across and had he not been inebriated, would have seemed to have taken forever. The last swell bashed him against the launching ramp. He scrambled out of the boat and dropped the loop end of the rope onto the bollard.

The underside of the pine plantation was dark and only the edges of the water were lit by the storm. Isaac had no idea where he was going but started to jog along the waterline, feeling for it. He could make out the water's edge on both sides of the small bay, and for some unknown reason he veered into the forest avoiding the lower branches as best he could. The ground was covered in pine needles with only a few tufts of grass to impede him. He was puffed blind and soon reached an embankment and slid into the edge of the water. Isaac lifted himself and pushed backwards out of the water and sat on the narrow course sand beach, his legs still immersed, puffing and glaring at the turbulence before him.

A scream burst in Isaac's head. A terrifying end-of-life scream unearthed a violent memory. As it crumbled to a gurgle the word came forth,

"NOSCITABUNDUS."

This was an echo of the professor's death. That is all Isaac could think it to be. An ear-splitting crack of thunder ended his consciousness. A bolt of lightning struck the water in front of him searing his legs, jump starting him onto the bank. His head pounded, blurring his vision until all he could see was the redness of his interior. A floppy white hat flew across the velvet. The hat tumbled back into view and slowed and as it rolled over, and Isaac saw the professor's head beneath it. His old piercing eyes looked directly into him and Isaac cried with joy.

"I will placate the storm, Isaac," said the Professor tenderly. I once before beseeched it to do so and failed. 1 paid with my life, but in so doing, gave you what you are."

Isaac sobbed. Through quivering lips Isaac spoke,

"I have so missed you."

"You are the knowing, Isaac," reminded the professor.

"What am I to do with this knowing!" Isaac yelled in frustration, quickly retracting with an apology.

"Antiquity will lead you to the future and you will know what so few have learned. Not even I know what you will know."

"Like more Latin riddles, professor, so many for my head to burst?"

"Isaac, the ancients, one among your ancestors will guide you, but you must be brave and believe you will be heard, and in turn be advised."

"You, professor, and only you would I believe," replied Isaac, and after a pause, much welled that he wanted to say to him. Rain continued to splash in waves across Isaac's face, lit up by intermittent flashes of light.

"Professor, I saw you die, I was there. I was little and I've lived my life no other way, than by what that tragedy brought to my life. I know not a clear head, nor a moment of peace."

He gathered himself for a diatribe withheld for a lifetime, and summoned the words to continue,

"I am driven by both passion and pain ignited by your loves. Love of being human, love of dignity for all, love of freedom to be, and to grow. Love of the greater human more than the sum of every living man, woman and child. Love of learning. Love of reason and love of the solutions beyond reason, and the gift of serendipitous fortune. Love of greatness and humility. Love of this earth."

And the questions.

"What of the great division, the chasm of space, the separation of time, the boundaries of infinity and the length of eternity where the realm of passion and pain rest. Are passion and pain inseparable? Can either one end the great divide within humankind, and the great divide of space to fulfil what we think is our destiny as life. Life has a destiny does it not? If not individually then collectively?"

"You have learned so well, Isaac," said the visage beneath the hat.

"I believed in you as a child, your family history, and the nature of yourself. You will find what you seek, my dearest." And the professor's image began to quaver.

"Stay with me, a little longer!" and the image returned without words, until it faded.

When he accepted that the professor was no longer, he looked across the water and all around him, everywhere was still and lit by bright moonlight. This night the professor's call to calm was heard. The sky had cleared and the storm was stilled.

The butler banged on the door and Isaac woke, still soaked in his formal clothing. He showered and changed. When he returned to his room, he saw that the mess he must have left on the floor during the night had already been cleaned. At breakfast, no one spoke of this, offering only the hope that he had had a good night's sleep. Isaac excused himself preferring to rest for much of the day. He was still shaken by the physical and mental effort expended during the night, and needed to collect himself and his thoughts for what would no doubt make or break his mission.

At 6 pm Isaac's evening clothes were returned to his room. The shirt was washed and ironed, shoes polished, and his suit and tie cleaned and pressed. Dinner was at 7:30 pm and being a Saturday, extra places were set for other guests.

Sir Angus Moreton and his Lady Beckett Moreton were so awe struck on learning why Isaac was present that they directed discussion to matters of the Ruling Class, and the effect of its undermining by immigrants who simply don't want to go home!

Isaac's spirit and confidence improved through the course of the meal. The barbecue aged beef was splendid. At the conclusion of the main course, Sir Henry and Isaac took leave from the table and withdrew to the boardroom table. There he laid out Isaac's chances of acquiring the additional funding. They were better than expected but still short of committing further government resources to the project. Isaac was well prepared for this situation.

"If I may, Sir Henry, I would like to present compelling evidence which I feel sure will help remove any doubts as to the investment."

"By all means," responded the Minister taking yet another sip of forty-year-old scotch.

Isaac produced a document marked *Confidential* titled, **The Futuris File.**

Compound Eye, Cognition, And the Social Contract

"The findings in this document are a by-product of our Hand-Fly-Capture program, the central theme of our research. Without this program and its practical benefits for stricken populations around the world, very little of what you are about to witness can be accessed. It is yet another example of pure research yielding unexpected, perhaps even unpredictable yet beneficial outcomes."

The Minister's fingers rapped the American cherrywood edge of the table as if he had heard all this before. Isaac moved his arms closer to the centre of the table and allowed his hands to feel the parquetry patterns of the burl-wood top, a gesture replying to the Ministers rapping and replete with expectation.

"The female Xenos peckii fly lives inside the common paper wasp and feeds on innards. She is sightless and flightless and exists only to be impregnated. Her male offspring emerge from the wasp and fly away. Using their olfactory senses and their eyes they seek another wasp, embed themselves in it searching the female within the wasp.

"Most compound eyes have hundreds of smaller facets each focusing on a handful of photo receptors producing only a single point of interpretation in the insect's visual field. Each of Xenos' one hundred eyelets on the other hand is a complete eye in itself, each with its own retina thereby delivering a visual field of one hundred receptors. This array produces an image of exceptionally high resolution."

"Is there anything we can do with this knowledge, Isaac?" Sir Henry queried.

"We are still searching adaptations for this particular fly's eye, however, we have made substantial progress on an even more bizarre case. Forty-five million years ago a tiny, now extinct fly was trapped in gooey tree resin. The amber capsule was delicately removed by technicians at Warsaw's Museum of the Earth. It was a typical compound eye with scores of dome receptors. But it is the strangeness of the parallel ridges etched on the domes that has led to new applications. Over the aeons, every design challenge has been met with a solution."

"What are some of the problems this particular fly's eye has solved for you?" queried a straightened Minister.

"The height and spacing of each ridge are half the wavelength of visible light, which ensures that light can move in a smooth transition from air to eye, with little disturbance or reflection. The eye ridge pattern can efficiently absorb light falling from an angle as low as eighty degrees from perpendicular making it a great anti-reflector."

"And the uses, Isaac?"

"Coatings made in its likeness have important military applications. Air force bombers and spy planes using these coatings in combination with profile shaping can conceal the aircraft from detection by radar. Simply, the high absorption rate prevents reflection, and in a word, stealth. The fly eye-design might also help improve the efficiency of photovoltaic cells used in solar power generation. Window coatings could improve light transmission while removing glare, and cut out annoying internal reflections in double and triple-glazed windows.

"A coated television or computer screen would give a crystal-clear image even if impeded by the light from a background window.

"Night vision glasses to help soldiers see more safely in the dark, improved optical disk performance and safer car dashboards to cut sunlight glare on the driver's eyes, and so on." The Minister's eyes clouded over as his mind raced across the possibilities. Isaac watched politely. He reached for a glass of water brought to the table by an invisible butler all too good at his job.

"And what about the social contract?"

"We believe we can reduce the fly population in crowded cities to the extent that European outdoor cafe and dining experiences can be safely introduced by Local Government by-laws. We also see these changes as having a positive influence on public health and a magnet for tourism." A smile broached his face – as if in acceptance of Isaac's proposals.

"Isaac, you must see I'm quite taken aback by what you have said," sounding somewhat apologetic.

"I'm going to authorise the funding you seek for the outback program and further, in consideration of the success the Chinese have had with their fly catching decree, I'm also recommending that the World Health Organisation support you in establishing a similar program wherever you choose, based on your experience in the Outback. You certainly have your work cut out for you. Unlike the Chinese you do not have the numbers to take out enough flies to make so great a difference. How you do this is up to you."

"Minister! Thank you!" glowed Isaac mixed with relief, joy and purpose.

The massed canopy of cypress limbs hovered above him as drove to the narrow road-crossing that separated the small peninsula from the hill. On reaching the highway he turned left and drove along the tranquil wooded hillside of the Inlet to the bridge. He stopped the car midway and looked along the water to the lake, and the shoreline where on that tumultuous yet exhilarating night, he reconnected with his beloved professor, unencumbered by time.

He lowered the window and paused to breathe his spirit.

Chapter 8

The Campaigns

In celebration of Isaac's achievements, a banquet was held in the Great Room of the house our brother Isaiah built for his wife and four children. Isaiah was successful and baronial. His cool store operations released him from the seasonal dependency of farm production and on this he grew rich.

The long table reminded us of the long table in the forum of the old farmhouse and Isaiah thought it his calling to keep the tradition alive. Like then, the table was laden with food and at the tinker of spoon on glass, Isaac was invited to share his dream with his family.

Isaac called the gathered to remember the dearly departed of their family. Grandfather and Patriarch Ezekiel, Grand Uncle Felix and our grandmother Rebekah who Isaac called Avia. For her he reserved his most profound praise,

"To Avia, for the gift of my life," and Isaac went on to describe how as a young boy she had taught him to catch flies in his hand without injuring the creature. It was this humble beginning that led him to the theory and practice of hand-fly-capture and his quest to restore human dignity across all the lands of the world.

When we had eaten the main course, the woman Isaiah married to bear his children, rose and ordered all the guests to assemble in the courtyard for photographs before coffee and cake would be served. Her name was Philomena, and she had prepared the greatest banquet any of us had seen since our days in the forum, and it was apt that she was so named after Philomen, the old Greek man who with his wife Baucis, shared what little they had with the disguised gods, Zeus and Hermes. The assembled re-arranged with each photo when at last I, Ignatius, stood with my brothers Isaiah and Isaac to be framed in memory forever. The bulb flashes lighted, as evidence that our moment together was duly recorded, and when Philomena was satisfied, we returned once again to the table.

"Annuit Coeptis" – God has smiled on our undertakings.

Ignatius.

***

The plane carrying Isaac and Julia landed in the centre of the continent. The airport at Alice Springs was as remote as it was central. To the greater population which clung to the coast lines this was just somewhere outback. In seeing its isolation from the air, he could already sense the spirituality for which it is was known.

As they stepped from the plane, one of a menacing pair of fighter bombers that Isaac spotted during the landing, took off with a thunderous roar, tearing a rift in the air, to a destination who knows where. Wherever, it would be quick.

The large number of black people in the terminal building highlighted how white the rest of the country was. It was different but the same. This is where Terminus, the god of boundaries had come to rest, at the junction of the ancient and new world.

Rex, who had arrived a week earlier, helped pack their luggage into one of three four-wheel-drive vehicles he had rented for the mission, temporarily emblazoned on its sides 'SNAP-ZAP Solutions'.

He talked fast about the preparations and provisions he organised, and how ready it all was. The road from the airport followed the river as it meandered through the mountain range like the serpent of the dreamtime. Isaac was struck by the beauty of the Papuana trees that lined the river bed. Sunlight dashed off the lime-gold leaves that stemmed from the white branches and trunks that nourished them. They were beguiling, like a tale unfolding, and looked fragile against the red backdrop of the ranges.

The image of Aneus Marius, the fourth ruler of Ancient Rome and the King responsible for extending Roman power, tumbled into Isaac's mind and announced in a bell-like sound so clear and loud, *"Fax mentis incedium gloriae,"* and Isaac understood it to mean what was now required of him. The passion for glory is the torch of the mind. He must yearn for success and visibility, for that is the glory which must remain the focus of his mind. He related this incursion to the Minister's endorsement of his programs. The comfort and confidence Isaac derived from these endorsements, was potent and blissful.

Rex had masterminded the Outback program. He had ensured that the white stunning boards, squash boards, stomping paddles (footwear flappers), soap and wash buckets, towels, scoreboards, pegs, lines, bunting, signs, a generator and megaphones could all be packed into trunks to be loaded onto trailers. In his genius, he also configured the trunks to open in three hinged parts so that they could be harnessed to a horse or camel.

Four dozen of Isaac's converted whisky flasks were packed including a stack of sticky cartridges and sanitary napkins. Further, three electric insect zappers, modified with a funnel attachment for use by the over-fifties, ensured that the competitions were inclusive and able to produce the highest number of kills.

When Isaac and Julia arrived at the motel, the carpark was littered with equipment. The other two Land Cruiser troop carriers were scattered among the debris. A team of four under-graduate students were packing the vehicles and trailers, recording the provisions in the order of use. The quantities were carefully assessed to ensure adequate supplies were available for the duration of their field trips. One trailer was fitted with refrigerated compartments for food, water and refreshments. Accommodation outside of towns, though rough was secured.

The under-grads arrived two days earlier and looked a little worse for wear. The boys needed little excuse for binge drinking, and the heat was a good as any. The four-week tour was to be a crash course in theory and practice, and they were expected to catalogue all empirical data without reference to scientific principles, with the aim of identifying any deviation of theory from practical application.

After their evening meal of egg-topped steak, chips and lettuce, quelched by schooners of lager and one gentle wine, they retreated to the motel meeting room. Jack Ladder known as 'beanstalk' and the oldest of the group, surmised that it might have been a better route if they had gone south.

"On what basis would you proffer that Jack?" asked Isaac, chipping in ahead of Rex.

"I heard a report that the boss-drover of the cattle run from Marree to Birdsville would be arriving in four weeks give or take a day. Can you imagine the fly population on their sweatshirts?"

"And I suppose the pub at Birdsville is where you've always wanted to sink a few?"

"It's not just that, Isaac, look at the towns." Un-scuffling a map, Beanstalk began to reel off their names.

"Leaving from here, we'd take the Finke Road through the MacDonnell Ranges and onto Ewaninga, Mt Polhil, Ooraminna, Deep Well, Rodinga, Maryvale, Bundooma, Engoordina, Mt. Squires, Rumbalara, Musgrave, Finke, Crown Point, Duffield, Wall Creek and that's just to the border!"

"Gee, Jack, that must be nearly two hundred people. What's on the South Australian side of the border?"

"Thank you for asking Rex Abminga, Bloods Creek, Ilbunga, Mount Emery, Pedirka, Alberga, Oodnadatta, Mt. Dutton, Algebuckina, Warrina, Edwards Creek, Boorthana, Anna Creek, William Creek, Strangways Springs, Coward Springs, ah…something murka, Bopeechee, Callanna and Marree where the cattle stock route to Birdsville starts!"

"That's gotta be another six hundred people. Think of the flies in the wake of all that shit. We'd cream it by the time we did the five hundred and fourteen kilometres between Marree and Birdsville!"

"Oh, Jack! A little less colour please!" begged Julia. "Anyway, that's another state border crossing – Queensland."

"Too late now, the plan is to go north," said Isaac and Rex took up.

"Thank God we dropped the Tanami Road route. Yuendumu is 269 kilometres west of the highway, and another 315 to Rabbit Flat, with its population of four. Camel and fly country it is, but we need people not just flies. Our job is training people to get rid of the flies. Let's not forget our mission!"

"Rex is right," said Isaac. "Our route north is fine. By doing this loop we get to really damage the fly population in the region. We turn east at Tea Tree, along the Sandover Highway to Ammaroo. Then we turn north to Elkedra and west again in time for the Murray Downs Rodeo. Think of the flies there, Jack!"

"I like Jack's idea of finishing at the Birdsville pub though," said Julia. "I would like to have taken a plane flight back to Alice and watch you guys drive through the Arunta desert."

"Look, we go as far north as Daly Waters and that's it!" stopped Rex. "There's an historic pub there! Goes by the local perverted name, Hydrant Hotel, i.e., the Daly Waters Pub, and from what I hear it's every bit as good as the Birdsville pub."

"You've organised something for tomorrow?" asked Isaac.

"Yes, I have," clarified Rex and pulled a flyer from his back pocket. "There's a carnival in town, out by the stockyards, perfect for flies, and by the sound of it it's well passed its use-by date. Here's what they offer:

Cannon fodder competition – avoid being hit by medicine balls and you win a stuffed toy! I bet the littlest guy wins that one.

This stand also features the human cannon ball, just returned from rehab. He squeezes backwards down the barrel of the cannon wearing only a helmet, an oiled suit and thick leather platform shoes.

"Will he hit the mattress on descent! " asks the flyer. "I bet he comes out steaming," imagining what might ensue from the blast.

Boxing of course – a good slug fest. Bar room brawlers welcome.

Get this!

The human fart.

The bearded lady kissing competition.

The human penis (peep show).

The human breast (peep show).

Since we leave the day after tomorrow, I took the liberty of booking the remaining stand for a practice run."

"Let me guess, right next to the freak show."

"As a matter of fact, yes, Julia, but the good thing is the wrestling ring is on the other side and the camel rides are behind us. There should be a steady supply of flies. It's going to be extremely hot and the fresh patties will be steaming alive."

"A little less graphic please!" exhorted Julia.

***

A mighty banner unfurled and was stretched high across the stand.

'FLYCATCHING COMPETITION'

"Roll up, roll up, roll up. Hear here how you can catch flies! Hear here!"

Megaphone Rex was hot!

"Our team of trainers will teach you how, and our great mentor Isaac, will read you the rules! Roll up. Come forth and destroy, before they go forth and multiply!"

This last hurrah got a stare from Isaac. Taking the megaphone off him Isaac took the stand.

"Sic 'em Rex get everybody up here!"

The comment got Isaac a glare from Rex.

"Jack, you've got a team of young kids practicing the slow motion and sweep technique. As soon as they're ready, stand each contestant in front of the white boards, one behind the other."

"The boss's fired up but I get the feeling that in this country you can make a sport out of anything," observed Julia in her analytical way.

"Below the stunning whiteboard is a flat stomping board. To the right and left of the whiteboard you can see soiled linen hanging from the frames. You can see just how attractive they are to flies. We've got good cover and if you're good enough you'll be able to take multiple catches or encasements as we prefer to call them.

"Remember, the linen represents an innocent bystander and if you touch it when you sweep over them, you lose two points. You must not touch who we call the victim, that is the person under attack by the fly.

"The points are awarded for each fly, one point per fly, successfully felled by the impact on the whiteboard and stomped on, using the foot paddles we supply you with.

"After a sweep and encasement, Rex will demonstrate the pitching action against the white board. The fly must be unharmed until it belts against the white board. If the pitch is strong enough the fly will be sufficiently stunned to drop straight down onto the stomping board where you can use the foot paddle to crush it. Each kill will be counted by a team member and will be added to your tally.

"Beside each soiled garment there is a bucket containing soapy water for washing your hands. If you fail to wash your hands after completing your tenth sweep, you will lose three points. Remember, it is vital to winning that you wash your hands!"

By now the alleyway between the stands was crowded. People were hanging off adjacent stands to get a look. Three lines of excited kids were facing white boards. The intrigue was electric and it was getting as noisy as it was hot. The spectator's arms normally swaying flies off their faces, took on a snappier action.

Isaac looked at the first three contestants standing on the platform.

"On the count of three, One, Two, Three, Go!"

Board-line 1 hit the shirt and wasted the first point. Board-line 2 contestant successfully swept, pitched and stomped his first catch, as did Board-line 3.

At the completion of ten sweeps, Board-line 1 had a tally of five. Board-line 2 had six. Board-line 3, eleven, the first to achieve a multiple catch.

"Next!"

The under-grads marshalled the lines with each contestant getting ten sweeps. The third kid on Board-line 2 managed two multiple encasements followed by two simultaneous kills. A large encasement of four flies failed to strike any kill, too many for just a small hand, and too many for such a young pitch strength. By the fifth group Isaac was calling for shirts from the spectators and in a masterstroke decided to have them stand with the backs to the contestants to continue supply. Julia topped up the soap and water buckets which were being vigorously splashed empty.

After the eighth group completed their ten sweeps, Rex called a halt as it was becoming difficult to verify the kills because of blood and gut smears saturating the stomping boards, but they did have enough to record a result. A large number in the audience were now swiping each with excitement and Isaac had to restore order that unless they could take the flies away, pitch them against a wall and wash their hands they should desist.

"We have a result? Rex, if you could pass me the totals, thank you."

After a pause, for the most part grinding in suspense, Isaac announced, "The winner in the Board-line category is Board number 2! Congratulations to the eight flycatchers in line two!"

The parents of their young charges screamed with joy and the rest cheered with delight, grinning at the very sight of the flies around them.

"Each contestant will be awarded a prize! Board-line 1 members will receive a cake of soap to practice the game at home and Board-line 2 and 3 members will received a cake of soap and a brand-new singlet to help work up a sweat that will make flies easier to catch when you are playing backyard fly catching.

"I now have pleasure in announcing our outright winner folks, and first champion with no less than three multiple encasements, the very young, fast learning Livingstone West III, who will receive in addition to the soap and singlet, and a brand-new white shirt. Go forth, sweep and destroy!

"Congratulations again to all our contestants, the grubby shirt volunteers, and this wonderful crowd for making the inaugural Flycatcher contest such a great and rewarding experience. Keep up! Sweep and destroy! and remember, what do we do?"

"WASH YOUR HANDS!" the chorus rang.

Isaac's first day in the field was glorious.

The next day the convoy left for a three-week tour of the towns and settlements of the Northern Territory. Their fame grew by the day and the competitions made the Territory News Bulletin three nights running, even making the results a regular feature on the sports report, cementing what Isaac knew was vital to the success of the program, to capture the human competitive spirit of participation. The over-fifties funnel-zapper events were a special treat, a must watch on Morning Breakfast Shows.

An important part of the program included maintaining contact with the interest groups they left behind to ensure that the rules were kept, and that the hand washing principle would be enshrined as paramount by those who practiced the art. These groups would eventually form district leagues, responsible for match scheduling, competition policy and sport promotion.

The Murray Downs Rodeo attracted a massive following. An entire tent city had been set up for the event and at the end of three exhaustive days of competition a remarkable indent in the fly population had been achieved. One man became teary, when he experienced the first fly-free hamburger in his life. The continuous sound of zizzing around the latrines fragmented into sporadic terse zizzers. It even seemed cooler with their diminished presence. The body language of people softened, less vigilant and more at ease.

Success left its imprint in towns and stations like Tea Tree, Woolla Downs, Harper Springs, Utopia, Ammaroo, Elkedra, Murray Downs, Wauchope, Singleton, Greenwood, Tennant Creek, Banka Banka, Helen

Springs, Renner Springs, Elliot, North Newcastle Waters, Dunmara and finally Daly Waters.

On the day of the last event of the field trials, the mayor was scheduled to hand the awards to the competitors at the famous Daly Waters Pub. His aircraft was late due to official business in another part of his vast shire.

Nonetheless, outside the pub, Isaac presented the awards with aplomb, fitting the moment and with above all, dignity. Aneus Martius was right. *"Fax Mentis incedium gloriae."* The passion for glory is the torch of the mind.

The long-awaited outback pub experience was now at hand. A hub had formed in and around the pub, like bees to the honey pot. Established in 1893, the building, like most remote structures had a roof made of iron sheeting originally painted red and now faded. A low-slung veranda cooled the entry to the pub.

The building nestled in an oasis of planting and a corrugated iron tank perched on a spindly steel-framed tower, stood out among the treetops, an oasis of spring water, a watering hole and cold beer on tap.

Inside, stools and table tops lined the perimeter of the large plain room. A few framed pictures of famous racing horses at full gallop crossing the finishing line graced the humble walls. The only decoration was reserved for the side and rear of the bar which consisted of old bank notes pinned crazily over each other. They were the conversation pieces, souvenirs and calling cards of visitors, many from the world over, some from countries that no longer existed. Free-flowing beer wetted bush yarns, a place of restoration, joy and the odd bar brawl, the patrons found completely satisfying.

Being unaccustomed to bars, never mind this one, Isaac sat up at the bar just as Rex told him to. The logic was that Isaac would pass the drinks through the crowd as they came from the barmaid and pay for them. It was noisy. An old codger perched at the bar to his left, gently tugging the wet toweling on the bar top, looked up at him and through his yellow rimmed pupils queried, "Keepin' busy mate?"

"Ah, yes, plenty to do thanks, how 'bout you?"

"Aw, yuh know, as long as yuh still peein', yuh must still be get'n a drink, eh!" all the while the pupils roving with little control.

From barely within earshot the barmaid offered her insight on her bar-bound patron.

"Got an IQ of seventy-five on a sunny day, haven't you, eh?" clearly out of fondness, with the old roustabout, responding,

"She can charm a copper head snake out of its skin, can't yuh love, eh!"

Isaac looked at both of them with several turns of his head and asked quite earnestly, "Do you always talk like this, in sayings I mean…eh?" adding the now familiar ending which could be a question, an explanation, agreement or just a statement depending on the inflexion of the voice.

A ruckus burst through the saloon door and the crowd started to peel away as the awesome figure of Mayor Donald Key and his entourage broke into the hotel rather than so much as entered it. Leaning towards him, the old codger grabbed Isaac's left forearm with his right hand and gripped, warning,

"Go easy on the EE-ORRR jokes," and just as he said it, the old codger winced, as a high- pitched mule sound screeched from somewhere along the wall on far the side of the room, under a photo of a prize-winning nag at the Birdsville Races.

Isaac, Rex and Julia were taken aback by presence of this big outback mountain of a man, rethinking the wisdom of inviting him to officiate at the closing ceremony. Perhaps it was fortunate that he didn't show up in time.

Don Key loved the exercise of political power as much as the physical crunching of bones, and before the dying squall of… ORRR! was through, the fearsome form of a wounded razorback turned to where the sound came and pushing the crowd of patrons aside, made his way to the wall. The expression on the two culprits perched on stools below the picture of Big Red, the sixty-nine-champion thoroughbred, turned from smirk, to guilt, to fear.

Mayor Donald Key, as those who wished to remain safe always addressed him, extended two giant hands at each throat and lifted both bodies, biffing them against the corrugated iron wall. They fell gracelessly over their stools and onto the floor, one landing on the shattered glass of his beer. Surveying the damage from his vast height, the mayor bellowed,

"If you don't like it, vote me out at the next election!" The mayor, spun around with the swiftness and glare of a goanna. The drinkers parted yet again as the mayor, spotting Isaac, approached the bar, deducing him from those he didn't know. Looking directly at Isaac he leaned on the old codger with the unspoken message to vacate the stool, showing what little respect he could to an elder of his constituency, all the while eyeing Isaac.

After lowering his left butt onto the stool, the mayor leaned forward, his face to Isaac's face, well within either's personal space.

"I wanna word with you," and after a pause,

"Isaac, is that you?"

Isaac confirmed with an almost imperceptible nod.

"Isaac, eh? Jewish, like the Jew in the Bible, eh," continued the one-sided investigation, and Isaac responded,

"I'm more Roman than Jew if you need to know such detail."

The mayor looked puzzled until he figured it out.

"What, like Ben Hur, chariots and stuff?"

"Something like that," said Isaac hoping to defray the line of questioning. It was becoming clear to Isaac that the mayor was not here to apologise for being late, nor for officiating, and Isaac was feeling more that he was about to be run out of town.

Rex, Jack and the others were getting twitchy and the bar patrons were becoming transfixed by the potential encounter.

The mayor then said what he came to say.

"I wanna know what you mean by coming into my territory."

Isaac stared breathlessly, his insides squirming under the pressure of Don Key's quiet violence. "You're implying my land and the land of my constituents is full of shit, stinking maggot-ridden shit!"

Still no comment from Isaac.

"I suppose your shit doesn't smell!" breaking momentarily into a crazed malevolent smile and Isaac couldn't take any more. At a distance of ten inches Isaac began to tell the mayor that in fact his shit did not smell, and in no uncertain terms, far from it.

"If I were to break wind in your face, the warm sweet air passing into your nostrils would be intoxicating if not hypnotic, so much so that you would wish it to never end."

The mayor's face dropped with disbelief. His pupils dilated into madness, his nostrils flared with rage, and as fear would have it, Isaac saw there was plenty of time to reflect on his life, to recall the science of smelling, how the varying flow rates of air entering each nostril picked up differing scents within any given odour, producing a stereo olfactory image of the nature and texture of it, leading the whole smell to be able to be catalogued for recall at any time in life, and associating smell, with any mood or sense of place the individual had experienced in his or her life. Isaac even had time to reflect on how amazing the recalling power of threatened life was.

The big man's right arm recoiled, flattening the diminutive Town Clerk, before propelling itself towards Isaac's head. Rex got to Isaac first, pulling him backwards off the stool as the mighty fist flew past his face with the full weight of an ox behind it. Don Key's arm could not stop, and propelled towards the beer tap, knocking it off the keg stand.

A hydrant of beer sprouted and danced in the air as the mayor's wrist shattered. Rex threw Isaac to the floor as six patrons jumped onto the bar, two of them standing on the fallen mayor, lapping and swallowing at the fountain of their dreams. Rex dragged Isaac along the floor while Julia and the others skirted around the room until they got to the doorway. Once Rex got him half way onto the veranda, Jack helped him to his feet. As they ran to their vehicles, Rex scolded Isaac for starting the fracas.

"Just as well Julia organised a flight back to Alice Springs and she's packed the basics for you, Jesus, what happened to your diplomatic skills back there!"

Just a few minutes up the highway, Rex pulled over onto a track leading to an airstrip. A small plane sounding like a mosquito revved ahead and Julia and Isaac boarded. On take off the plane jerked sideways while still maintaining its forward bumpy ride and Isaac asked of Julia, "I don't suppose you've got any Kwells with you?" Adding, "These things make me airsick!" Julia reached into the seat pocket.

"Here's a leak-proof puke bag, use it only if you have to."

***

By every measure the Outback field trials were a success and after cataloguing the results, and the first month's district league results, Isaac received a quicker than expected commission from the World Health Organisation. Could Isaac please arrange a similar campaign within the narrow strip of the Southern Mediterranean coastline, north of the Sahara Desert?

With the assistance of a United Nations delegate, Isaac and Rex mapped out the North African Campaign to which Rex obtusely referred to as 'Roman Holiday', incorrectly ascribing the saying to the annexure of the land by the Roman Empire.

Rex studied the territory from the ancient maps of the IMPERIUM ROMANUM which included the original and modern names, Vaga (Constantine, Algeria), Utica (Tabarka, Tunisai), Cathargo (Tunis, Tunisia), Zama (Gafsa, Tunisia, Thapsus (Sfax, Tunisia) and east to Cyrene (Shahhat, Libya) and Alexandria (El Iskandariya, Egypt).

The principal deserts available to them from these centres were, the Grand Erg Occidental, Grand Erg Oriental, Tripolitania, Cyrenaica and the moist Qattara Depression.

It seemed logical to follow the Australian experience, as they could be applied to the torrid, dry zones of Africa. Rex chose to plan the expedition, and while Isaac felt some foreboding, he did not object to his proposals. The U.N. scheduled Rome as the centre of operations for the campaign and Isaac, as commander of operations, was to be stationed in Rome.

He appointed Rex as field commander and Julia as logistics comptroller and chief statistician reporting directly to Isaac. It was Isaac's task to stall or speed up the program after assessing the effectiveness of the campaign.

The U.N. envoy in Rome arranged for Isaac's lodgings, generously inviting his wife Luteesha to join him. The stay included all costs for three months.

"Hand-fly-capture!" The envoy grinned, not yet a convert, but in awe of Isaac's mastery.

"You will be staying in the Fontana Hotel, directly opposite the Trevi Fountain, and I have secured two rooms in the office of a publishing house, just a five-minute walk from the hotel. I am sure you will be very comfortable, and the history, oh the history will amaze you. You'll be right in the middle of it!"

Isaac placed the suit cases on the bed and parted the gold and calico drapes to open the shutters of the hotel room. An embroidered cloth-covered round table, and two chairs were well placed next to the window. A tall, glass tray holding a fine selection of fruit thoughtfully centred on the table, had a still-life quality.

"Isaac, I'm exhausted! Let's go to the rooftop bar, sit down, and have a drink. It looks fabulous in the brochure. We can unpack later."

They climbed the stairs to the rooftop, Luteesha leading the way, and walked across to the iron balustrade overlooking the Trevi Fountain. Tourists everywhere, some in the water and others preciously holding their spot to take in the fanciful wonder of it all.

Isaac took in the parapeted vista of this historic place, domes, turrets, distant hills, Renaissance, Rococo, Greco-Roman architecture and the extraordinary sculptures adorning them.

The bar was a concoction. Oddly, splayed terracotta tile flooring had a pinkish tinge. Dark stained tree-trunk beams that spanned the full width of the space, supported raked timber roof rafters and ceiling boards. On the walls either side of the chimney breast, black and white tiles were laid in a diamond pattern, a layout usually reserved for floors.

Aperol Spritz, Peroni, prosciutto and fresh figs were served by an understanding waiter.

The window of their room looked onto the fountain. The night lighting deepened the blue hue of the water and lit the monumental facade of the Palazzo Poli, and the marble statues and rock falls that spilled water into the fountain pool. It spoke of the past, present and future, material and immaterial, eternal in its reach.

In the early morning sun, the memory of Grand Uncle Felix came to mind, telling him how he and his grandfather Ezekiel in their youth visited Rome.

He stared out of the window with the sun warming the side of his face. He kept it this way for some minutes as he pondered the view before him. The inscription on the entablature of the Palazzo Poli, hovered above the turmoil of the central figure of Oceanus, standing atop a chariot pulled by sea horses, and accompanied by Tritons. "PERFECTUM. BENEDICTUS XIV. PON MAX," even without translation, the pronouncement was made powerful and perfect, chiselled in stone.

In niches to the left and right resided the figures of Abundance and Health. In a bas-relief was sculpted the legend of the Aqua Virgo, the name Agrippa gave to the aqueduct he built in 19 BC to supply water for his baths. The source of the spring was revealed to Roman soldiers by a virgin and to this benevolent omen, Marcus Agrippa paid homage by the naming of the virginal water.

Isaac's sight became lost in the blue waters of the fountain. The warmth on his neck nourished the nostalgia for his family bonds. The bustle below increased, and he retreated further into history.

He was filled with unease and belonging, as if his demons and benefactors melted into one. How he came to be in Rome was some kind of fate or destiny, a malicious benevolence of his distant ancestors, softened by the sweet and sorrow loss of his grandfather and uncle.

Coincidence was becoming expected and transparent without subtlety, and as much as he found it unsettling, he as much loved it.

After breakfast, Isaac found his way to via Santa Maria and Piazza San Silvestro. At the Posta Centrale he turned right into Via della Mercede, and a few buildings to his right Isaac stopped to read.

'Associazione Stampa Estera in Italia, via della Mercede, 55–00187, Roma'. He entered the doorway and walked tentatively into a wide unadorned corridor, unsure how many people working there had a reasonable command of English. The sounds of people moving within the building echoed down the open stair well. The painted plaster and concrete surfaces were devoid of decoration, even spartan, reduced to the simple function of cleanly accessing the floors above.

On the second floor a small round man with an embryo moustache greeted Isaac and directed him to his rooms. He stopped abruptly at a doorway from which he clumsily introduced Isaac to co-tenant office workers. The spaces were filled with counters and filing cabinets, desks, computer screens, fax/photocopiers and glazed office partitions. Light fittings from high above hung so low they looked like office equipment. Despite the clutter Isaac felt conspicuous.

Within a week, the first field results were coming through from Julia, and Isaac worked through them diligently. What he was particularly concerned about, was the impact cultural differences would have on the program compared to the Australian results.

When he was not working Isaac devoted his energies to exploring historic locations, and learning as much about the city's ancient past as is free time would permit. Luteesha would meet him for lunch at various caffe's and ristorantes' when they could easily enough reach each other. He wanted his wife enjoy the best possible experience, encouraging her to visit the many galleries, museums, and churches. On one outing, she walked through the Via dei Condotti on her way to the Spanish Steps to meet Isaac at Babington's Tea Room. In this street, stores brimming with designer clothing and luxury goods captivated her, and she returned often. Just a four-minute walk from the hotel was the Rinascente Department Store, the best in Rome. Here, she could buy clothes for her husband, having gotten used to his ambivalence for the finer art of dressing let alone shopping.

Isaac immersed himself in the patina and enclosure of the narrow streets that regularly yielded to small, shapeless piazzas, and admired the inventiveness of the building forms, sculpted around comers of awkwardly random intersections.

The buildings were old and solid, the walls and doorways heavy as though reluctant to allow entry. Arched alleyways secured by decorative iron screens accessed internal courtyards, blotched walls passing as having the patina of age. In the floors above, windows some with shutters perforated the walls, ultimately revealing the sky above the narrow streets.

It was some weeks before he could wander the maze of streets, lanes and passages with any certainty of knowing where he was and how to get back, without reference to a map.

In its parchment, he learned to differentiate the architectural and artistic periods. The remains of the Roman Empire now had a physical presence, even more real than had been made known to him in his mind.

In the sixth week of the program Rex requested that they bypass Sfax in Tunisia and move directly to Cyrene and Alexandria. Isaac agreed subject to rescheduling the itinerary to include two additional bazaars, one casbah and deleting one oasis to bring the finishing date back on line. Sports administration emerged as a major issue. It became evident that volunteer base clubs would not work here as they had in Australia.

He made enquiries about private interest groups, keen to secure 'sporting contracts', or seek U.N. funding to meet the needs of volunteer programs. He left it to Julia to follow up.

Isaac studied the epoch of the ancients who invaded his mind. As well he committed to memory the faces of Caesar, Marcus Antonius and Marcus Lepidus, Brutus and Cassius. These were the central figures in the assignation of Julius Caesar, a jumble of figures he gleaned from the play of Shakespeare mixed with the historic record of the period.

This conspiratorial malice, contrasted with Hadrian, the Great Constructor and Emperor who promoted and treasured the value of peace.

The facade of the temple his son Antoninus Pius erected to honour his father's deification, stood in the Piazza di Pietra, a short walk from Isaac's hotel.

The eleven massive columns of fraying marble reminded Isaac of the strength and companionship of the cypress trees of his boyhood, and he came to see the columns as the touchstone of the ancient reality of his mind.

Just as he was deified after his death, Hadrian had honoured others before him. As emperor, he replaced the temple of Agrippa with the more imposing Pantheon, dedicating the inscription on the pediment above the columns to his memory.

M.AGRIPPA.L.F.COS.TERTIUM.FECIT.

And before him, Agrippa built the original temple in dedication to Augustus, his father-in-law and friend, but he declined the honour, and Agrippa dedicated it to the gods, Mars, Venus and Julius Caesar.

These people and their gods were the crust of Isaac's mind.

On one of his walks, Isaac ascended the Mons Capitolinus. From the top of the escarpment that overlooked the Forum, Isaac fixed his gaze on the Curia, the house of the Senators and the People of Rome. The Arch of Septimius Severus stood adjacent to the Curia, a distant relative of Isaac as told to him by Grand Uncle Felix.

Below, to the right of where he was standing, the ruins of the Templum Iovis, flaunted its proud position. The Temple of Jupiter, the God of Lightning and Thunder, responsible for the taking of the professor from him stood there. Isaac paused in remembrance, trying to come to terms with his taker.

"Fulmen Brutum," a senseless thunderbolt, striking blindly. As he looked over the temple of Jupiter, he wondered whether the strike that took the Professor and almost killed him, was as senseless as it seemed. Destiny is not senseless. If it was not pre-determined, why was it that he should find himself in this place of Jupiter, and, by the most improbable

path that had led him here. As his thoughts closed in on his senses the words, *"Fumum et opes, strepitumque Romae,"* entered the quiet perimeter of his mind, where the smoke, the riches and the noise of Rome lay silent. In this stasis Isaac knew that only one enormous thunderbolt from Jupiter would bring the city to life again.

Luteesha became concerned with the time her husband was devoting to his search for answers. As strong and understanding as she was, her awareness to the seriousness of his condition heightened. To her, he seemed to have succumbed to his increasing distress, nearing the irreversible.

The campaign in Africa had gained momentum. Julia's records of before and after fly-program were stunning enough, but reports of the first of many medical breakthroughs heartened Isaac. In a bazaar in Zama a blind man stood and walked one hundred paces through the tumult without stumbling, the infestation in his sockets having subsided in the near absence of gnawing secretions. Stories like this and many others were being heard all the way to New York and talk of extending the campaign into the Horn of Africa and the Middle East, were now being considered for funding and the hiring of additional field operatives. In another age, the results would have been the work of miracles.

Near the end of their stay in Rome summer had passed into autumn. The days shortened and the heat of the night cooled. The peak of the tourist season had now passed and the restaurateurs resumed calling their patrons by name. In a city used to the influx of tourists, a newcomer who stayed longer than a week could be accepted as local, and he took great pleasure in hearing his name called by staff.

In the week before their return to Melbourne, the bust of Marcus Junius Brutus descended into Isaac's mind. The familiar holographic image, hung still and whitened in the red velvet retina of his eye, a face that came with guilt. His lips moved and Isaac heard it said,

"Hannibal ad portas,*"* Hannibal before the gates, which in Latin meant, the enemy was close at hand. "He who had murdered his wife is upon us.

From the quiet of the forum, the pious fraud will rise, to be killed again for the good of Rome."

"Hunc tu Romane caveto in extremis," Roman, beware of that man, at the point of death. Isaac's legs turned numb and his insides squirmed as he lay beside his wife. This man Brutus, of all the tyrants that tormented him, had about him the wanton desire of repetition, to repeat the same ill over and over without contrition, for eternity.

"Mali Principii malus finis," and Isaac knew this as reference to the murder of Caesars wife that 'bad beginnings have bad endings'. And in a final tirade Brutus mouthed,

"Ne Jupiter quidem omnibus placet," not even Jupiter pleases everybody.

"Ecce Brutus, filius nullius," behold Brutus, a son of nobody and illegitimate son of his despised father, Julius Caesar.

"Permittere lis litem generat!" Let strife beget strife!

Isaac's neck was lathered and a run of sweat roused him from the nightmare. He could not lie any longer and rose slowly. He pulled a light-weight gown off the chair and strapped sandals to his feet. He left the room quietly. Luteesha did not stir.

It was after midnight when Isaac left the foyer. Lovers, insomniacs and beggars lingered by the waters of the fountain and Isaac tucked his head down, allowing himself to be guided left towards the Via del Corso.

There he swung left to face the great monolith of Victor Emanuel, raised in honour of Rome's Imperial greatness. The monument loomed and beckoned, drawing Isaac like an insect to the light. The image of Brutus ate at him, and it was only by running that he could diminish its power. Still, his words of warning, of imminent danger, rang on in Isaac's jogging head. He felt like a knowing lamb to the slaughter.

Towards the monument he paced, in fear of death, fear that he would perish and that his life would come to nothing. The fear of a violent and untimely death, as in the taking of the professor, propelled him onto the roadway of the Piazza Venezia. A screech of wheels and an angry horn shook him from his trance and he steadied to a walk across the grass island in the middle of the square.

He puffed, breathlessly unconscious of whether he was heading away from danger or towards his peril. He approached the huge colonnaded monument, passing between two bronze statues mounted high on stone pedestals, one representing thought and the other action. The broad flight of steps loomed, but Isaac stepped back and away, deciding to take the stairs leading to the natural depression between the two peaks of the Capitoline Hill. Along this crest called the Asylum, he walked to the rear of the Palazzo Senatorio, and descended into the Forum.

As before, he made his way to the humble roof that sheltered the concrete pile encasing the ashes of Julius Caesar. In the darkness, sheet lightning lit the path causing a panic to well in him, swelling his stomach with fear. He could be grateful for Jupiter lighting the way but it always came at a cost. Isaac stood before the mound. Thunder clapped in the distance and rolled towards him.

A vapor coalesced in front of him, and like the writing on a steamed window pane, words and numbers formed on the shroud of mist.

'Eid Mar', the ides, the fifteenth of March, 44 BC, floated above the mound just as a mighty bolt of lightning careened earthwards. The roof buckled as it took the strike, the loud boom jolting him. The rain abstained. The forms of two men emerged from behind the mound, glowing into shape as they stood up. Isaac reeled back tripping over rubble and falling out of sight.

He rolled onto his belly and twisted to look upwards at the of the draped body of Julius Caesar and the gladiatorial armour of his general Marcus Antonius as they walked towards the Curia. Isaac bounced his adrenaline-charged body to his feet and followed, keeping out of their sight. The very act of taking this precaution caused him to question his own sanity. The three walked through the Templum Vestae and at the Templum Castoris turned into the Via Sacra past what were the shops at the rear of the Forum. At the Basilica Aemilia, all three turned left passing over the Cloaca Maxima and stopping at the door of the Senate House, the Curia.

Isaac overheard them speaking about the change of venue for their meeting with the Senators. Caesar agreed to the attend, despite not being officially required. The Senators would now be meeting in the in the *Templum Divus Hadrianus,* the Temple of Hadrian that Isaac knew in the Piazza di Pietra.

They left the Curia, and as they walked under the Arch of Septimius Severus, Isaac recalled Septimius as being a distant relative as told to him by Felix. That this oblique recollection should come to mind, staggered him, given the predicament he was now in.

The men Jupiter had exhumed, talked as they climbed the Clivus Capitolinus and passed the Temples of Concordiae and Saturni. At the top of the hill, they stopped to pay homage to Carmentis the prophetess, mother of Evander, who came with her from Greece to Latium. Here Julius Caesar confided to Mark Antony of his wife's pleas to stay at home today.

"Antony, before Carmentis, I say fearlessly, Caesar ignores the wild dreams of Calpurnia and the findings of the Augurers. I will not be shamed into cowardice with talk of drizzled blood upon this Capitol. But I do fear for her, for the dreams of horrible sights, of the whelping lioness and graves that yawn and yield their dead."

In his unwavering reply, Antony, the true friend and protector, secured Caesar's faith. Isaac followed them down the steps to the Via Marcelus, in full knowledge of where they were going. Isaac had formed a bond with the marble columns of the temple, for the grandeur and power they exuded.

As they passed the Basilica of the evangelist San Marco, he thought of the chapel in which the remains of Spaniard, Ignatius of Loyola, the namesake of Isaac's older brother, lay in an urn.

Caesar and Antony walked from the square into the opening of the narrow and straight Via del Corso. Sensing the danger that lay ahead,

Isaac raced forward and confronted the men not knowing what he was going to say or whether they would even see him,

"Caesar, beware Brutus and the Senators! He has warned me, and I must you! Let strife beget." Before Isaac could finish, Antony pushed his right hand to Isaac's shoulder pulling the night gown off his shoulder. Isaac reeled back into the dark. An apparition and what looked like nothing more than a ghost, physically attacked him. The resurrected figures of Caesar and Antony moved on.

Isaac withdrew into a lane and ran the back streets parallel to the Via del Corso. He could still feel the imprint of a hand on his shoulder. In chronic disbelief, Isaac jogged in uneven steps to the end of the via Collegia Romano and turned into the Piazza San Ignazio, entered the Church of Saint Ignatius and therein walked impulsively to the yellow marble disc, embedded in the floor.

Here Isaac stood and looked up into the vortex of Baroque cloud formations that swept all before it into an infinite, celestial glory. From the disc the universe was correct, masterful and eternal, a perfect universe. From the disc absolution was complete, a place unconsummated by sin or crime.

For Isaac to step out of this perfect universe and into the distorted madness of the world of his demons, would require only that he step off the marble disc and walk a few paces. From this displaced viewpoint the same perfect after-world would distort into chaos, uncertainty and instability. By the stroke of an illusion, the restless world of the Roman afterlife spiralled into an eternal fall, where peace could never be known. How small a step it was between the eternal choice of harmony and the mad space of the abyss.

Isaac felt the very same distortion. A distortion of time and place, in which the dead are awakened only to be killed again. A world in an eternal cycle of torment played by Jupiter with his wretched, anything but senseless thunderbolts, that he dispensed for the murdered to relive their fear, shock and death, and for the murderers to live over and over again, the guilt of their deeds.

Through these demons Isaac had stepped into this god-ridden, distorted void, a void now in name only. Isaac was part of it, the third substance in the void he thought, beyond simply hearing and speaking, and onto the full consequences of interference.

When these gods and long dead tyrants behaved like his benefactors what did it mean of him? Was he part of the distortion or was he really distorted himself? Was he evil by association? These questions troubled him deeply, and when he could no longer bear to think about it, he sprinted out of the church. Julius Caesar must be getting closer to his meeting with the Senators and he made straight for the Temple of Hadrian.

He ran into the piazza and spotted Caesar and Antony talking in front of the Temple. On seeing Isaac closing in on them Antony shouted,

"You, *Sortilegus* – fortune teller, for the second time what business have you!"

Isaac pulled to a standstill facing them.

"Let us hear it before we have you slit and drawn," ruled Caesar as he raised his regal arm.

Isaac implored, "The Senators, the assassins and Brutus lie in wait – Antonius, do not leave Caesar's side, or..." On the mention of Brutus, Julius Caesar succumbed to the falling sickness, swooning and collapsing to the pavement. Knowing this as an affliction of Caesar, Antony fell with him to catch his head before it hit the iron railing.

Caesar's eyes were glazed open and Isaac looked so intently into them he could see the reflection of the eleven white columns soaring above, curved by the roundness of his eyes. Between the columns, Isaac could see the redness of his mind. The familiarity of the image surprised him, and in that instant, the stricken man lying before him had an overwhelming affinity for him.

In that moment, Isaac recognised that Caesar inhabited another world. He wondered if in that place, Caesar was conscious of his presence. As he revived consciousness, Antony raised Caesar and then he drew his knife, directing the lucent blade at Isaac.

"Caesar! I beseech you! Show me tenderness, I know you know me," burst Isaac for his life, cutting through to Caesar. Julius Caesar's right hand brushed against Antony's clenched fist bearing the weapon, summoning him to hold.

"I beg you to spare me an untimely death and entrust me to make my life complete," implored Isaac, and bravely stepped forward to hear from Caesar,

"Amicus humani generis, friend of the human race, go back from whence you came. There, you will find what you seek."

Mark Antony stepped between them nudging Isaac back with his chest plate ending the confrontation.

Isaac backed away reassured, but mortified that he could not stop what was about to happen. Mark Antony walked away and Caesar disappeared between the columns, and a stunned Isaac stared at where Caesar had lain. A few bystanders watched Isaac's bizarre motions. It was in the early hours of the morning, the curious and dispossessed, unsurprised, moved on.

Isaac's brief elation drifted into guilt at having failed to stop Caesar from entering the building. His heart raced and he needed to retreat. He could not yet go back to the Hotel. Distraught, tired and frightened, Isaac walked the pathway of the narrow Via dei Pastini and entered the Piazza della Rotonda, the Pantheon. He approached the great portico. The massive double bronze doors were closed and Isaac sat at the base of one of the sixteen columns, and squatted there as if he were resting at the base of the cherry tree.

That the great rotunda behind him was constructed to reflect cosmic and earthly order did not soothe him, and before the thought resolved itself, Isaac felt a terrible blow to his neck. He clasped his hand over the pain and another blow struck him in the back. Two more blows rolled him off the base of the column and Isaac knew the Senator's knives were mauling Caesar.

Casca, Decius, Metellus, Cossius, Cinna and others dealt blows each and every one of which Isaac felt, all in the name of the good of Rome.

The last stab came from his beloved Brutus, and Caesar allowed himself to fall, dedicating to him his deification. As Caesar's dying pulses depleted his veins, Isaac rolled onto his knees and shaking cold, vomited on the stone floor of the ancients, and between each retching, gathered himself to think how many more times in eternity, must Caesar be killed in the name of the Senate and the People of Rome, consoled only by his deification. His head pounded and on his last reflux lost consciousness, and fell hitting his head on a stone pedestal.

At first light, Isaac woke shivering. The grit and stench of his mouth was disgusting and he got up and walked out from the Portico towards the fountain in the middle of the square, his gown in tatters.

A homeless man shaving an office worker stood by a small brass tap on the side of the fountain wall. Isaac walked around the fountain and approached them. The homeless man leaned down to wash his cut-throat razor under the running water. Isaac covered his own stubble not wishing to be shaved. When the unkempt man wiped the blade, Isaac bent down to rinse his mouth and wet his eyes. As the cool water ran into his mouth Isaac looked up suspiciously and saw the blade holding still against the worker's face, and the homeless man staring down at him. Behind the rancorous smile, the obelisk from the Egyptian Temple of Isis stood like an accomplice. Trusting it safe to do so, Isaac finished washing, raised himself and walked away.

***

The sun had not yet risen when Isaac returned to the Trevi Fountain, and stepped into the quoined archway of the Hotel Fontana. He walked the narrow entrance between the marble- topped wooden reception desk and the mirror wall, adding a reflected confusion to the night, and clambered up the stairs. He mindfully entered the darkened room only to find his wife sitting up. "Isaac, I just woke and you weren't here. Where have you been?"

He walked to the bathroom dropping his gown to the tiled floor. After pausing there, he made his way to his side of the bed and sat down with his back to her.

"I saw him, and I've been with him, Julius Caesar, and now I'm really tired and need to rest."

"Visions?" asked Luteesha.

And all he could offer was, "Yes, but now they're real."

He lay down where he had left the bed, and she covered him like a child. Isaac passed into black sleep. An hour later, Luteesha sobbed in her sleep. Her face rested on Isaac and the tears rolling down his shoulder woke him. He moved to see what was wrong,

"What is it, 'Teesh, what?"

She swallowed hard so that she could speak.

"I dreamed a rag doll, Isaac, I dream a rag doll."

Isaac could not fathom what she meant, and began to clear the falling tears off her cheek with his thumb. He could see she needed time.

"I dreamed the beautiful head of a baby child on a padded body dressed in a red and white check shirt and light blue trousers…

"I picked it up by the back feeling the stick of its spine that held the padding of its body, and as the doll sat straight up in my arm, the beautiful porcelain lips moved, and its cheeks raised as its mouth opened to speak to me."

She began to shake, panting to hold back the tears.

"I only heard through our minds, yours and mine together. The baby child asked if it could eat something, taste something with us, and I could still feel the stick of its back in my hand. Its soft tongue moved and I could see it was searching for food and I reached down for a teaspoon of custard and gently held the spoon to its mouth, placing some on its tongue. The tongue moved from side to side as if trying to work out how to eat it, but still tasting the food. The warm bliss of sharing food overcame us and its mouth and its eyes closed and opened with quiet joy."

Isaac wondered.

"Then I realised it could not swallow so I gently collected the custard with the spoon, the baby child thanking me, us, as it moved its tongue from side to side placing the food onto the spoon from its mouth.

"It's loving thanks crushed me and I began to cry with the joy of sharing the love we received. I washed the baby child from my mind with my tears all the while feeling the stick of its back.

"And now even awake I can still see, feel the pleasure of its mouth and the joy of us, and the thanks for the food we gave and shared."

Isaac was awestruck. He knew this was about him, as well as her and each together but could not say a word overcome by the emotion of the dream.

"The baby child looked briefly in my eyes, twice, Isaac, lovingly." Isaac could only hug her and a tear welled in his eye for the beauty of her dream. She had dreamt a rag doll, a life not begun, a life yearned the way women dream.

After they had showered, they sat closely together to eat breakfast and Luteesha often looked to her side, as if the baby child might be there, not wanting to let go of the dream.

"What's happening to us?" asked Isaac not really expecting an answer.

"You, Isaac, you, my darling. My dream is understandable but I worry that your health is deteriorating. Your visions are becoming impulsive and what you hear now, you act on. When we get home, I want you to see a doctor."

The logical fabric of Isaac's mind agreed with her and yet in light of the night's events, he could not shake it as a truth, and then Calpurnia's dream flooded his mind.

Caesar's wife dreamt her husband's effigy, punctured by a hundred spouts, running pure blood. Romans bathed their hands in the airborne rivulets of her husband's life fluid, smiling with blood lust. As vivid as Luteesha's, Calpurnias dream was not of an unborn, but of a life to be ended.

The way women dream, pondered a deeply troubled Isaac, *the way women dream.*

Ab incurabulis, ad finem... From the cradle, to the end

A die, ad infinitum From that day, to infinity

Adsum I am present

Chapter 9

Luteesha's Lament

On their return, Isaac made an appointment to see Dr Olga Niesohn, a clinical psychologist recommended by a colleague of Luteesha, specialising in psychiatric/psychology categories at the State Library. He was reticent, believing his condition to be an unshakable truth, but it had become bigger than himself. His wife was struggling with her experience and he thought it best to appease her.

On her part, they agreed she should visit a Buddhist Temple in Tokyo, devoted to the unborn, and infants who had died early in life. One thousand Guardian Deities of Children in the form of little statues dedicated to the safe growth of children, was also a memorial to stillborn and miscarried children. This place struck at the heart of Luteesha, and she needed to suspend herself in its healing.

There, she hoped to find solace, to ease the pain brought about by her profound dream.

Her movements had become mechanical and her voice was often muffled by the grey haze of sadness. She had not been the same since her baby-child dream, and had replayed it over and over not wanting to let it go.

She fell into despair, and it was in pursuit of closure that she planned to spend as much time as needed in the Zojo-ji Temple, to be in its setting of expansive treed gardens, to pray to Jizo, Guardian Deity of Children.

She had agreed not to have children, but the taunt of "waiting too long" loomed in spite of her commitment. She had bonded with her unborn child, at odds with everything she believed about her life choice. Her baby had nonetheless coalesced, somewhere along the continuum, the threshold between life and the ability to have life.

The plane landed at Tokyo Haneda Airport in the northern hemisphere autumn. Luteesha checked in to the Shiba Park Hotel, located within an easy walk to the Zojo-ji Temple. She did not intend to stay beyond her search for emotional closure, even though she believed it to be unattainable, so deep was her grief. The in-house restaurant was convenient for her short stay, a place of least distraction.

The flight, with all the security and customs checks had been tiring and she retired to bed, thankful that jet lag would not upset her body clock.

She wished to be centred and at peace for the next day.

In the early afternoon, Luteesha approached the imposing entrance of the Sangedatsu-mon gate, two stories tall, the upper level being perched above five wide bays. The centre three openings allowed entry to the temple grounds. Known as the Temple Gate of the Three Liberations, passage through it freed the visitor from greed, hatred or foolishness. Luteesha stood beneath it for a few minutes, thinking deeply about absolution from these negative afflictions. When she felt she had absorbed these freedoms, Luteesha ventured onto the broad flagstone pathway towards the four-hundred-year-old Zojo-ji Buddhist temple. Unmissable, the relatively recent Tokyo Tower, counter to historical traditions loomed high above the hip roof of the temple. She did not allow it to disturb her focus.

In a courtyard she stopped to pray before Kesodate Kannon, Goddess of Compassion, Protectress of women and children. In her divine wisdom, she embraced even her most unruly children with kindness and mercy. Before her, younger women hoping to become pregnant, prayed for fertility and safe delivery of their water-child.

Luteesha chose not to pray to the Goddess thinking it unhelpful to wish so profoundly for a child, and respectfully watched young women deep in prayer.

She moved on to the Ankokuden and the Mausoleum to find the guardian deities. There she found the beautiful, serene faces of the infant

Jizo statues, aligned in long stepped, rows. She melted at the sight of so many stone babies standing proudly upright, covered in red crocheted caps and bibs.

Their eyes were closed and their lips pursed, as if wanting food, just as she had dreamed the porcelain head of her doll. Brightly coloured pinwheels and flowers, lighted the stillness.

Some had stone vases beside them, filled with flowers or smoking sticks of incense. A few were surrounded by juice boxes or sweets. A cap had slipped off one tiny head and Luteesha picked it up, and before replacing it, she stroked the bald stone head, which felt like a new-born.

Women came here, to place toys and food as an offering on behalf of their lost dreams, and in that likeness, Luteesha had brought a small toy.

The offerings were made to Jizo, who watches over the unborn, the miscarried, and aborted fetuses. The statues, with their hands clasped in prayer and their eyes closed, appeared as child and monk, human and deity.

Her dream was right before her. She caressed a bib, and placed the toy beside a statue.

She smiled rapturously before wishing it on to a netherworld she did not know, but trusted. Her love glowed as her grief eased, remembering Mizuko, the water-child, whose existence flowed into being, slowly, like liquid. She took comfort in the belief that children only solidified gradually over time, and in this culture were not considered to be fully in our world until they reached the age of seven. This was meant to make it easier for her, though she did not accept the gesture, believing her baby-child would not forget her, even if her body had never been its host.

A breeze carried the waning scents of the lavender bushes in the garden they shared with wild irises, azaleas, fleabane and camellias. She stayed calm until the movement of people leaving, heralded the falling twilight. The garden turned cold as if telling her it was okay to leave.

Luteesha, brimming with emotion, turned left onto the parkway, walking in small steps. She passed the Le Pain Quotidien cafe. Headlights reflected in her tears like fleeting diamonds, an incongruity to behold. She had the foresight to not apply eye shadow, only lipstick.

She succumbed to exhaustion, not able to continue a longer walk, and turned towards her hotel for a light meal and early night. She took a seat at one of the regimented tables of the restaurant, and ordered the Gomyo chilled soba dish and a small bottle of sparkling wine.

She pulled back the strands of dark hair that had stuck to her cheek and reached into her handbag, picking up the phone to set it in her hand, ready to make a call. Her eyes were too moist to see clearly, the delay causing her to rethink talking to her husband.

She put the phone back in her bag just as her meal was served. The restaurant was busy, and a man sat opposite her, a commercial traveller, she thought. They exchanged a polite acknowledgement, and beyond that nothing.

The tables were reasonably separated but the odd eye contact was difficult to avoid. The meal seemed to take forever. In an unspoken dialogue, Luteesha prepared to leave and retire to her room.

She left.

He followed.

In her abandonment.

Touch, craving, hunger, fulfilment, ended in tears.

He left.

***

Isaac read from Shakespeare's *The Tragedy of Julius Caesar*;

Fierce fiery warriors fought upon the clouds,
In ranks and squadrons and right form of war,
Which drizzled blood upon the Capitol;
The noise of battle hurtled in the air,
Horses did neigh, and dying men did groan;
And ghosts did shriek and squeal about the streets.

Calpurnia's dream of what happened above the clouds righted in Isaac's mind. He feared clouds. Images of their formations unsettled him, the floating forms, taller than mountains and as broad as a continent, defied the natural laws of gravity.

In their plumes resided angry, interfering gods. Principal among them, Jupiter, whose image was cast on his grandfather's seventh Roman coin. He remembered Ezekiel holding the coin up high for all to see at the banquet celebrating the family's migration to Australia.

"The coin of the Emperor Antoninus Pius is made of gold!" emphasised Ezekiel.

"It is inscribed to Iovi Statori, to Jupiter Stator. The God is holding a sceptre in his left hand and a thunderbolt in his right!"

Isaac's flesh had felt the fire of his thunderbolt, and his heart the tragic loss of a loved one. The torment of his mind was unrelenting, and worst of all was the doubt Isaac felt when the recalcitrant God behaved as a benefactor. Could fear of a tyrant ever be benign, let alone a saviour?

The clouds that harboured Jupiter and provided the energy of his senseless thunderbolts, occupied Isaac's mind. He began to see as sinister and subversive, the way they gathered and frayed. Cirrus, Cumulus, Stratus and Nimbus, each sounding like the names of Roman Senators, each with dagger at hand to plunge endlessly into a trusting moment of vulnerability. In Julius Caesar's calculated, frenzied stabbing, the fiery warriors upon the clouds of Cirrus, Cumulus, Stratus and Nimbus, drizzled blood upon him.

Isaac could not even find comfort in the distorted clouds painted on the ceiling of the church of St. Ignatius, nor in the whirling of angel wings that climaxed them into a blaze of light and glory. On and on Isaac waited, to be guided, to be told, a saying, that would direct him next.

***

It was barely three weeks after she returned from Japan, that the nausea and occasional vomiting began. She was forty-two, and wasted no time in seeing a doctor. She had managed to keep her condition from Isaac, but it would be increasingly difficult to conceal.

The doctor confirmed her pregnancy, and for six weeks she hid her discomfort from her husband.

After a morning tea break, Luteesha developed severe back, and abdominal pain. When she could no longer bear the pain and anguish of losing the baby, her work friend rushed her to the nearby hospital emergency department, aware of the cause of her sudden distress. Luteesha was triaged in time to receive full medical treatment for miscarriage.

In the late afternoon, while under mild sedation, she called her husband.

Prepared for the expected questions was one thing, but the betrayal beyond a dalliance, that of having a child, would crush Isaac. It was after all, a solemn commitment broken.

Over the coming week, Luteesha rested at home. Isaac spent more time with her, spent by his anguish, but he had not forsaken her. He committed to seeking help to resolve this conflict, and promised he would do so, mindful of the context of his fragile mind, and the rationale for remaining childless.

He made an appointment to see Doctor Olga Niesohn, psychologist.

The psychologist welcomed him warmly, to make him feel at ease.

"Please sit, Isaac, if I may call you by your first name."

"It's fine, doctor. Do I call you Olga?"

"Perhaps," while reading his referral letter. Until she knew what she was dealing with, Dr Niesohn kept the relationship intentionally awkward.

"You are feeling unwell from what I see as a significant number of reasons. You have powerful visions, even hallucinations as we refer to them. And there is the trauma of your wife losing the baby."

"Can I ask where you would feel more comfortable starting?"

Isaac had already decided how this would go.

"I am trying to resolve with my wife something not disclosed to you, an arrangement to not have children." Olga listened. Isaac stopped talking, visibly emotional.

"What was the circumstance of Luteesha's betrayal, as you have stated?"

After a pause, Isaac looked down.

"Pregnant to a stranger."

"And in the aftermath?" the doctor pressed.

"She needed me to understand, she implored."

"Isaac, is it the cheating or that she wilfully sought to get pregnant, that is the main cause of your distress?"

"Here, you should understand the nature of our commitment to be childless. It comes back to the 'hallucinations' as you call them, and this is something I don't believe you will ever understand." He went on to say, "I expect I could be wasting your time."

They talked through more on this, and Olga concluded by advising Isaac to give his wife more time and care, setting him a goal of trying to understand her loss.

"I feel sure that she will respond in kind, to give you the encouragement and the love you both sought in marriage."

He would follow up only once more.

***

The campaign in Africa had been judged an important success. As with the Australian program, participants took their new found experience into their homes. They taught others in their communities, and made humorous advances in removing flies from kitchens, bathrooms, living spaces, streets and villages far and wide. The all-important hand washing principle was generally observed and the World Health Organisation was becoming actively involved in establishing a world program.

Isaac found it difficult to move in these circles. His health was now an issue and Rex had matured into a commanding role. Isaac and Luteesha had talked of his relinquishing directorship of Snap-Zap Solutions, and were considering establishing a Foundation to attract donations.

The funds were to be used to lobby government leaders and educate department heads, responsible for budgets and health portfolios. The sales angle associated with this work suited him. Corporate governance of a large enterprise did not.

Six months after their return from Rome, Luteesha encouraged Isaac to seek medical help. Her fears for him in Rome, were founded on his state of mind, but there now appeared to be signs of physical illness. His childhood lightning strike was tested for physical injury, but none could be found. He underwent the usual medical tests prescribed for men of his age, and these were deemed normal.

In all the time these consultations were being undertaken, Isaac had recurring dreams of the towering columns of Hadrian's temple, curved in the reflection of Julius Caesar's eyes, but it was the redness between the marble pillars that captivated him.

He had known the familiar redness since childhood, the velvet interior of his eye that hosted the tumbling statues of distant forebears and ancient kings. What Isaac saw in the glazed eyes of Julius Caesar was vastly more remote, yet at once, in the forefront of his mind.

Caesar had called him, "Amicus Humani generis," friend of the human race, the man so powerful he could save him by simply raising his hand to Marcus Antony, saw in Isaac something only Caesar could know. And Isaac thought of the name handed to him at the professor's death, Noscitabundus, the knowing. How apt it was to apply the word to Caesar.

Friend had said Caesar. Friend as though Caesar saw Isaac that way personally, and not just of the Human race at large. In the space between the reflected columns, Isaac saw that Caesar was in another place, an other-world that now drew him into its domain, wherein Caesar was conscious of Isaac's presence. The link between them was undeniable.

And here Isaac was in the place where Caesar had directed him months ago. He felt no closer, nor received clear direction, as to how or where the place might be.

Between medical tests and light duties at work, Isaac sat at home pondering his place and reason for being. How does Julius Caesar fit his life? What had the professor given him, that he should become what he was? What part had Iovi Statori, Jupiter, played in transmitting that giving to Isaac? Was it all coincidence or, was it destiny? Was he selected?

He had to be patient. The directions, at times almost instructions, had come to him in the past. Why should it be different now?

He sought to be more comfortable with the clouds that gathered, in the hope of diminishing their power over him, and to understand them not just meteorologically, but what they did. They obscured light and in some mysterious way they observed the world they hovered above.

It explained why, for periods in his life, his visions and hearing had been sparse, unpredictable and sporadic. Had he not understood them properly when he needed direction and he needed to understand what clouds did.

They conceal the sun, the moon and the heavens, and rain fresh salt-free water on the land. They were mindless, reacting to every nuance imaginable that the sun, the earth, the air and water, and all its living things could generate. The creation of Cirrus, Cumulus, Stratus and Nimbus and the like, were not choreographed, even though the plumes that begat more plumes looked that way. No matter how reasonable Isaac was about their creation, he felt they obscured much more. They conceded the winds that roared through them, the embryonic life forms they sucked from the oceans and lakes, the thunder until it was time to be heard and the lightning in all its malevolent forms. Above all they concealed the realm of gods, gods who could form senseless thunderbolts into a play for life and death. Most were random but in Isaac's life they were directed. The professor's taking and his return to Isaac so many years later, the bolt that awakened Caesar and Antony in the Forum, were brazen acts of design.

In concluding this, he determined to spend more time outside. He would go to parkland on a high ground and observe their formation to conquer his fear. Initially, Luteesha would drive him and sit with him for a while, and when she was comfortable that he was right, she would go to the car and read where she could keep an eye on him. In some small way this pampering helped to soothe her mothering instinct.

On a bald hill save for one single solitary tree, Isaac sat on a darkened late afternoon. Cumulo-Nimbus had grown miles high above him. On this day he was sitting on a fold-out seat, alone, without his wife to take him to safety. The city around him lit up under its darkness and Isaac challenged Jupiter to strike him. "Dead or tell me!" he screamed.

Within seconds a massive bolt of electricity fractured the cloud above and frazzled its way to the tree, Isaac's sole companion on the hill. The tree cracked in two just as the thunderclap burst, sending the sound wave crashing down flattening the tall grasses of the bald hill. Isaac felt the faintest tingle through the metal legs of his chair and he smiled.

The electrically charged atmosphere scuffed his face and long hairs stood and waved. The forces of Jupiter were with him again.

The very next day the saying *'Mens sana in corpore sano'* came into Isaac's mind. He took great comfort in the assurance that he was still of sound mind living in a sound body. By now the doctors were struggling to find any serious illness but accepted that his condition was still unstable.

Isaac's void was peopled. As a child he only heard them. As a man he made himself understood to them, and in Rome Mark Antony physically pushed him as surely as Caesar did know him. No wish or want would deny him, nor treat him differently. This is the way it had to be and it was right.

And came to him the words,

"Caelum non animum mutant qui trans mare currunt," they who cross the sea, change their sky but not their feelings. And the water-milk bust of Julius Caesar hung in the red and its lips moved to speak, and after some time the words Isaac needed to hear were heard by him.

"Exegi monumentum aere perennius," I have reared a monument more lasting than brass, and continued,

"Hic sepultus in vacuo jacet veritas," here, buried in a vacuum, lies the truth.

Buried was the underground. Vacuum, the coldness of space. The truth? Was this truth the monument Caesar founded and raised, more lasting than anything that could be built or greater than any law passed.

"Credo quia impossibele est," and Isaac believed it because it was impossible, and further,

"Credo quia absurdum," he believed it because it was absurd, and beyond this travesty of logic, Isaac remembered,

"Ignotum per ignotius," the unknown explained by the still more unknown.

***

On a blistering hot summer's day, Isaac entered the Degraves Street Subway, where he would find the vacuum of space. This instruction he intuited as being that which he received from Jupiter.

He was heavily dressed in thermal underwear, thick socks, woollen trousers and under shirts, pullovers, gloves and a heavy black woven overcoat. A thick woollen cap covered his head and ears. As he approached the subway, he was acutely aware how bizarre, perhaps even stupid, he must have looked to everyone else, scantily dressed for the heat.

He waited in the arcade for an event he was sure would emerge. He soon noticed a vapor forming in front of him. As it thickened, people in the subway thinned out until he was alone.

The colour intensified to azure, the colour representing Jupiter and he knew to allow himself to be taken.

The vapor took his breath away. It was freezing and his clothes now became a haven. What breath he could draw hurt his lungs and formed plumes of cold vapor as he breathed out. Within the cloud floated the swaying image of a man, dressed in the regal white of a Patrician Roman family. Isaac's hands were tucked well within his pockets. He had never experienced such cold.

The image relied on the density of the vapor for its sustenance. From within the vapor Isaac could not see out. The mouth moved and Isaac heard his name to be Paulinus directing him to follow this vapor wherever it condensed. This connection also indicated where Isaac should go next, to a gothic building near the corner of Collins and Queen. The image faded as the vapor thawed.

Isaac, sensing urgency, did not have time to reflect on what had happened. The proximity and shortness of the encounter indicated he must move now. He climbed the stairs at the northern entrance to the subway and continued along the busy narrow section of Degraves Street, filled with cafe tables, a testament to Isaac's life work to eliminate the fly population enough to permit outdoor dining. Those who caught a glimpse of him as he passed the crowded tables developed instant theories as to what or who he was. He crossed Flinders Lane and into Centre Place and through to Collins Street, attracting more unwanted attention. His dignity was not a priority.

Helped by following a pale vapor, he found the nineteenth century Gothic Bank, two blocks west along Collins Street.

Here he stopped at the tall gothic archway leading to a flight of steps. The pale vapor had intensified to a deeper blue.

"Under the watchful eye of a stone griffin embedded in a column holding a shield, Isaac entered the building, now immersed within the vapour. He ascended the stone steps and entered through a timber framed doorway into the lobby, and climbed yet another staircase to a large chamber. The high ceiling was supported by tall granite columns on which sprung skeletal iron arches. He was now invisible to the outside world.

He sat on one of the timber screen booths aligned along the side wall bank clerks used to interview clients, and steeled himself for what would come next. The vapour was now cold and dense, a full azure colour.

He wrapped the overcoat around his legs and fluffed the two scarves around his neck and pulled his cap firmly over his ears. A white frost began to form along the top of the wooden partition and settled onto the small table between chairs.

An image of a young girl dressed in simple grey cloth, formed in the seat opposite him. The apparition danced and hovered until it came to rest.

And like the lucent busts of his mind, the girl with dark blonde hair, braided in two strands tied to the back of her head, moved her mouth and Isaac heard words that did not belong to the lips that spoke.

"Amicus Humani Generis," the lips kept moving even though there was a pause in the voice.

"Cucullus non facit monachum."

"Friend of the human race, trust not to appearances," the words Caesar had uttered to him in Rome. Isaac was now trance-like and a rapture gripped him.

"Before you, sits the girl Mercia, whose time occurred six hundred Earth years after the death of Julius Caesar." Mercia was staring at Isaac without passion. Her lips moved slowly without hesitation, unrelated to the form of the words spoken.

The voice continued in its measured way.

"We are friends of Caesar from Azuria, the aqua-planet that is home to us in the void. At this moment is the rare confluence of our occupation in the same continuum. This is now the third commune, and it will be of short duration, and we cannot know when the next confluence will occur."

"What news have you of Caesar?"

He answered, "Julius Caesar was assassinated by the Senators on behalf of the people of Rome." A pause. "We are saddened to hear this. He was a friend of the people of Azuria. The monument we erected in his honour is revered. Next to him stands the diminutive figure of Mercia."

"How is it we are here, now?" asked Isaac, his voice quavering.

"My name is Isaac Marcu Moritz," he quickly added, fearing his introduction was belated. In the flashes that sped across his mind, his life questions began to pile in front of him.

The response came, "In this age of conjoin our worlds occupy the same location. Our worlds are separated by phase, and are not synchronous. In the first conjoin, it was possible to meet Caesar. In the conjoin after, it was possible to meet Mercia. In the now conjoin, we greet you, Isaac Marcu Moritz."

The image of Mercia speaking blurred, as Isaac exhaled a heavy fog. The voice, straightforward and unemotional, continued.

"You belong to the first great expansion. Our world is the afterbirth of yours, resulting from the implosion of that which could not escape. The second expansion, with a different space-time signature, invisible and unknowable to the first expansion, filled the vacating space of the first."

The information stopped, as if to give Isaac a moment to comprehend the mechanics of creation then continued,

"The conjoin is the proximity linked with compatible intellectual purity. This is the Great Alignment, when the Pillars of Creation in your Eagle Nebula of Serpens become clear to us. As our universal motions vary, we cannot expect such conjoin conditions to remain beyond this cycle."

" Isaac detected the first sign of an emotional stall in the speaking.

"We have known Humani Generis through Caesar, Mercia and now you, Isaac."

"Of God, what of God, the Creator!" burst Isaac not wanting it to end.

"From Caesar we learned of your many Gods. We learned of humans made into Gods. From Mercia, you have one God and an Anti-God and the stone tablets prescribing manner of life." Mercia's eyes barely wavered from subservience as she continued her irrational movements.

"The Book of Crystals, found by our first space traveller, Zeernon on the planet Pelagus I, speak of the Creation, and the Observances, the guiding acknowledgements. The manner of life, how it should be carried out, was left to the non-binary Azurian people to devise, for and unto themselves. The Book of Crystals gives us custody of the Manner of Life.

On the first tablet made of sapphire crystal is,

The Beginning
The Creator was not created and
From infinite wisdom created the Sphere and the Passage of Time, Energy and Substance, The Orders and the Elements
The second tablet of sapphire,

The Observances
The Creator is not Azurian nor Human and
Leaves to chance not destiny to Beget life, Abundance and Paucity, Good and Evil to beget intellect
Only the Created can Love

Isaac was stunned by the explicit nature of the pages of sapphire. His words came slowly, his mind raced.

"The existence of Human Beings was revealed to you? and this has been your search," stating rather than asking.

Isaac then asked the inevitable, "What of Life, the meaning of Life?"

"The question is incomplete, and should be stated as what can I bring to the meaning of Life?

"The bridge of life is to be crossed, and the path made."

Isaac understood that action and purpose were inherent in the word crossed. The next question gathered,

"What can I possibly bring to the Table of Creation?"

"The offspring of intellect, insights, and the influence of their myriad number upon the creation, this is your obligation."

Mercia's image began to waver and the mist around her developed a small vortex. Isaac feared the end of the conjoin was near.

"What of the Afterlife?"

"Insight alters the natural state. The altered states you create become part of creation, to the extent of your insight's sphere of influence. The so altered state of the universe becomes home to the mind."

The conjoin was fraying. Isaac could not think beyond all that was said. Mercia faded as the temperature warmed. Would, could this happen again and if it did, what more could be said?

The white frost on the top of the wooden screen vaporised and feeling warmer, he loosened the scarves around his neck. He looked at the gothic splendour around him, silent and past.

He stood up and began to disrobe. As he left the banking chamber he passed a security guard, realising that in his conference, no one had had the presence of mind to enter the chamber, nor had the guard the sense to query his intentions, dressed as he was.

This condition must have been an effect of the transmission, a word Isaac thought not good enough for what just happened, and then remembered the word conjoin. That is exactly what it was.

He continued to strip off layers of clothing as he walked the street, his mind elsewhere. Feeling exposed, he turned into an arcade and found a quiet place to sit in a small cafe before the lunch rush.

Having risen from the waters of their planet, Azuria, the Azurian people occupied the blue atmosphere from which they took their name. He remembered that the name Azuria in Hebrew meant 'God's help'. The colour azure, the color between cyan and blue, not one or the other, distinct and purposeful, to be the colour ascribed to Jupiter.

How Earth-like the process of their creation had been. Isaac thought over the similarities and intertwined meanings. The repetition of evolution would ingrain itself in knowledge beyond measure save for what Caesar might have known. What was he to do with it? Who would direct him now? To what end? *Noscitabundus,* he was the knowing now in more ways than he could have dreamed. He was the knowing, whose breadth was beyond the Professor's history, his languages and social conscience.

A true knowing would find a way. A knowing alone has no partners, no scholarship, no ministry, no government. But he had a place and only deliberation over time would allow him to sanely and believably reveal what he knew.

A new race had now developed for him. The race to resolve the action needed to take in the revelation and disseminate it, against the deepening irrationality of his mind. Luteesha had been at her husband to accept, and at least consider, his mental condition to be abnormal. But still, the insights came and the signals pointing to them, continued to be offered by the crazed dead.

Isaac sipped his coffee, likening the sensation to pinching himself. It was all true.

***

In the beginning was the word
The word was be
And thereafter
All was being.

Chapter 10

The Third Confinement

In the weeks following his encounter, Isaac studied the astronomy of the Constellation Serpens. He had first seen the snake, Serpentis, when stationed in Rome. Within its celestial field, Isaac imagined what the Eagle Nebula might look like from different directions across space, how the Azurians would monitor its movements, for potential alignments of when a new conjoin with our world might emerge.

The massive volumes of stellar gas held great meaning for him. He had been told countless times that an eagle does not catch flies. The eagle was the irritant in his journey, the unhelpful piece that did not fit. Its persistently negative intrusions seemed to question the value of his life's work, that of catching flies. Was the eagle a harbinger of doubt?

Isaac continued to search through what was known of the Eagle Nebula. Recent images of the nebula revealed giant gaseous columns to which were given the title, 'The Pillars of Creation', and Isaac recognised the mutual locus for him and the Azurian people of the other world. The eagle had directed him to the place of the conjoin and the Harbour of Gods, the likes of Jupiter.

He could see the first fires of light, dense gases combining to form the critical mass of new stars. Those that had come to an end of their lives, released the elements they had made that would beget life. It was within such a vision that the image of Tarquinius Superbus, the expelled tyrant King of Ancient Rome, drifted out of the cloud and floated forward to address Isaac. Tarquin the Proud hovered in the glow of creation and after a time, his pearlescent lips moved and Isaac heard,

"Eo Nomine Noscitabundus, posse exegi monumentum aere perennius?" – by that name Knowing, can you rear a monument more lasting than brass?

"In disjecta membra ex arcana caelestia, aquila non capit muscas."

Isaac recognised the tyrant's advice as meaning, in the scattered remains of celestial mysteries, an eagle does not catch flies. After making sense of the role of the eagle, this statement confused Isaac. What more could there be? Before he could assimilate the information as a direction, the figure proposed to Isaac,

"Epulis accumbere divum," – to sit down at the banquet of the gods.

"Coram Nobis, tu posse esto quod esse videris," – in our presence you can be what you seem to be.

The image of Tarquinius Superbus moved sideways to be replaced by the bust of his predecessor Servius Tullius, the King renowned for the re-organisation of people. The sturdy face moved and the mouth opened to form the words,

"Consilio et animus, gutta cavat lapidem non vi, sed suepe cadendo," – by wisdom and courage, the drop hollows the stone by frequent falling, not by force.

The role of time as a force caused a rush of nerves. Isaac felt sick. He was running out of time and Servius Tullius rendered this delivery as a reminder of his weakening condition. Frequent falling takes time to hollow the stone but it also takes careful placement. Locus also meant placement. It all fell together to prove his worth, all except for time.

Isaac fell into a gnawing sobriety. The thought of legacies beaten by time took on a new level of meaning. Time had about it a power of affliction. Caesar's untold secrets were shrouded by the falling sickness. Mercia's knowledge burned at the stake, wrongly taken as a child witch. And now, what of Isaac's very same knowledge. Would he be beaten by time only to languish as a lunatic?

The questions plagued him, and the time that made up the day shortened. Luteesha more and more held them together. She was now suspecting that his childhood lightning strike to be the cause of his increasingly physical illness, knowing how sensitive he was about questions of his mental state. She did not broach it directly. Unrelenting, Isaac stayed true to his presence of mind.

In this illness Isaac resorted to his childhood, the beautiful, lonely place of his dreams and the wellspring of his learning. Surely, he had achieved what no man had done. He had incubated the lives of the ancients and their truths and insights. He had been made privy to the existence of the Azurian people in an invisible world. He knew of the Book of Crystals, the telling of their Creator.

And in this world, his miracle of hand-fly-capture, the means to health and dignity for millions of people, he wrought from his passions for learning and altruism. He had devised a health program for harsh environments and given it to the world.

He had made real a great challenge, and all this was still not enough. His restless mind needed more, a mechanism. He had invented a game when he needed a vehicle to employ his theories. Now he needed a mechanism. A mental, mind mechanism. A freezing, a mind channel to the other world that could be accessed by all. It should not be too difficult as it was already matched, awaiting on the other side.

This emergency distracted Isaac from his illness. He thought about the guidance the Gods and the ancients had given him and in particular the direction Julius Caesar had given him. *"Go back from whence you came."* Perhaps he had not yet completed this journey. Did Caesar also mean for him to go back to the farm, to the Forum, the place of his childhood?

The more he thought on this the clearer it became. The mechanism had something to do with the place of his origin, and he determined that when he felt well enough, he would return to the farm. He had spent months pondering this next step, and now some certainty of action had attached itself.

After failing to convince Isaac to let her drive him, Luteesha accepted that he needed to go alone. He had been alone in the place of his first memory and her presence might deny him access to whatever awaited. She left it that this was his to do.

On a hot December morning, Isaac left the city and as he drove through the middle ring suburbs, he reflected on how much it had changed since his first drive to the city with his father and uncle. He could remember sitting in the back seat of the Pontiac sedan, how eager he had been to see it and how deeply it affected him. The urban sprawl continued.

Over the years its growth had rivetted itself to the surrounding districts, absorbing towns and engulfing forests, orchards and grazing land. The Drive-In theatres that once flickered between the trees were consumed by subdivisions.

What Isaac remembered most about this drive were the vivid veins of light below the night sky. Under its spell the road lost its physical presence, becoming a continuous orange glow of highway lamps, the illuminated signs, shop lighting, traffic lights, and the sinuous lines of head and tail lights, detached from the unseen surface of the earth.

The illusion transformed the road into a wavering ribbon of light, like a trace of the Milky Way in the night sky. Within its serpent likeness, the chambers of commerce hoped to attract customers to its counters, like moths to the light. To the weary passengers in the darkened cabins driving the highway, the lighting was part of a bigger picture, that of the ever-increasing size of a city mesmerised by light, the promise of jobs, security and wealth.

In less time than he thought it would take, Isaac reached the steep incline into the commercial centre of Lilydale, a view framed by the distant Warburton ranges.

The distinguished cover of elm leaf above the main street of the town was still there. He crossed the railway line and soon climbed the broad open street of the shopping centre. Through the tree canopy, he caught glimpses of the old landmark steeples and towers, and behind the renewed shopfronts, the tree lined side streets still retained their majestic stance.

As he past, he recognised the streets where he first attended school, the grandeur of the classical buildings still there, the banks, the Lilydale

Athenaeum Theatre that hosted Dame Nellie Melba concerts, the Mechanics Institute, Masonic Temple and the Old Courthouse set among Catholic and State schools.

He wound the window down and breathed in deeply. The heat and the deep scent of eucalypt fleshed out his childhood memory. He now knew how much he needed this.

Beyond the township and the horse studs, the fields of market gardens opened up the vistas of the nearby mountain range. The sun, the soil and the sight of crops struck him with a deep connection to the people he missed from his young life. The farmhands, his youthful mother and the Professor came to the fore.

At Wandin North, Isaac made a right turn off the highway and descended towards the timber church that had become the spiritual home of the family. The Sacerdos, Pater Seneca Levit, walked from the side of the building and stepped into the porch just as Isaac passed. Neither was aware enough to acknowledge the other. Seneca had survived the ridicule of local Christian groups and managed to retain a small congregation for his Church of the Prophet Jesus.

Isaac reached the intersection at top of the hill, and scanned the inscription on the Jubilee arch of the primary school as he passed. From this vantage point he could look over the orchards, crops and mountain range.

Just a mile further, he rounded the bend that gave him his first view of the farm in many years. His heart raced. Much of the bushland by the creek was now gone and as the road curved around again, the hill on which young Filius died, rose to his right.

He stopped short of the corner of the Queens Road and looked at the back of the Post Master's Cottage. Most of the hedge was gone but the fence which claimed the Professor's life was still there, and he saw how close it was to his family's home. As a child everything seemed so much bigger and further away.

The farmhouse looked different and at least one cypress tree had been removed. Of the large extended family that once lived there, only Uncle

Cato remained. He had never married, vowing to wait for the goddess Diana to 'mortalise' as he put it.

The cottage at the corner was no longer a post office. The ground around the corner was now a jumble of unkempt plants, the remains of a pride in a garden whose caring had died.

He turned left and stopped where the red pillar box once stood. The double door entry to the office was still there, long disused. Just one hundred yards further Isaac turned into the driveway. It was deeply rutted and overgrown, the house neglected. At its end he turned, raising dust in the yard. The shade of a large cypress bough covered the car.

He got out and before he could shut the door he fixated on where the barn had stood. A messy patch of seeded vegetable plants grew in the soil amid five stumps that originally supported the floor of the building.

The small guard dog yapped as it roved in an arc at the end of its chain. Isaac ignored it. Disturbed by the barking, the squat figure of Uncle Cato ambled towards him.

"Be quiet Tullius! Shush!" he warned, and the dog cowered, dropping its ears before it began to reach for his master's leg.

"Hello, Uncle Cato. It's me, Isaac," noticing the lugubrious expression on his uncle's face, that feigned not to know him.

"Where you been, I haven't seen you in ages?" And not really expecting an answer continued, "Your cousin Anton and two friends were here last week. They told me how good you're doing. Good to see you. Come. I just made coffee. It's too hot outside."

"Maybe a cold beer too, Unc. It has been a long time, and you've got more hair on your face and neck than you've got on your head since the last time I saw you."

They walked towards the new house that looked worn out the day it was built, whereupon he realised that demolished too, were the washroom block and the wall of his grandfather's bedroom, leaving a gaping hole in what used to be the Forum.

Three battered steel posts held up what was left of the grape vine. Cato wrecked the forum ten years earlier for lack of something better to do in the winter. Isaac looked for other areas of damage wreaked by his ageing uncle. First, the barn that housed the immigrants, now the forum where they held banquets and where his grandmother packed strawberries and caught flies.

Before he could absorb the mess of it all, Isaac noticed two massive tree stumps. Two grand cypress trees had been felled. Isaac was beginning to liken his uncle to the Emperor Titus whose iron rule was responsible for the destruction of the second temple in Jerusalem.

"Like it? I cleaned up the place."

"Uncle Cato, you're a disaster." The old man grinned in acknowledgement.

"I chopped the trees in the creek and built this long open shed. The dirt floor works much better. But, true, I'm no Hadrian."

Isaac declined the coffee and tossed the beer straight down, impressing his uncle. He then walked through where the wash-house once stood and down towards a copse of scraggy looking fruit trees. Cato followed him. After locating his memory of the place, he stopped at the cherry tree where his mother had comforted him, the day he learned about going to school. A hollow had formed at the base of its trunk. Had he sapped its strength so that he could use it in his own life, he wondered.

His focus drifted as he tried to take it all in. High up in the next tree Isaac saw something that looked like offal caught in a thicket of twigs. As he did so the old man wheezed an almost inaudible giggle.

"Piss bag," he said, "pigs piss bag."

Cato then turned Isaac's attention to an amputated bough on a butchered cypress tree.

"I lift him up there with the block and tackle, hanging upside down. Then I cut his throat," signalling the motion with the slide of his index finger across his neck.

"Should hear him squeal."

With his facial expression changing from mock surprise to a grin, Cato confided, "He didn't like it!"

Isaac just took it all in and again initiated a move and walked to the covered roof area sheltering the implements. The wine press was still there. He stepped over a rusted hand-plough to look for the cellar door when he noticed a shot gun leaning against the wall.

"Is that loaded, Unc?" Isaac questioned.

"Yeh. Just in case that woman comes. It's for her," not specifying if a love gone wrong.

Isaac stopped himself from going into the cellar. It looked abandoned and he had had his fill of disappointment, and he did not want to risk anymore.

"I can't get under there. My back. I took the barrels out. They're under the new house. Beautiful wine! Try some," all said as if Uncle Cato had to explain something.

While his uncle spoke Isaac's gaze fixed on the cellar door. The farm he knew had disintegrated along with the pride of his grandfather, Ezekiel. It gestated there in the cellar of silent pigs. Isaac recalled its revelation. An un-enlightenment pit, inelegant and artless.

He could only wonder at what other preciousness had been desecrated.

"Later, Unc, we'll try the wine later."

Uncle Cato, taking the lead, headed to the field that lay between the house and the creek, expecting Isaac to follow. He looked the part of the innocent ignorant. His hair scuffed over his balding pate like tumbleweed clinging to the desert. The crops of hairs protruding from his ears extended across the top of his cheekbones and his moustache started from deep within his nostrils. It was as if he was already dead and the nails and hair on his body continued to grow. The glint in his eye seemed like a ploy to repulse the inevitable. For all this, he enjoyed himself, and his life.

Halfway across the yard, Isaac looked back over his left shoulder towards the cottage that was once the home of the Professor and his wife Victoria. Across a small neglected crop, he saw the iron fence and in a flash that can speak of a lifetime, the tragic summer afternoon that took the Professor from him rushed back, and with it the scrambling, muddied fear of his running home. The same event framed the visions that brokered his life and now it threatened his very existence.

Isaac gathered himself and picked up pace to catch the crumpled, yet spritely figure of his uncle. Cato was standing in a broad aisle between two different crops. When Isaac came to him, he pointed to the hill beyond the creek, summoning him to see,

"Decius, Laz and Quin are picking up there. They come every other weekend to help me."

Isaac warmed to the very sound of their names. Little Quincunx, Lazarus and Decius, his arm wrestle hero, the sound of Isaac's young life. They were all old men now.

The top of hill looked different. The pine windrow that lined the crest was gone and the view was bald and soulless. Isaac wondered why Julius Caesar directed him to return to these ruins for the answers he needed. Perhaps he got it wrong in coming back here. Memories, sanitised by time can be good, and sometimes they are better left that way. Isaac was in an emotional free fall as he lowered his head. He steadied, a pile of greying timbers on the edge of the escarpment caught his eye.

"You've still got the pig sty, Unc."

"I keep only one or two now." Cato was a pig keeper and always would be.

The sun blazed high above and both men agreed to go inside, but not before Cato insisted on trying the produce straight of the bush. As he looked down, sweat dribbled along his forehead and dripped off his bushy eye brows. A couple of flies circled above his head.

The old man bent his knees and dropped onto a raised clod of earth to break his fall. He burrowed out weeds from around a pepper bush with his strong sausage-like fingers. Isaac looked down on him.

"It's not the same anymore," puffed the old man. "The money grabbers have taken over farming. They don't grow the produce, just collect it in big trucks and take it to the market or storage. I get nothing for all this work!"

Holding a hand full of weeds, his uncle looked up at Isaac.

"Your brother, Isaiah, he's got a big cool store, makes a fortune!" The last word rang in their heads as the old man tossed the weeds into the next aisle.

"Crescit amor nummi, quantum ipsa pecunia crescit – the love of money increases as wealth grows," sighed the old man.

Isaac sympathised with his uncle's pain with the tilt of his head. Life seemed to have left him behind. He thought how great it would be for his uncle, if his beloved Goddess Diana, materialised into his life. But his uncle looked beaten, as if his failure to accumulate wealth drove her away from him.

'*opem copia fecit* – Abundance has made him poor," admonished Cato of Isaiah, trying to reconcile his loss.

In an attempt to cheer up him up, Isaac quoted,

"Vera incessupatuit Dea – The real goddess is made manifest by her walk."

Cato smiled at the thought of his goddess walking beside him.

As his love sentiment wore off, Cato slapped at a fly crushing it against his thigh, and in the same movement he wiped his hand on his soiled trouser leg.

"You did a good job, Isaac. Not many flies left now. The local flycatching club has two piggeries to practice on, and organises trips to the Outback to compete in the Central Australian league." Still kneeling, Cato's hands ruffled under a bush. He snapped off a shiny green capsicum, and in the same movement brought it to his mouth and chomped half of it off. As he chewed it, he looked up at Isaac and offered the rest to him.

"Have some."

"No, it's okay. I'll have a tomato." Isaac bent down to pick a near ripe tomato off a plant in the next row. He wiped it and took a considered bite to avoid spraying its juice over his shirt.

"I remember the day you picked your first case of tomatoes, when you were little. Still like 'em, heh?"

Isaac stayed with his uncle, and together they picked as many peppers and tomatoes as they could hold in their hands. On their way to the packing bench under a make-shift shelter, Isaac remembered where he used to run his hands in the dirt. He smiled as he re-lived swirling his hands in search of the cool damp beneath the surface. It was just visible through the matted grass, a sign of how few people now worked on the property. Its heyday had passed and so too was the world of his grandfather, the patriarch Ezekiel.

Isaac joined his uncle and friends for lunch in the hope of gaining an insight that did not seem so fruitless. He felt empty and as the minutes passed a thought found its way out. Is it possible for time to pass through a void without the carriage of substance?

The food was simple and always the same. Lazarus, Decius and Little Quin brought most of the cooked food with them, since Cato could not judge quantities much past what he needed for himself. His diet consisted of fried eggs, bread, coffee, aniseed liqueur and wine, pig meat and pig fat in all its forms. To save cooking and cleaning, he ate fruit and vegetables he picked directly from the crops.

The men were quieter and more tired looking than they were in the old days. The table was smaller and there were no women to serve the food and clean up. Life had changed.

One by one the helpers retired. Lazarus moved to a dust laden couch and Quin and Decius found beds in the dorm. Uncle Cato fell asleep at the table.

Isaac resisted the urge to nod off and pushed away from the table. He got up and walked through what was once the pride of the farm, the forum. As he ambled through the ruins, Isaac felt dazed. He was growing weaker and more unsteady, well beyond any effect of the wine. He sighed heavily and continued to walk beneath the cypress trees and into the yard. His vision blurred and his actions were becoming involuntary, and like acting out a memory he set off calmly and with deliberation, to trace the fateful steps of his childhood. This was the last thing he had to do in this place.

He staggered like a drunkard towards the fence at the rear of the cottage. The dried clods of earth crumbled under his feet, raising puffs of dust and the dry tussocks gave way as he kicked through them. He walked on his shadow, cast in brilliant sunshine squinting in its glare. He focused his gaze on the wire mesh fence and remembered chasing the kitten.

Isaac reached the iron gate as if expecting the ghost of the Professor to once more, placate the storm. It was here where his visions began. His skin tingled and he felt a rush in his arms as he gripped the hot rail of the gate with both hands, fearing he might lose whatever he was about to discover. Music flooded into his mind. A voice sounded a pristine declaration, pronouncing the strains to be those of Romanus Weichlein's *Encaenia Grave*.

Its measure of discord and triumphant exchanges, of gods talking and answering each other, both thrilled and unnerved him as it stammered with contrasting clarity, hesitation and uncertainty. His eyes screwed shut as the trumpet soared, lifting his spirit onto a firmament of air.

The voice boomed, Romanus! Romanus! Romanus! The name was familiar, strong yet tenuous. The man, who answered the call to inspiration, lived three hundred years before Isaac.

His ancestors were distant relatives of Isaac's family, and when they recognised the musical talents within them, left Dacia to settle in Vienna. Isaac absorbed the harmonies of his ancestor, the distilled, shameless nervousness of its passages strangely appeasing him.

The refrain returned, Romanus! Romanus! Romanus! An apprehension separated each ascension from its cadence, a moment void of breath in which trust was the need not to have to trust. Isaac was beyond questioning.

The bald head of Numa, the second King of Rome tumbled into Isaac's mind dissipated the music, and with the announcement of one final taunt,

"*Vox et praeterea nihil* – a voice and nothing more, sound but no sense." Isaac collapsed.

Lying on the baked earth, he fell into the absence of light, a starless, moonless dark, a blank, an unknowing, unfeeling darkness.

In this state, Isaac was neither dead nor born.

And God saw the light, that *it was good;* and God divided the light from the darkness.

Gen. 1,4.

***

Luteesha consoled her husband in his convalescence. She took six weeks leave to help him with medical appointments, and in the home. Brain scans for possible causes of his black-out confirmed the tumour to be benign and concluded it was not a direct cause of his condition.

This did not surprise him knowing within himself, the causes to be the real occurrences of the cohort of visitors from time past, and the immediacy he experienced in the distant realm of the conjoin.

Explaining to others of these connections proved fruitless, and he avoided elaborating, fearing being committed against his will. Only his wife had an intimate understanding, an understanding, privy to his actions. He hoped her trust and devotion to him, was out of unfailing love, and not a consequence of her transgression in Japan, though that may have been partially true.

He in turn showed love, respect, and kindness and as he gained strength, helped in the everyday duties that had been defined for her as a woman.

If ever the visions and their actions ceased, Isaac believed it would be an abandonment, not a saviour. He knew Jupiter as a villain, but also knew him as a benefactor. Could he be both?

By the fourth week he had recovered well enough to resume tutorial sessions at Newman College.

He attended a day-long conference on advances in bio-degradable spraying of insect infestations, specifically for use in coastal holiday resorts. They all but decimated his life's work, but he still felt pride in achieving relief for areas not deemed commercial enough to warrant such an expensive solution.

He felt exhausted sitting for such long periods of presentations, and catching up with colleagues. He walked home, mulling over the technology and Council resources, expended to secure their rate base.

He entered the house, placed his briefcase on the side-board in the hall, and called out to Luteesha.

He walked through the house to look for her in the yard. Perhaps she was shopping. He climbed the stairs for a rest and opened the door to the bedroom. Luteesha appeared to be in a deep sleep, and he went to the side of the bed to check if she was okay. She didn't respond to him being there, and he gently put his hand to her face. She was cold and did not move. He reeled back, standing upright. He drew a sharp breath and could not exhale. Shock silenced him. He noticed that she was lying on her side in a tight foetal position. An envelope was partly tucked under the pillow. He could not bear to look at it, then collapsed to the floor screaming in grief.

***

A group of extended family members, work colleagues and friends gathered in the Necropolis of the Melbourne General Cemetery.

Isaac stood alone nearest his wife, choked with doubt, his mind clear.

The sun came and went with the passing of the clouds as the service unfolded, ending with the lowering of the casket. What good was the sun now?

Isaac returned to read the inscription on the headstone.

Luteesha Moritz, nee Veranova, lies here.
Beloved wife of Isaac Marcu Moritz, Mother to her Unborn,
Loving Sister to Suetonia,
Aunt to Livy, Diana and Suetonius.
Rest in Peace

Her birth and death dates arced above her name. She was fifty-two.

Isaac, for weeks filled with contortions of blameless guilt, and the growing alienation by Luteesha's family, sought clarity, some kind of justice he could live with.

He made an appointment to see his therapist, Dr Niesohn, to recount his life in the hope of understanding the demons that plagued his mind. She had helped him to show compassion and forgiveness for the loss of Luteesha's baby, and to settle the hurt it caused him.

His day of resolve came, and he climbed the stairs to the waiting room.

Presently, Dr Niesohn opened the door of her consulting room and greeted him. He went in and sat on the couch, now a vehicle for truth and redemption.

The doctor reviewed the report she had on file. An addendum showed that his wife had died, circumstances distressing.

"Isaac, what have you?" A question with a thousand ways to answer, implying where do I start with you.

Neither did Isaac know how to begin. After a numbed pause, he reached into his jacket pocket and took out an envelope, the one Luteesha left for him under the pillow. It was crumpled from being opened and closed so many times. She had addressed it to him, to her husband, with love and a sprinkle of her favourite perfume.

He took out two pages of the well-worn paper of countless readings, and handed them to the doctor.

"She left me a poem. Luteesha was creative with words. When she wrote, she would do many drafts, and I suspect this one was well crafted."

"I sense a belittlement, in that this poem attests to her suffering a long period of anguish, unbeknown to you."

Dr Niesohn unfolded the pages and read,

First time I saw you, you made me ache
To be, to you, beholden
For my children to be forsaken,
I promised

In our embrace, I committed

To being an empty bride, always
Rethinking, unthinking
Our lonely nest for my love of thee.
While you chased Caesar's ghost
All over Rome
I dreamed a rag doll
I held it close to me
To be the host of our love

A beautiful head, made of porcelain
Dressed in red and white
I hold its spine
Beholding its proud and loving
Luminous smile

Looking into me
The child's lips moved without speaking
To share some food with us
I raised a spoon and pressed its lips
And in my waking
It was gone

In the temple of Zojo-ji
I passed through the gate
To free my foolishness
In a place given to the unborn
To set my burden free
I walked the streets
Yet to shed my dream
Through my tears
Headlights reflected like diamonds
No eye shadow to run,
Only lipstick

I dreamed a rag doll,
And still,
I ache, I ache, I ache

Olga stilled to take it in, so profound were her words. Isaac raised his head, having silently repeated the poem, almost word for word.

"How do I live with this love and pain?" he asked, and went on to say,

"My wife died broken, and I am sliced with guilt. This is how I have thought it over and over, and it is not trite, to say so."

To his therapist, this was a deep low. She offered to look into his past, born of such an unusual history as he was, that a better understanding would help her to better counsel him in reconciling his grief.

He agreed.

Dr Niesohn allowed him to rummage through his recollection of good times, to express his wife's warmth, and the support she gave to his unconventional mission. But it was enough for one sitting and she wound it up before the session became a negative experience for her client.

***

On the doctor's advice, Isaac took a three month stay at a health resort to quiet his mind, to grieve, refocus and restore a sense of dignity.

The facility also had indefinite, long stay accommodation. He attended wellness breaks and group exercise to little avail.

Isaac withheld much from staff and the guests, most of whom had very short stays of a week. He often missed sessions, preferring the solitude of the opulent grounds of the retreat. At the edge of a manicured lawn, a track led through a stand of pine trees and up to a small remote clearing on a hill in a far corner of the property. Most days he spent seated on a bench with a high backrest.

It was high ground relative to the surrounding landscape, quiet and at times breezy, and neither did he mind the blustery gales that buffeted him.

The outer broad branches of a single oak tree reached above the seat. Through the eucalypt trunks, he could see undulating canopies of bushland, extending well into the distance. The further he looked the grey-green plumes merged to a silhouette below the cobalt blue of a mountain range, that appeared to hover when mist separated their stark differences.

Isaac thought about how different cypress, pine and eucalypts were to ornamental trees, unencumbered by the self-absorbed prettiness of liquid amber, ash, maple, pinoak, elm and silver birch. The moment of reflection brought a warmth of memory, of Victoria, the professor's wife who first told him of the ornamental tree in the garden of the post office. Three months of his stay had passed and with his movements becoming constrained, a nurse had been assigned to him. Nurse Kretski knew where to find him on his usual observation post, that he sometimes accessed with the aid of an electric wheelchair.

This day, as was her usual practice, she sat on the bench seat next to him. She stayed quietly for a couple of minutes before she spoke:

"Isaac, I'm going to meet with your doctor. I will show her the way to you and leave. I'll be about twenty minutes. Okay?"

Isaac turned his head slightly and closed his eyes for a moment, acknowledging that he understood her and asked, "Olga?"

"Yes, Isaac. See you soon. Enjoy the sun."

She stood up and paused to look at him before heading towards the administration building.

A fly landed on Isaac's right hand. The insect adjusted its stance before moving onto the back of Isaac's index finger. There it settled. Isaac could barely feel the sticky, itchy balls of its feet when it started to move in a tight circle over his skin. He watched it, thinking how many of them he had personally killed and how responsible he had been for their declining numbers. How things had changed for him. This fly was getting comfortable and there was very little he could do about it.

A glancing angle of the sunlight glistened off its wings. The fly squatted on its four hind legs. It lifted its two front legs into the air and tilted its bulbous head between them. Like a bow of a violin the fly then zithered its legs along the back of its head, alternating each leg to one stroke at a time.

He resisted the temptation to shoo it off. The fly stopped rubbing and retracted to a stance position. It then leaned its body forward, lifted its two back legs and rubbed them against each other. He could see that the fly was enjoying itself.

When it finished with its back legs, the fly squatted on all six and spread its wings apart revealing the centre of its back to the sun. In all the years he devoted to this creature Isaac failed to examine its personality. In neglecting to do so he may well have missed the opportunity of making important discoveries about nuances of its societal and cultural patterns, perhaps missing a second avenue towards its ultimate elimination.

This fly was clearly enjoying itself. That it was doing so amused Isaac and his face broke into a smile of admiration. In these few minutes had seen the fly in a way he had never done before. This was the same creature he had hated all his life and here he was trying to come to terms with the possibility that he might come to like it.

Isaac dwelled on this newfound reality. A kindliness welled from deep within him. Isaac felt an overwhelming freedom. A freedom to repair his illness. This strange new love struck him. What would his life have been if he had loved it from the beginning? Would he have been plagued by visions? Would he have been tormented by the dead and the crazed, and to stoop so low as to wantonly receive their guidance?

Isaac found new strength. Without hesitation he pressed his forearms onto the edge of the seat, dislodging the fly. He lifted himself enough to move his body forward and apply pressure to his legs. With his weight firmly planted above his legs he stood strong, the blanket covering his legs falling to the ground.

Nurse Anna Kretski and Doctor Olga Niesohn approached him. The nurse quickly moved to stabilise him, and helped him back onto the bench seat, saying,

"Oh my god, Isaac, well done, but you should have me beside you when you want to move like this. Dr Niesohn is here and I will leave you with her."

The nurse moved aside to allow the doctor to sit bedside Isaac.

"Hello, Isaac, I'm sorry it's been a while, but I have some news I think might be helpful."

She stopped to make sure he was attentive enough to continue.

"The medical specialist has diagnosed your condition as being one of an extreme case of auditory hallucination. He has prescribed a new drug regimen that combined with regular therapy he feels confident will restore you to a level of independence, possibly sufficient for you to reside at a facility of independent living. This is good news, yes?"

Isaac looked vaguely pleased, but still unbelieving. His experience was stubbornly real as far as he knew.

Olga continued.

"You will remember we talked about my searching into your family upbringing, and you agreed? I want to be sure you approve as there are privacy issues involved."

"Yes, I remember agreeing to it," addressing his doctor's concerns.

"Then you know about your two older brothers, Ignatius and Isaiah."

"Yes, the first was miscarried at three months. And, the second, Isaiah, was stillborn. I am the first to be born, and the third confinement of my mother Johanna. It was to Ignatius I turned, in whose voice I chose to recount my life, as you suggested I do."

"Yes, I did ask you to recall, but why, Isaac, did you construct this history?"

"I have two older brothers, and I know them to be real. Can you see, that my being the closest born to them, that it was not only my duty, but a moral obligation to give them a life.

"Other than for me, they would have been denied any life at all."

Olga noticed him drifting, and called him to stay with her in conversation.

"Look at my lips, Isaac. Do you believe you've known about this all along rather than as a subconscious insertion into your life? To put it another way, could you intuit that you were not the only pregnancy, that you may have had older siblings?"

"I think I did see them, real, even though I was never told."

Dr Niesohn searched deeply, cautioning herself momentarily before Isaac interrupted her thought. "The gift of life is, that it's yours," he said, and continued, "They could not have it to themselves. It was for me to give it to them, and now they can rest."

"Do you think you can now rest too, Isaac?" she asked and he replied,

"The bridge of life is to be crossed. *Omnia vincit amor* – love conquers all things."

"Isaac, I think you are crossing your bridge. I am very pleased with today's progress. Focus on my lips. I am very optimistic that we can help you recover.

"It is very important now, to work together such that you can properly say goodbye to them. The sooner you reconcile this, the sooner the voices and visions will diminish in their intensity. Of this I feel sure.

"I will call again tomorrow, Isaac, keep well." She stood up and smiled, saying, "Nurse Kretski will come back and stay with you a little longer."

When the nurse returned, she fussed over getting his blanket taught around his legs and tied the shawl to his shoulders. A bird flew onto the grass in front of them.

"Ooh! That's an unusual little bird!" she said, surprised she had not seen it before.

"It's a Satin Flycatcher. It has quite a full blue-black head. There's another I see sometimes, but only the top of its head is black. It is called the Restless Flycatcher. Together though, they don't catch enough flies to make a difference. They only eat what they need and leave the rest to us."

"Look at me, Isaac. You're on about flies again. You'll have to reconcile with them too you know, though I shouldn't be giving you advice. What has made you so fixated about flies?" Isaac responded from the readings of the bible that spoke to him.

"In the Book of the Prophet Isaiah is the vision of Isaiah the son of Amoz – which he saw concerning Judah and Jerusalem in the days of the kings of Judah.
Therein it is said,
'And it shall come to pass in that day, that the Lord shall hiss for the fly that is in the uttermost part of the rivers of Egypt, and for the bee that is in the land of Assyria.'
That is what is apparent about them. So, the visionary said,
'For my name's sake will I defer mine anger, and for my praise will I refrain for thee, that I cut thee not off.
'Behold, I have refined thee, but not with silver; I have chosen thee in the furnace of affliction.'"

Anna Kretski asked,
"Is that how you feel?"
"Yes. In the furnace of affliction, so I am made."
"You talked to Dr Niesohn about giving life to the unborn. Is that something from the Book of Crystals you sometimes talk about?"
Isaac continued to quote the scriptures,

"Behold, the name of the Lord cometh from far, burning with his anger, and the burden thereof is heavy; his lips are full of indignation, and his tongue as a devouring fire.
For the stammering lips and another tongue will he speak to his people.
To whom he said, this is the rest wherewith ye may cause the weary to rest; and this is the refreshing; yet they would not hear.
And they said unto him, thus saith Hezekiah. This is a day of trouble, and of rebuke, and of blasphemy; for the children are come to birth, and there is not strength to bring forth.

The living, the living, he shall praise thee, as I do this day; the father to the children shall make known thy truth.

Fear not: for I am with thee: I will bring thy seed from the east, and gather thee from the west;

I will say to the north, give up; and to the south, keep not back; bring my sons from far, and my daughters from the ends of the earth.

Even everyone that is called by my name; for I have created him for my glory, I have formed him; yea, I have made him."

Anna continued asking about the book of crystals,

"Isaac, you missed what I asked before, about the Book of Crystals."

"The creator created to create, that is what they say in the other world and..."

Isaac appeared to forget the tenets of that world that only he, Julius Caesar, and the girl Mercia knew, and resorted to the intent of the scripture, ending with,

"To bear the furnace of affliction for the children who did not have the strength to come forth to be born, is tiring."

Before leaving him to be, Anna said,

"If it is at all helpful, my mother used to say that prophecies are too easily fulfilled. Isaac, look at me, I think you will find your recovery, and a life of your own, the one you love and the one you have always wanted. I believe it is within your reach."

"Nurse Kretski, that would be wonderful. Is that too strong a word?"

"Isaac, no word is too powerful to describe the life you love."

The next day as promised, Dr Niesohn returned, finding him in his usual place on the clearing at the top of the hill. He was sitting on the bench seat, leaning on the backrest, looking across the long view. She again sat next to him and leaned forward to face him.

"I thought about our discussion yesterday, about your siblings, remember?"

"Yes, doctor."

"Then, what of your life, and your life's work I'm speaking of?"

Isaac had thought through this question for two years of gnawing review of his mission, and had at the ready the response she sought, and asked of her pointedly,

"Is life a lie?"

"A lie we tell ourselves, when the how of we want to be is exhausted, finding ourselves exposed to the holistic and rewarding alternative we failed to see."

Olga did not flinch nor speak, expecting to learn, to suspect, a radical shift in his thinking.

"Is the life I have lived a lie, when the burdens I undertook to run the race, to fall and rise again and again to burst across the finish line, only to find I ran the entire length on the wrong track, to face humiliation."

"Isaac, if I may, this doubt, as strong a derision as it is, could apply to many people, not just you. A life's work, however humble, becomes a truth by force of, indeed, the power of time. It may well have enshrined itself by decades of what you have concluded to be a misplaced devotion, but it's disappointments can be diminished by an achievement of something you undertake beyond that journey, however short the remaining years may be."

She could see him reckoning with this truth, and hoped it was a rethinking, a breakthrough for him.

"On my way in today, I spoke with Nurse Kretski, and she told me of your conversation about love and wonderment. She also mentioned a revelation you had about a fly, the strength you gained from seeing it as a creature deserving of its own life, that in a different life, you may have loved. The strength of love, as some would have it. This is not to say that access to such is not difficult or insurmountable, but it is a forgiveness and a blessing to strive for."

He answered, "Given the lengths I went to for the creature's eradication, your logic for my healing seems unattainable. The gods have shown me more guidance."

He neglected to say that it had been a long time since the last of their interventions, and that he missed them, thinking how they had forged themselves as an essential part of his life, the good and the bad.

"Isaac, have they abandoned you and left you destitute?"

The doctor reserved a story in circumstances of this moment, recalling,

"In fear of eternal hell, a troubled Hindu man came to Gandhi, and confessed to killing a Muslim boy. Gandhi replied knowingly that he could find his redemption, by taking a homeless Muslim boy into his house on the condition that he raise him as a Muslim."

On hearing this, Isaac contemplated the extremes of crime and absolution, and this frustrated him, leaving him feel more abandoned. Dr Niesohn's ploy had backfired.

He protested,

"No, they are with me still, I know it, and they will give me the strength to recover from my afflictions."

Olga Niesohn could see he was becoming unhelpfully agitated, and sought to wind up the session. "Isaac, I think a stay on our working relationship is advised. I respect that you still need time to come to terms with the decline of the visions and voices, and the contact you are so sure are part of who you are. I will arrange to see you in one month. Stay well, Isaac."

He mumbled a thank you, as much for her leaving as for her advice.

On her way back to the administration building, she passed Nurse Kretski returning to check on Isaac. In the space of five minutes a dry thunderstorm floated above Isaac, packing a towering, cumulonimbus cloud, filled with menace.

Sheet lightning lit its underbelly, the flashes lighting the darkened landscape below. He looked up and wondered.

A deafening crack of thunder pulsed a wave he could feel. It was electric and dry. Again, another clap, this time sending a bolt of lightning hurtling towards him, and he was fearless.

Jupiter in his awakening descended, splitting the tree in two, one side crashing over him.

***

Anna Kretski squealed! In panic, without thinking for her own safety, she ran to the fallen tree and parted some of the lighter branches from the bench seat.

Ignatius Moritz was slumped with his head over the backrest of the bench seat, bleeding from a gash on his scalp. He was unconscious, stricken by the lightning bolt.

"Ignatius! Ignatius! It's Anna, Anna Kretski. Stay with me! Can you hear me?"

She lifted his head into an upright position, and he started to moan. Ignatius soon responded and Anna helped him to his feet, and taking his weight, motioned him to walk with her.

They cleared the branches and hobbled slowly across the grass towards the clinic on the ground floor of the administration building.

Crazy George ran across the expansive lawn and started to pull backwards on the stricken man's arm.

"CG, you're not helping. I saw a dingo run into the ditch by the Ha-Ha wall. Go find it!" instructed Anna.

Crazy George dropped the arm, shouting, "Dingo! Dingo!" his eyes oscillating left and right. He took off, galloping to the wall, arms flailing, almost bumping into 'Laughing Jimmi' who was bent over in an uncontrolled laughing fit with his fists jammed in his jacket pockets, at having looked up to see the cloud.

They approached the imposing three-storey Italianate-Style buildings of the State-run Beechworth Hospital for the Insane and Mayday Hills Lunatic asylum, set in an arboretum of soulless stands of conifers the locals called 'The Sunburst Mental Asylum', even though five hundred towns-people worked there, serving twelve hundred patients and inmates.

A stupidly narrow door accessed the clinic. Anna managed to get in with her patient and sat him in a chair by the first-aid cabinet. She cut his hair away from the wound and cleaned it with alcohol swabs.

Ignatius was now fully aware of being with Nurse Kretski, but still unhelpfully looking around the surgery, not knowing how or why he was there. The cut was not deep and she was able to pad and tighten it with tape.

She waited with him for ten minutes to see if he had recovered from the blow well enough to take him to Superintendent's office to explain what had happened to her charge. She fitted him into a wheel chair, squeezed out of the door and into the hallway.

They passed through the activity tables set up in the vast foyer. Three inmates lying on the broad steps of the grand staircase, heads resting on their elbows, stared at them with vacant musings, the bottom man with his head to the left and the two further up the staircase with their heads to the right.

A huddle of men surrounded the hot water urn, excited by the tea break.

A supervisor was trying to separate them and restore order after a scuffle broke out over tea mugs. An island of sanity in a sea of madness, Peter Rosethorn's blank face ceased to show emotion, so vigilant had his work demands been.

'A rose among thorns,' he often remarked, being the only vaguely, humorous comment he offered socially.

The Superintendent's room was high ceilinged, long and wide, with a tall bay window. He greeted them and stood up from behind his huge desk, pointing to the seating area by the window. Nurse Kretski sat Ignatius in the deep leather couch, and introduced him to the Superintendent, explaining what had just happened with the lightning strike and the tree collapse. He remembered Ignatius as one of the more reserved patients and being at peace when working in the maintenance shed with the ground staff. Handy with a range of tools, the facilities manager was comfortable enough to provide materials for him when he asked, after being satisfied with his intended use for them. A project for Ignatius was as good as respite. He was intrigued by his peculiar disposition, his profound engagements with historical figures and other worldly scenarios. Perhaps this violent accident could help him where electrotherapy had failed. with a peculiar disposition, his profound engagements with historical figures and other worldly scenarios. Perhaps this violent accident could help him where electrotherapy had failed.

Superintendent James Munro sat in an armchair opposite him, and asked Nurse Anna to sit in the other chair, thinking that her presence would be calming.

"Ignatius, do you recollect your family upbringing, your brothers specifically?" he asked, not wanting to waste time with the usual preambles.

Ignatius was surprisingly lucid given the impact of the lightning strike.

"Yes, I do," he said cooperatively.

"Go on," invited the Superintendent.

"I was lying up high on the bough of a cypress tree. I looked down and saw him, Isaac. It was hot and," he thought, then continued.

"I could see that he was ploughing his hands in the dirt."

James Munro interrupted,

"Ignatius, we know your family history, you are an only child, you have no siblings. How do you account for this obsession?"

Ignatius took umbrage at his rude bluntness, and replied as if to quell the interrogation.

"I know them. Our mother had me, and two more pregnancies. One, Isaiah was still-born, and the next, named Isaac, miscarried at four months."

"Yes, we know this as well, so why the allusion?"

Ignatius ignored the pushy Superintendent and continued,

"It was my duty and obligation to give them a life. The cost to me has been great, but I love them, always have loved them.

"To Isaiah, I have granted a big family and financial success.

"To Isaac, I have granted the highest achievement ever attained by any member of our family in all of our history, the greatest flycatcher there ever was."

With this, Ignatius rested.

Epilogue

Jupiter, god of the sky, father of gods and men;
The patron of Rome, his temple on the Capitol;
Sent the rain and thunder;
His weapons were the thunderbolts forged for him
By the Cyclopes, giants who toiled in the depths
Of the roiling lava of Earth

His wife, Juno, goddess of Marriage bore him a son, Mars
The raging god of war and savage fury;
Whose conflicts could bring about lasting peace

In the aftermath of Isaac's affliction
Jupiter made peace with his son
And embraced his daughters; The three Graces
Aglaea – Brightness
Euphrosyne – Joyfulness
Thalia – Blooming

His anger so appeased
Jupiter
Rested his thunderbolt